"Who's going to want to mentor a Hoffman?"

Wade shook his head and added, "C'mon, Lori, you know how people in this town must feel about me being back. You're my only hope."

She looked at Wade for a long moment. What he was proposing was dangerous. To her heart. To the regrets she kept locked away so they wouldn't overwhelm her. But he was trying to make something of himself. Trying to prove himself. She understood that—she was living it.

"All right. We'll try it." She was crazy to agree, but how could she say no?

"Thank you," he breathed, relief written stark across his face. "I promise I'll try to take as little of your time as possible. And I'll pay for Bill Cooper's time when he helps us figure out the water share. I'm truly grateful, Lori."

He was looking at her like she was his guardian angel, his salvation. And then the reality of this, of *them*, sent anxiety washing over her. How would he look at her if he knew what she'd done?

Dear Reader,

Return to Marker Ranch started out as a short story about two young people caught in a snowstorm together and forced to come to terms with their past. I entered the story in a contest, which it didn't win, and then set it aside. But the characters, Wade Hoffman and Lori Allen, so in love, and so torn apart by the past, haunted me. I couldn't stop thinking about them and the issues they were grappling with. I realized that they had to have their own book. But when I started writing, it quickly became clear that their story was much bigger than one book. So that first short story grew into the Sierra Legacy series.

I loved writing Wade and Lori's book. And along the way it became so much more than a story for me. Wade's attempts to fit into his hometown felt similar to my own struggles growing up in a troubled family and feeling like I'd never fit in anywhere. Lori's efforts to never show weakness, and to work so hard to seem perfect, also felt familiar. Wade's PTSD broke my heart as I read articles and learned more about the challenges that veterans face. And Lori came to represent all of the brave people who love our veterans and stand by them, even when it's difficult.

I hope you enjoy Wade and Lori's story of love, forgiveness and healing. To find out more about PTSD, or how to help veterans, please visit the resources page of my website, www.clairemcewen.com. And thank you for reading *Return to Marker Ranch*. I hope the story touches your heart the way it did mine.

Claire McEwen

CLAIRE McEWEN

—

Return to Marker Ranch

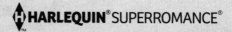

HARLEQUIN® SUPERROMANCE®

Recycling programs
for this product may
not exist in your area.

ISBN-13: 978-0-373-60995-6

Return to Marker Ranch

Printed in U.S.A.

Claire McEwen lives by the ocean in Northern California with her husband, son and a scruffy, mischievous terrier, whose unique looks and goofy hijinks provided inspiration for an important character in *Return to Marker Ranch*. When not dreaming up new stories, Claire can be found digging in her garden with a lot of enthusiasm but, unfortunately, no green thumb. She loves discovering flea-market treasures, walking on the beach, dancing, traveling and reading, of course! Claire enjoys Facebook, Twitter, Pinterest and Instagram, and likes musing about writing and all things romantic on her blog, *Romance All Around Us*. Please visit her website, clairemcewen.com, for more information.

Books by Claire McEwen

HARLEQUIN SUPERROMANCE

A Ranch to Keep
More Than a Rancher
Convincing the Rancher
Wild Horses

Visit the Author Profile page at Harlequin.com.

For my stepsister, Heather: a brave and dedicated soldier and pilot, a rescuer of cats, and a light in my childhood. Memories of her warmed my heart while I wrote this story.

And for animal lovers everywhere, who know that when we rescue an animal they rescue us too, and grow our hearts a few sizes bigger in the process.

And for Arik, who makes it all possible and keeps me believing in love.

CHAPTER ONE

LORI ALLEN TUGGED at the brim of her hat in a futile attempt to shade her eyes from the relentless blue sky. It was way too hot for this late in the fall. She scanned the granite ridges that towered behind her ranch. Heat waves shimmered between her and the peaks. No clouds. Again.

But heat or no heat, Lori couldn't put it off any longer. She needed to get this pasture ready. The cattle she'd summered up in the high Sierra meadows had to come down. The Bureau of Land Management didn't care that summer never seemed to end anymore. They'd fine her if she let the herd stay beyond the terms of the lease.

Leaning forward in the saddle, Lori nudged her mare up the rutted dirt road that bordered her upper pasture. She glanced at the neat rows of barbed wire with pride. There'd been plenty of time to mend fences last winter when the snow never came. Though she'd happily trade this perfect fence line for a few snowstorms.

Thanks to the drought, the only forage up here was brush and brown stubble. Maybe if she turned on the irrigation for a few days she could get some new grass started before she brought the cattle down. She glanced at the sky again. It was her only choice. Irrigate or pray for rain. And she'd been praying to deaf ears for a while now.

Dakota's short, choppy gait took them quickly up the hill toward the well and the irrigation valves. The flaking gray metal of the storage tank came into view. Lori veered the mare alongside it and peeked at the gauge. And felt her heart stutter. "No..." she breathed, staring at the gauge. "You've *got* to be kidding me."

Dakota's ears flicked back instantly, as if the little quarter horse was trying to comprehend the sudden change in her rider's mood.

Lori blinked, looked and blinked again. But nothing changed. The tank was empty.

No. No, no, no. The words hammered along with her heart. She'd heard of wells running dry a little south of here, but this one was supplied by mountain runoff, and there had been some snow up on the highest peaks last winter. It would make sense for the well to be low... but empty? Impossible.

The gauge *had* to be stuck. Lori reached

over and tapped its thick, clear surface with her knuckles, waiting for the numbers to jump. Nothing. She smacked the gauge hard with the palm of her hand, wincing as the impact jarred her wrist. She willed the numbers to change. They didn't.

Four-letter words she rarely said hung ugly in the afternoon silence. She couldn't deal with this. Couldn't afford this. The threatening heat of tears slicked behind her eyes, but she blinked them back. She wouldn't cry. Not even up here, alone in the most remote part of her ranch.

Solutions. Focus on solutions. She knew how to handle his. She slid off Dakota's back and led the mare in a circle around the tank, looking for broken pipes, dripping water, cracks in the tank, anything that would explain what was going on.

Everything looked just fine.

"Okay," she said to Dakota, her voice sounding foreign in the deep mountain silence. "We'll ride up closer to the mountains." She put her foot in the stirrup and swung up onto the saddle. "Let's take a look at the creek up here. Maybe we can see what's going wrong." It was silly to talk to her horse, but it kept the panic at bay.

Maybe a new spring had pushed its way out somewhere. The east side of the Sierra Nevada was known for its hot springs. Water wandered deep under the still-forming peaks and met up with all kinds of heat and pressure, then popped out of the earth in unpredictable places. If a new spring had surfaced, it could change everything.

A flicker of hope had her urging Dakota through the brush behind the tank, following deer trails until they were in the shadow of the higher peaks. There'd been an earthquake last week. Not a big one, but maybe enough to shift things around. If that was the cause of the problem, it might be an easy fix.

It was probably wishful thinking, but she could allow herself a few hours of wishing before she went home and called up Bill Cooper, the local driller.

She let Dakota have a loose rein so the horse could pick her own way up the hill. Arching her back, Lori stretched in the saddle, trying to let some of the stress go. A ride on a hot fall afternoon would normally relax her. The drone of insects and the crunch of dry brush under Dakota's hooves melded in a soothing rhythm that should have made everything feel hopeful and okay. But the tension that had been buzzing in the back of her brain ever since her father moved away clamped claws onto her shoulders, making them ache.

Taking over the ranch had been so much harder than she'd ever imagined. She had a lifetime of experience and a degree in animal husbandry, but that hadn't prepared her for the pressure of making all the decisions, every day. She'd always respected her father, but that respect had grown tenfold since she'd tried to fill his shoes these past couple of months. She rolled her shoulders, wincing at the stabbing pain. Her well was dry and *damn*, she needed that water.

Dakota took them over a rise, and Lori turned her onto a faint path that meandered along the summit. From up here, Lone Mountain Ranch looked tiny, a distant patchwork quilt rather than the busy operation it really was. But it wouldn't be busy if she didn't have water. Panic threatened again and Lori bit it back. She looked up at the mountains instead, their fierce grandeur a reminder to keep her problems in perspective.

And then she saw it, on the next hill over. Something white and shining—and unfamiliar. The closer she got, the more it took shape—a large metal water tank, brand-new and gleaming in the sun.

"What the…" She stood up in the stirrups, trying to get a sense of the size and scope of the thing. And then she jerked Dakota to a halt at the sight of barbed wire. They'd reached the rusted old fence marking the far northern boundary of her family's ranch. The new tank was on the other side. On Marker Ranch. The Hoffmans' land, abandoned for the past decade.

But apparently not abandoned anymore. She stared at the overgrown pasture. Native shrubs had overtaken most of the grass. Marker Ranch hadn't been maintained when the Hoffmans lived here, and ever since they'd run off, nature had been busy reclaiming the land.

But now they were back. Or someone was. She glanced down the hill. Far below, she could see the top of her tank, downstream from this new one. Typical Hoffman underhanded behavior. They'd drilled a well and stolen her water.

She stared out over the parched landscape. It didn't make sense. Why would the Hoffmans come back? Everyone said they were hiding down in Mexico ever since they fled arrest for drug dealing years ago. They couldn't come back.

Could it be Nora or Wade? The two younger Hoffman kids had stayed away from the shady family business. Nora had left for college and Wade had followed his older sister a few years later.

Lori shivered despite the heat. She wasn't

going down that road—wasn't going to think about Wade Hoffman. She made a habit of not thinking about him every day. The jerk had stolen her heart, her pride and her happiness. She'd often wished he'd just followed family tradition and swiped her car instead.

The tank squatted in the field, all shiny and new. If she had her gun, she'd shoot it. Lori ran a hand over her eyes, but when she opened them, the tank was still there. This was really happening.

No. It *wasn't* happening. Memories and old hurt turned to outrage. This couldn't happen—wasn't going to happen. She wouldn't allow it. Lori turned Dakota and pressed her into a jog, heading back along the ridge.

Thoughts swirled in circles of fury. She'd worked for years so she'd be ready to take over Lone Mountain Ranch. She'd pushed herself on every exam, every paper and every lab in college. She'd handled all the challenges life had thrown her way. And worst of all, she'd put herself through a heartbreak so big that it still ached. All so she could achieve her dream of running this ranch and her father could retire and finally find some peace.

And now that dream was in serious peril. No water on her upper pastures meant half her grazing land would be useless. Which meant she'd have to sell off her cattle. Which would mean that all she'd gone through, all she'd sacrificed, would have been for nothing.

They passed her empty storage tank and picked their way back down the hill. Lori asked Dakota for a lope the moment the mare's hooves hit the packed dirt road at the bottom. She was going to take care of this today. Somehow.

I can do this. It had been her mantra for months, but this was her biggest test. No way was she going to fail it. She faced down bulls, delivered calves and took care of herds of cattle every day. She dealt with disapproving ranch hands who questioned her every move. Compared with all that, a little chat with the lowlife, water-stealing Hoffmans would be easy.

CHAPTER TWO

EVEN THOUGH MARKER RANCH was just down the road, Lori had never actually been there. She'd grown up with Wade and wasted her teenage years in the throes of a tortured crush on the bad boy he became. But no one she knew had ever set foot on his family's ranch. Wade's dad and older brothers hadn't exactly encouraged visitors. In fact, they'd been downright scary.

She squinted at a weathered sign nailed to a post at the start of the driveway. The faded black letters read Keep Out. Lori wasn't usually one to break the rules, but today was different. Her ranch was at stake.

Her truck pitched and bumped through the minefield of potholes that passed for a driveway. The place was a mess. One entire pasture was filled with rusted-out cars. The main barn was leaning and sagging, tired and gray, its paint long gone. The farmhouse was in a similar state. Roof shingles were missing and the porch looked like it was about to fall right off the house. It was a shame because it had obviously been a lovely home long ago.

The place looked deserted. There was none of the bustle you'd find around a typical ranch house. No dogs barking, chickens fluttering or livestock clamoring for dinner. The silence made her uneasy, and suddenly she wondered if she should have brought someone with her. She stepped out of the truck, keeping one hand on the door. "Hello?" she called.

Her voice disappeared into the dry heat of the late afternoon. "Hello?" she tried again.

She shut the door and took a few steps toward the house, but a noise coming from a ramshackle plywood shed to her left stopped her in her tracks. There was a clanking and a scraping, and then a skateboard came flying out the shed door and landed in the grass with a thud. As Lori watched in amazement, a Weedwacker followed. Then a chain saw. Then another.

She took a few steps toward the shed. A car wheel rolled out of the dim interior, and she dodged out of its path. "Hey!" she yelled. "Anyone in there?"

There was silence, then the crunching of boots on gravel. A man stepped out of the shadows, and Lori's heart hit her stomach with a soft, sickening thump of recognition. *Wade Hoffman.*

He had the same dark brown hair, but it was shorter now. The same dark eyes and high cheekbones. She'd traced her fingertips along them the night they'd spent together. *Don't think of that.* She bit down on her lip, the sharp pain a reminder of all the pain he'd caused. *Don't* ever *think of that.*

"Lori?" he asked, and his voice sounded kind of hoarse. "What are you doing here?"

"I didn't know you were back." And then she felt the impact of her own words ramming into her chest. "How long have you been here?"

"About six weeks."

It stung. She shouldn't care what he did. Or where he went. But it stung. He'd come home and hadn't even bothered to get in touch. For six weeks.

He reached up on the door, pulled a battered straw cowboy hat off a nail and clapped it on his head. Then he walked around the scattered junk to stand in front of her. Close up he was bigger than she remembered. He'd always been several inches taller than her—most people were. But now he was so solid that even through the faded gray T-shirt she could tell he was all muscle.

As a teenager he'd been good-looking. Since then he'd gone from good-looking to gorgeous.

She didn't want him to be gorgeous. This day was getting worse, if that was possible.

He was waiting for her to say something, but it was hard to think when his eyes were the same deep brown she remembered. They'd gone almost black when he'd kissed her. Her voice came out as a weird squeak. "You're here to stay?"

"Yup." He looked wary, his jaw set with tension. But she knew that if he gave one of his rare smiles, it would change everything. Light him up. It always had.

Don't think about his damn smile. He'd been here long enough to build a giant well above hers. Long enough to use up all her water. And he'd never once contacted her.

"Oh." It was all she could manage and still get oxygen. He'd always done that. Crowded her, sucked up all the air just by standing close.

"You hadn't heard?" he asked. "Did the Benson gossip machine break down while I was gone?"

She gave the expected smile, but it felt stiff. "I haven't been to town much the past month or so. My dad retired to Florida. There was all the packing to get him ready and then…" How to explain the last couple of months?

She'd dropped into bed exhausted every night. There'd been no time to go to town and hear the gossip. "Well, it's been busy, what with all the fall cattle work starting."

"I've got a few cattle of my own here now," he offered.

"Really?" She made a mental note to count her stock very carefully when she collected them from the mountains. Wade used to be the lone honest Hoffman son, but things could change.

"Yup. I'm planning on fixing this place up… turn it into a real working ranch."

"Oh." What was she supposed to say to that? "That's great." Suddenly the last bit of the resilience that had kept her going over the past hard months melted away. She had an overwhelming urge to lie down in the oily dust of Wade's junkyard ranch and give up. Wade was her permanent next-door neighbor? Who'd taken her water? She knew life wasn't fair. But sometimes it doled out bits of unfairness so cruel they felt like cuts to the soul.

"You okay, Lori? You look kind of pale." Wade stepped forward and put a hand on her upper arm as if to support her. But the strength of his fingers, and the memories they sent burning to the surface of her mind, had the opposite effect. Her knees felt shaky and she pulled away from him.

"I'm fine." But she wasn't. This wasn't okay. Wade, here, was not okay.

"Let me get you some water," he offered.

Her laugh wheezed like a mule's bray. "Water. Yeah, I'd love some water. *My* water."

Wariness crept like a cloud across Wade's eyes. "I'm missing something here, Lori. Look, you need to sit down."

He obviously thought she was crazy. She felt crazy. Felt like she'd crossed through some time warp and crashed right into that naive girl she'd been back when she'd slept with him.

"I'm fine, really." She forced her back muscles straight, her hands into fists, digging her nails into her palms so the pain would wake her up, sharpen her traitorous mind. "I'm here because you built a well. And ruined mine."

He stared at her. "How…"

"Up on the southern edge of your ranch? Well, the way our boundaries are, your property is above mine. So your well is uphill from my well. And mine dried out."

"Oh, crap." He had the grace to look stricken.

She nodded. "That just about sums it up."

"What do we do now?"

At least he wasn't going on the defensive, trying to deny it or bully her or any of the other worries she'd had on the drive over. "Shut it down and give me my water back."

He looked past her, uphill and south, in the direction of the new tank, though they couldn't see it from here. "I can't do that. I spent most of my combat pay on that thing."

"Combat?" Pieces of this new version of Wade—the muscles, the poise, the calm, curt way he was speaking—all fell into place. "You were in combat? Fighting?"

"Yup."

He didn't say more and she didn't ask. How did you ask about something like that? And it was none of her business, anyway. He'd made that clear by his silence in the weeks since he'd come home.

That silence hurt, but maybe the hurt was good. It would add another layer to her carefully honed resentment. A resentment and a regret that had carried her through so many hard times it had become a part of her. A strong part, kind of like a second skeleton. "Look, I'm sorry you spent your money on that well. You should have checked with me first. That water belongs to my ranch."

"I looked into that. You don't own the rights."

His words were little earthquakes, shaking her world. She'd always assumed her father had taken care of that when he first drilled. "That can't be true."

"I wouldn't lie to you."

"I'm not saying you would." She studied the ground at her feet, frantically going through her options. "It's just a lot to take in."

"I didn't mean to cause you harm, Lori."

"Ha." She blurted it out without thinking. He was walking, talking harm. She swallowed hard, getting her misfiring mind under control. "I'm sure. But here's some advice. It's best to check in with your neighbors before you start a big project like that. We're all connected out here."

He looked away for a moment before he spoke. "I guess I didn't realize it."

"I guess you didn't." Everything he didn't realize sat on her shoulders in an oppressive weight. Their night together had changed her life forever. And he had no idea. She pulled the keys to her truck out of her pocket. There was nothing for her here.

"Look, I'm sorry about the water."

"Sorry doesn't help. And if you were truly sorry, you'd shut down that well."

"I wish I could, but I can't."

"Then I'll have to figure out what to do next." She needed to get out of here. Needed to get far away from this new betrayal and these unearthed memories and all her endless, useless wishing that they'd both done things differently. "I'd better go."

"It was good to see you." He held out his hand to shake hers. She didn't want to take it. Didn't want to feel that strength ever again. His strength had always been her weakness.

She grabbed his hand and there it was. All wrapped around hers, fingers long and strong and warm. As compelling as she'd dreaded. *Damn him.* She yanked her hand back. "I'll call the driller. And if he can't help me, I'll call my lawyer." There. That felt better. She was strong and fierce when she let the old bitterness drive her. He'd been careless with her when they were young, and now he was being careless with her again. With her ranch, her career, her livelihood, her life. But this time she wouldn't crumble or let him destroy her. She'd fight back.

"A lawyer? Lori, come on…"

"No, *you* come on. You can't just come back here after all these years and sink a well that uses up all my water. I'm in charge of Lone Mountain Ranch now, and if I need a lawyer to get my water back, I'm damn well going to call one."

"I didn't know my well would dry yours out.

And my guess is that you don't know for sure that it has."

There was truth there, but she wouldn't admit it. Not when he was digging in his heels. "I checked around up there and didn't see any other reason for it."

He shrugged. "Well, let's wait to hear what the driller has to say. I mean, we're friends, right? We can solve this problem."

"Friends?" She let him see her cynicism. "Is that what we are?"

He looked at her carefully, like she was some kind of feral thing that might reach out and bite. "I always thought so."

"Do you even remember…" She stopped. There was no use talking about it. No way he could know the pain he'd helped cause. No way she wanted to tell him. "I've got to get back." She started to turn away when something caught her eye. "Hang on." She stooped and picked up one of the chain saws he'd left on the ground. "That's my ranch's logo. The Lone Mountain. It's scratched out, but…see?" She shoved it toward him, blade first.

"Easy there." He stepped around the blade and moved closer to see where she pointed. "You're right. That's yours. Want to take it? I'll throw in a Weedwacker, too." He picked one up and held it out to her, a humorless smile tilting the corner of his mouth. She didn't want to notice the way it creased a bitter dimple into his cheek.

"How can you joke about this? Is all this stuff stolen?"

"I reckon."

"That's all you can say? *You reckon?* When you've got stolen property from half the county here?"

"More like half the state, I think."

She stared at him, looking for shame, or remorse, or some indication of what he thought about it all. But he just stared right back at her, not a hint of apology in his eyes. She couldn't care less about the stolen chain saw. Her water was the real crime here.

"Well, I'll leave you to your illegal junkyard, then."

He stilled. Her blow had hit home. "That's just low. You know I didn't steal it. Don't be like the rest of this town and judge me because of my family." His smile was gone and his voice was quiet. "I'd expect a little more kindness from the Lori I used to know."

"Kindness?" Her voice went shrill, and she stopped herself. Tried to breathe. Tried to bring her words lower. "This from the guy who didn't even bother to knock on my door before he drilled a well over mine?"

"I'm new at this. I didn't know."

"It was your *responsibility* to know." *Kindness.* Her rage made her breath catch. How dare he call her unkind, when he'd been so cruel the last time they'd seen each other? "I'll give you some kindness…by telling you a hard truth about ranching. There is no room for excuses. If you screw up, you've got to own up to it and fix the problem right away. Because your land, your animals, your staff, your family, they all need you not to screw up. They rely on you for everything, and your mistakes can affect them in huge ways. So don't waste your time on excuses. Just fix the problem."

"Sounds like you've got a lot on your plate."

She gaped at him. He'd always done that. Seen right through her into what was really going on. Lately it felt like every move she made had an extra weight attached to it. The weight of all the people who needed Lone Mountain to survive this damn drought. Who saw ranches going under all around them and were counting on her to pull a miracle out of her pocket.

Tears hit the back of her eyes—an acid burn. No way was she going to cry in front of him.

"I'm doing fine." She threw the old chain saw in the back of her pickup and jumped into the cab, slamming the door and rolling up the window so she didn't have to hear him.

But he didn't speak. Just stood there, stolen Weedwacker in hand. She U-turned in his driveway and cursed when it turned into a bumpy three-pointer, the deep potholes rocking her truck back and forth and making her escape even more undignified. Then, finally, she got straightened out and clattered away.

With stolen glimpses in her rearview mirror, she could see him standing there, so still, watching her leave. When she got to the Keep Out sign, she allowed herself one more glance. Then she rounded the corner and he was out of view. That's when the tears overflowed—too hot, too much, so she had to jerk her truck to the side of the road and just sit, the back of her hand over her twisted mouth, trying to stop the ancient sobs from coming through.

CHAPTER THREE

THAT WENT WELL. Wade dropped the Weed-wacker and leaned against the wall of the old shed. Disappointment and frustration surged in a filthy wave that had him turning to slam his fist into the wall, sending splinters of plywood flying.

His dream of ranching was rapidly becoming a disaster. He hadn't anticipated the size of the mess his dad and brothers had left behind. Piles of stolen property hidden in the sheds and barns, or just lying around in the fields. Remnants of a meth lab in the old homestead cabin up in the woods. Every building in need of massive repair. Every pasture overgrown, every fence half-down. And now his one accomplishment, his brand-new well, had destroyed the water supply of the woman he'd loved since they were kids.

He shouldn't be here. Shouldn't have come home. Buddies from the service had gone home to parades, flags waving, the whole town excited to see them. But Wade was a Hoffman, which meant people from his hometown would be happier to see the back of him. Lori included, evidently.

But she had reason for her anger. He could assemble a weapon in seconds, creep through an Afghan desert without being seen, but he had no idea how to run a ranch. He definitely had no idea how to site a well. And now he'd taken her water.

He shouldn't have hired a driller from out of town. Someone local would have known about Lori's well. But the local guys were pricey, and Wade was just about broke.

She was right. He should have gone by to talk to her first. He was a decorated veteran, but he was also a coward. He'd treated her so badly when they were young. When he'd taken the comfort she'd offered for his loneliness and fear. And then shoved her as far away as he possibly could, so he'd have the courage to leave.

He owed her a mile-long apology. He'd driven to her ranch to try to make amends a few times since he'd come home. But the anxiety that had dogged him ever since he left the army had his hands shaking and his breath scarce as soon as her driveway came in sight. So each time he'd driven on past, not wanting to stand in front of her a weak and shaking fraction of the boy she'd known.

Seeing her today, he hadn't shaken. Instead he'd felt almost paralyzed. There she was, just like he'd remembered. Petite. Incredibly beautiful. Her sun-streaked hair whipping loose from her ponytail in the hot afternoon breeze. Her dark blue eyes fierce. So strong, tough, smart and good. And he'd stumbled around in his numb brain trying to find even the simplest words. What a fricking disaster.

All these years, all he'd wanted was to get back here and see her again. But what would she think if she knew he was broken, his mind fragmented by the insidious fault lines of PTSD? The pity in her eyes would be confirmation of his worst fear. That no matter how hard he worked, he'd never be whole. That he'd never be man enough for her.

His fist came up even as he tried to will it still. The urge to slam it down a second time was so strong. *Don't feed the dragon*, Dr. Miller had told him. *Don't let your mind go too far over the edge of emotion. It's the PTSD taking over, and you don't have to let it.*

But it was stronger than he was. Almost as if it belonged to someone else, he watched his fist come up and smash the shed wall again. And again. Over and over until he'd knocked a hole clear through and a trickle of blood ran down his wrist. Only then could he pull his arm back, sliding down the wall to sit heavily in the dirt, welcoming the pain that returned him to reality and brought him home to his body. He had no control over the damn dragon. It was running rampant inside. And it fed off moments like this, when he could still see the disappointment in Lori's eyes.

"IT'S DRY, LORI." Bill Cooper climbed down from her water tank and shook his head. "I'm seeing this all over. If this damn drought doesn't end soon, I honestly don't know what we're all gonna do."

Stay calm, Lori told herself sternly as stress twisted her insides. She was a rancher, and things going wrong was just part of the job description. "I don't know, either. But what can I do, right now, to get more water to this end of the ranch?"

"Well, you could pump water up from your lower wells. But that will put a pretty big strain on those, and you'll be in big trouble if they dry out, too."

"I don't want to take that risk." Just the thought made her palms sweat.

Bill nodded. "So you can buy water and have it delivered, or you can drill deeper."

"Deeper? How deep?"

Bill stared at the ground as if willing it to divulge its secrets. "At least another fifty feet. More likely a hundred or so."

"Seriously? That far? That will cost me a fortune!"

"Yeah, it's not cheap." He shook his head a little mournfully. "When I put this well in for your dad, we were swimming in water. Now the aquifers are so low, you gotta go far down to find it."

"Can you be sure we'll get water if we drill?"

"Nope."

"That's all you've got for me, Bill? *Nope?*" She slapped her palm against the tank and listened to the empty sound echoing back at her.

Bill took off his baseball cap and scratched his bald head. "I'm not sure of much anymore when it comes to drilling. Wells are drying out right and left because the aquifers are empty. No rain means we're all pumping water. No snowpack in the mountains means the aquifers aren't getting refilled. It comes down to simple math. We're in the red."

Lori took a shaky breath. *No water.* A rancher's nightmare. Only she was awake. "Well, it is what it is. I'm calling a lawyer. It's not right that Wade drilled up there."

"Yeah, I sure wish he'd called me to help him

out with that. But calling a lawyer won't solve the problem. You both need water."

"But he won't shut down his well. Maybe a lawyer could make him."

"But then how's Wade gonna make it without water? I know you're pissed at him, but do you really want to see the man ruined?" Bill paused, staring absently at her useless well. "You know, I think your only good solution is to work something out with Wade. Maybe a water sharing program. Use his well. It's so close, we'd just have to run a line down the hill to your land and you'd be set. Of course you'd have to agree on the terms. How much water you each get, how to split any maintenance cost on the well, an irrigation schedule, all that."

"What if he won't share?"

Bill shot her a look of fatherly humor. "Wasn't it you who trounced my boy Elliot on the high school debate team senior year?"

Lori smiled at the memory. "He was tough to beat."

"But you did it with style. We were all impressed. So just use those skills. You'll talk Wade into it."

She remembered the stubborn set to Wade's jaw yesterday. The steel determination in his eyes when he talked about the ranch. She didn't share any of Bill's confidence in her persuasive skills when it came to Wade.

And even if he said yes, would that be a good thing? Just seeing him yesterday had brought so much back. How alone she'd felt, away at college, a few weeks after he'd left her with his harsh words. When she'd found out she was pregnant.

Yesterday those memories had come back. And they'd made her cry, and she didn't want to be that pathetic girl, crying over him. The girl who'd been so lost, she'd made a decision she'd regretted ever since. But yesterday afternoon, sobbing in her truck by the side of the road, that's exactly who she'd been.

"I don't know if it's a good idea, Bill. Maybe you can help me get some contacts and look into bringing water in?"

"I can. But it will cost you an arm and a leg. Look, I know Wade is a Hoffman. And that family was hard and mean and wrong in their ways. But Wade was never involved in much of their activities, and a lot of time has gone by since then. Plus, I heard that he's served our country. It's a shame our town hasn't treated him better since he's been back."

Lori had never heard Bill talk so much. She just wished he'd decided to get loquacious about a different subject.

"All I'm saying, Lori, is that I think we're all going to have to work together if our ranches are going to make it. We've all cut our herd size, but a lot of people are talking about selling out entirely. So if you don't want to go bust, I think you and Wade should put your heads together and see what you can come up with."

Lori wasn't willing to put her head, or any other part of her body, together with Wade Hoffman. She'd made that mistake once already, with tragic results.

She watched Bill's truck rattle slowly down the dirt road back toward the main barn. When he was out of sight, she leaned against the water tank and stared up at the austere cliffs above her, looking for answers in the way the light and shadow played across the sheer granite slabs. She loved these mountains. Had always felt so at home here. But with the drought, her sense of home had never seemed more tenuous. Families were leaving. Ranching was becoming more difficult than ever. What if she failed, too?

People depended on her. Especially her sister—sweet, quiet Mandy. Worry churned inside. If the ranch folded, Lori could go east and work for someone else. But what would Mandy do without the ranch? Her whole world was the ranch house, her kitchen, her pets.

Bill was right. Sinking thousands of dollars into drilling deeper for water was a gamble. And with so much to lose, Lori couldn't afford to roll the dice. Trucking in water would bust her budget wide open. Which meant she'd just have to put on her big girl pants and head back over to Wade's. And beg.

CHAPTER FOUR

"YOU NEVER MENTIONED that Wade Hoffman was back." The words escaped the moment Lori stepped into the coffee-scented kitchen. She hadn't meant to say them. But dreams of Wade had haunted her all night.

Mandy's big blue eyes went even wider. "I didn't know he was back."

"Well, he is." Lori told her sister, "Right down the road, trying to get Marker Ranch up and running."

"I had no idea." Mandy went to the coffeepot and filled two mugs. She held one out. "Good morning, by the way."

"Good morning." Lori took the cup but couldn't let the topic go. "But you're the one who goes to town all the time. You do our shopping and you bake for people. You're constantly trying to talk people into adopting some stray animal or another... How can you not have heard the juiciest piece of gossip to hit the town of Benson in years?"

Mandy sighed. "I don't know... I guess I'm

not one for gossip. You know me…" Mandy's sentence trailed off, and she looked away, out the kitchen window.

Lori didn't need her to finish the sentence because she knew how it ended. Mandy was quiet—living in her own world of sweet domesticity. She'd been that way ever since their mom had died, and when Lori tried to talk to her about it, she always got that same line. *You know me… I'm just quiet.*

Which wasn't really true. Mandy hadn't always been quiet. She'd been bubbly and happy, a typical adolescent girl. But Mandy had been with their mom riding in the mountains on the day she died. Mom's horse had startled, rearing up and throwing her off sideways with her foot still caught in the stirrup. She'd been dragged. By the time Mandy caught the horse, it was too late. All these years later and that bubbly, happy girl had never come back.

But Mandy wasn't *un*happy. Just different. She spent her days concocting amazing things in the big farmhouse kitchen. Her baking was out of this world. Lori grabbed a muffin off the cooling rack and bit in. The cinnamon and walnuts were rich and a little tangy on her tongue. "Hey, if the ranch goes under, maybe you could open a bakery and support us. These are incredible."

Mandy's cheeks went pink. "They're okay. I'm still working out the kinks in the recipe. But is it that bad with the ranch? *Are* we going under?"

Lori's protective instincts kicked in. "We're just fine. But if this drought doesn't end soon, it's going to get harder."

"You'll make it work," Mandy assured her. "And if I can do anything to help, let me know."

It was a generous offer. Mandy avoided most of the ranch animals, except for the chickens she raised in the gorgeous coop she'd coaxed their father into building. Those creatures lived in ridiculous luxury under her care.

Instead of ranch work, she'd taken on all the domestic chores—which suited Lori fine. Without Mandy, Lori would probably be eating baked beans out of a can—she was that clumsy in a kitchen. For her, cooking meant burning things, breaking things and always wishing she were outside in the fresh air with the horses and cattle.

Mandy went to the sink to wash her hands. Lori watched her adorable china doll of a sister, wondering if she should be worried about her. They'd both had to grow up fast. Their dad had been so devastated by his wife's death that he could barely function. That's when Mandy took over all the house chores so Lori could take on more responsibility around the ranch.

And as the years went by and Dad's depression didn't really lift… Well, that changed Lori, too. She could see how much he needed a new start. How badly he wanted to go somewhere else, where memories of his beloved wife weren't waiting for him around every corner.

But her dad had also made it clear he wouldn't let Lori take over the ranch until she'd finished college and apprenticed herself under him for several years. So Lori had pushed hard to get through school quickly so she could work with him on the ranch full-time. And now here she was. In charge of Lone Mountain while Dad sent palm-tree postcards from his new home in Florida.

Mandy interrupted her musings. "You'd have known about Wade being back if you left this ranch once in a while."

Lori glanced at her sister, who'd pulled the cloth off a bowl of bread dough and was kneading briskly. "What do you mean?" Lori tried to remember the last time she'd been in town. "I leave the ranch."

"When?" Mandy asked. "And going to the feed store doesn't count. That's still work."

Lori shrugged. "I left a couple days ago to yell at Wade. He's sunk a well above ours, up by the northern edge of the ranch. And now we have no water for the pastures up there."

Mandy's pale skin got paler. "That's horrible, Lori. I had no idea."

"Yeah, well, I'm trying to figure out what to do. Bill says we should just share the water from the new well, but I can't imagine Wade will be happy about that."

"You don't know until you ask."

"I don't want to ask." The knot coiled again in Lori's stomach at the thought. She shouldn't have to beg for water. Not from anyone. Definitely not from Wade.

"I know you had some kind of crush on him in high school, but that was ages ago." Mandy covered the dough again and opened a carton of eggs, cracking them briskly into a pan on the stove.

Lori wished it had stayed a crush. She'd never told Mandy about what happened. About sleeping with him. About the pregnancy. About how she'd handled it. She probably never would. It would upset her sister too much. And the telling would bring no relief. "It's not that. When I talked to him about the well, I might have gotten a little upset. Said a few things I shouldn't have."

"That's not like you. It goes right back to what I was saying before. You need some time off. A few hours away from this ranch. I can see the responsibility weighing you down. I can't believe I'm saying this, but let's go out this weekend. I saw Sunny at the store yesterday. She mentioned that she's meeting Heather and Tina for drinks on Saturday. She invited us to join them."

Lori stared. "Who are you, and what did you do with my sister? You hate bars."

"I know you won't go on your own." Mandy turned off the stove and scooped scrambled eggs onto a flowered plate. She handed it to Lori. "If ever someone needed a night out, it's you. Taking on the ranch has been a huge job. You don't tell me much, but I know it's been hard."

Lori sighed. "It's just the guys, you know? They question everything I do. They wouldn't do that if I were a man. It bugs me. It's so weird to have worked here almost my whole life only to realize that no one's on my side."

"I think it's just an adjustment. They'll see how amazing you are once they get used to Dad being gone. And *I'm* on your side. You can talk to me about anything. I'll try to help wherever I can. Like by taking you drinking on Saturday night."

Lori smiled. It was just too funny, her homebody little sister trying to get her to go out drinking. It was probably the last thing on earth that Mandy really wanted to do. How could she say no? "You're right. We should go out. Tell Sunny we'll be there."

"And you need to apologize to Wade if you really were out of line. Eat some humble pie. It won't kill you, and you just might talk him into sharing his well."

Sometimes Mandy reminded her so much of their mom. Lori's heart ached a little. "Yes, ma'am," she said, and smiled when her sister giggled.

"You know I'm right," Mandy retorted.

"I hate humble pie," Lori grumbled, poking at her eggs with her fork.

"I'll make you a peach one when you get home," Mandy offered. "To take away the bitter taste."

"That's a nice offer." But even Mandy's prize-winning peach pie wasn't sweet enough to take away the bitterness that Wade Hoffman brought with him when he came home to Marker Ranch.

IT'S ONLY GROCERY SHOPPING, Wade reminded himself. *People do it every day. You get your wallet and step out of the truck and go into the store and shop.* But he stayed where he was, white knuckles on the steering wheel, because shopping wasn't simple anymore.

First of all, now that he was back in Benson, he never knew what kind of reception he'd get. Some places he went, people were fairly friendly. But there was still plenty of suspicion attached to the Hoffman name. He was tailed at the pharmacy as if the clerk thought he was going to run off with all the cold medicine. And whenever he went into the bank, the security guard provided a personal escort for his entire visit. A special perk they *provided* just for Hoffmans, apparently.

And then there was PTSD. Combat had messed with his perceptions. A loud noise like a motorcycle could suddenly sound like a machine gun. And once he heard it, he'd be on the floor, rolling for shelter, regardless of where he was or who was nearby.

Wade pried his fingers off the steering wheel and exited the cab. Leaning on his ancient truck, he stared at the Blue Water Mercantile. Its weathered sign with a grinning fish jumping into the air was a vintage monument to the 1960s. The Blue Water was out on the outskirts of Benson and far less crowded than the market downtown. But despite all that, Wade was on edge. He just kept imagining himself perusing the aisles, a shopping basket on his arm, and a

Harley going by on nearby Highway 395. The Benson gossips would have a field day talking about how poor Wade Hoffman hit the decks, firing a baguette like it was an M60.

He had to man up. A guy who couldn't even go buy a few groceries was pathetic. Plus, it was early, so he shouldn't have to worry too much about loud noises. His sister, Nora, who was hell-bent on fixing his PTSD, had advised him to shop in the morning, before things got busy. He had no excuse. It was time to find some courage and buy some food.

He shoved himself away from his pickup and strode to the market door, only to find it locked. He shook it once before realizing the sign read Closed. Feeling foolish, he pulled out his cell phone and glanced at the time. Seven o'clock. Sleep had eluded him last night, so he'd rolled out of bed at first light, relieved to be free of the nightmares that plagued him. But he hadn't realized it was still so early. Guess that was what happened when his day started at 5 a.m.

Frustrated, he turned to go, wondering what to do with himself in the hour before the store opened. The tinkling of a bell behind him had him turning to face Dan Sanders, the store owner.

"Wade, you're up early today."

He could feel his face flush. He was a former army ranger. Since when did he blush like a girl? "Yeah...sorry to bother you. Didn't realize quite how early it was."

"Why don't you come on in?" Dan asked. "You can get your shopping done now. It's fine. And I've got coffee brewing if you want some."

"Thanks," Wade said, following the older man into the shop. Dan had thick gray hair and a kind smile. He'd always been good to Wade and Nora, slipping them food and sweets when they were young and their dad forgot to feed them.

He accepted the cup of coffee Dan handed him and sipped it black. Its sharp taste was just what he needed to wipe away the last few cobwebs of the night before.

"How's everything out at the ranch?" Dan asked. He had a ledger open on the counter. Wade must have interrupted his bookkeeping.

"Coming along, slowly," Wade answered. And knowing he needed to make some small talk, he asked, "How's business?"

"Doing better," Dan answered. "It used to be that most of my customers were tourists, and fishermen getting supplies. But I'm getting more locals these days. I've improved my produce section. I'm trying to give the Downtown Market a run for its money."

Wade smiled, feeling a little more at ease

with the chitchat. "It's nicer here. Way too crowded at the Downtown."

"That's what folks have been telling me," Dan answered. "And speaking of that, I had a talk with your sister a while back."

Wade's sense of dignity went on alert. He was Nora's little brother, and she would go to great lengths to help him out. "Do I want to know what she said?"

Dan laughed. "Well, she's a little worried about you, I think. And I get it. I fought in Vietnam. I know what it's like to come home from a war. Getting used to civilian life again is tough."

Wade shifted his weight uneasily. He wasn't used to talking like this. Not to someone like Dan. Not to anyone, really, except lately to Nora and Todd. And Dr. Miller. "It's kind of a challenge," he admitted. "And starting up the ranch was a crazy idea. I'm learning pretty quickly that I've got a lot to learn."

Dan laughed. "Don't worry. I almost bankrupted this business a few times when I first started out. There's a big learning curve when you try something new."

Wade nodded. "Thanks for the sympathy." But he didn't really want more of it. It just didn't sit well. Maybe it was just his pride talking, but now that he knew his mind didn't work as well as it used to, pride was all he had left. "I'll just get my groceries, then."

He started down the aisles, filling his basket with soups and pasta and other staples. And a baguette that, thankfully, he never mistook for an M60. Then he was back at the counter and Dan was ringing him up.

Wade was just starting to feel relieved that they weren't going to have any more personal conversations when Dan handed him his receipt and said, "You know, when I first got back from 'Nam, loud noises bugged me a lot. And crowds." He sighed as if reliving the memory. "Honestly, pretty much everything bugged me. So if you want to come here early, before the store opens, and do your shopping like you did today, that's no problem."

"Thanks," Wade muttered, touched and mortified by Dan's kindness. Was his PTSD that obvious? Could everyone see it? He grabbed his bag. "I appreciate that."

"And if you ever want to talk about anything, I'm here. I'll probably understand. It's an adjustment, Wade. Sometimes it helps to have someone who's been through it on your side."

Wade squared his shoulders. He was an army ranger, dammit. Not some emotional ponytailed dude like Dan who wanted to talk about his feelings. "I'm doing good, Dan. I appreciate the offer, though, truly." Raising his cup of coffee in a brief salute, Wade pushed through the door into the crisp morning air. He could do this. He could shop and ranch and overcome this PTSD thing on his own. He had to. He'd come home to Benson to resurrect the Hoffman ranch and make his family name stand for something much finer than it had before. And that wasn't going to happen if he sat around telling sob stories with Dan Sanders at the Blue Water Mercantile.

CHAPTER FIVE

LORI SCOWLED AS she turned into Wade's driveway. Everything about him moving back to Marker Ranch felt unfair. Especially seeing Wade now. He was bent over, sanding the board he'd laid across a couple of sawhorses, his working arm muscles so defined she could see them from here. Unfair. He was dressed in a tight khaki T-shirt and low-slung faded jeans, with a tool belt hanging off his hips. And that was unfair, too. Because he was beautiful and he affected her like no one else ever had. It had always been that way for her, and it wasn't fair that despite everything that had happened between them, she still couldn't drag her eyes away.

She hadn't been able to stop thinking about him since he'd stepped out of that shed the other day. Which was *also* unfair, since she'd devoted years of effort to forgetting him. Obviously it hadn't worked. Maybe her old desire for him had been lingering this entire time like some kind of cancer, deep in her cells. Now that he was back, it was spreading through her system, and there didn't seem to be much she could do to stop it. But she couldn't let it get the better of her. She had to be strong today.

If Wade was surprised to see her, he didn't let on, just glanced up as her truck bumped down his driveway and shoved a pair of safety glasses up onto his head.

Maybe she was a coward, afraid of the emotions Wade drew out of her, but she was glad she'd brought Jim along. Her ranch foreman had known her since she was a kid. She was far more likely to behave well with him looking on.

"He needs to grade this road," Jim complained. "My old bones can't take this kind of jostle."

Lori forced herself to stop noticing the way Wade's chest muscles moved when he reached up to wipe sweat from his forehead. "That might have more to do with the state of the shocks on this old truck."

"Or the state of *my* shocks," Jim said with a grin. "I'm telling you, I may just heed your father's example and get myself a little beach shack down in Florida somewhere."

Lori glanced his way, wondering if he was serious. "I hope you don't. Or at least, see me through this first year. Please? It's a rough one so far."

Jim's face creased into a reassuring smile. "You're doing just fine."

"I don't think so. The guys hate me. I swear they roll their eyes every time I ask them to do something."

"They don't hate you. But they *are* testing you." Jim gripped his door handle with white knuckles when Lori navigated around a pothole so big it might have been a crater. "You've always been a spitfire, Lori. Don't hold back on those guys just because you're in charge now. If they give you grief, be a smartass and dish it straight back at 'em. When they see you giving as good as you get, they'll settle down."

"That's not the management advice they gave me in college."

"Well, maybe those college folks don't know everything."

"Maybe not. I'll work on my smartassness." She shot him a wink and he chuckled.

"I'll look forward to it. Now park this damn truck before we hit another one of these bumps."

They were at the end of the drive, where the dusty road widened into the dusty front yard. Lori put the truck into Park and stopped the engine. "You ready for this?"

"Let's get it over with." Jim shook his head. "Never did think I'd see the day when I came begging a Hoffman for water."

As they stepped down from the truck and slammed the doors, Wade came toward them. "Hey, Lori" was all he said. She couldn't read his expression. She'd never really been able to. Even when they were kids, he'd masked his feelings behind a wall of defiance and attitude—a magnet for her adolescent heart. And right now it was all back. Shielding him. Awakening all of that same ridiculous longing.

"Do you remember Jim Duncan?"

"Of course. Nice to see you again, Jim."

Lori marveled at Wade's polite tone, his calm, cordial voice. The military had certainly taught him good manners.

"Nice to have you back, Wade. I can see you've already made some improvements on the place." Jim reached out and shook Wade's hand.

Lori smiled at Jim, grateful that he was the one buttering Wade up. She knew bringing him with her was a good idea. He'd make sure she kept things professional.

Both men were looking at her expectantly.

She took a bracing breath. "Wade, I said some things the other day that I regret."

Jim looked at her sharply. She hadn't exactly

filled him in on the details of her and Wade's previous chat.

"Thank you," Wade said carefully.

"Your new well had me really worried. It still does."

"Is that what brings you out here?"

"I met with Bill Cooper about our water situation. He had an idea that might be beneficial to both of us."

Wade leaned back against the sawhorse behind him and crossed his arms. "Okay," he said, "shoot."

Lori swallowed hard. She remembered Mandy's advice. *Humble pie.* "He said that trying to drill deeper will only create new problems." She readied herself for the hard part. "So Bill thought... I thought...maybe we could share the water from your well?"

Wade stared at some spot on the ground in front of his battered work boots. "I don't know," he finally answered.

"You don't know?" It wasn't what she'd expected, and her voice came out in a squeak.

Jim touched her arm in a silent command to calm down. "Son, it's like this. The water in your well has been supporting the upper end of Lone Mountain Ranch for a long time. We're gonna need some of it back."

Wade nodded slowly. "With all due respect,

Jim, I didn't do anything wrong when I sunk a well on my property. And you don't know for sure that my well is what caused yours to dry up."

"But Bill Cooper said so!" Lori regretted the words the second they were out. She sounded like a four-year-old.

"Of course we'd compensate you for the use of your well," Jim went on as if she hadn't spoken. "Split any maintenance costs, for example."

"And it would help us manage the existing water in the aquifer more carefully if we were working together," Lori added. *There.* That sounded scientific and neutral.

"Look, I get that you guys are in a bind," Wade said. "But as you know, I'm only just getting started, and this place has been neglected for a very long time. I've sunk all I have into this ranch, and my sister's done the same."

"I thought I saw Nora the other day," Jim said. "But I figured my old eyes were playing tricks on me."

Wade brightened a little at the mention of his sister. They'd always been close. "She's working as a consultant on range management. But in her free time she's been here, helping me out."

"That's really great," Lori chimed in. "How

nice that you're working together to start up the ranch again."

"Thanks." Wade gave her a glance with eyebrows raised, obviously recognizing her chipper demeanor for what it truly was—desperation. He saw right through her—he always had. It was like he was born with a Lori Allen instruction manual and he'd memorized the whole thing. Back in high school, she'd tried to hide her crush on him, but he'd known the entire time.

"Lori, I want to help. I really do. But I'm new at this. I don't know how much water I'm going to need, and I don't want to take any big risks. I've got to turn a profit as fast as possible or I won't be able to make it."

"I understand that." Lori tried to calm the anxiety rising inside. "But I need to make a profit, too, and with this drought, we're on year three of loss. I've got cows and calves up in the mountains that I need to bring down, and I've been counting on my upper pastures for them. If I can't irrigate that area, what am I supposed to do?"

Wade shifted uncomfortably. "I'm not saying no to your idea outright. But I'm definitely going to need a little time to crunch the numbers and see if it will work."

"But it's not *your* water." Lori's clenched her

hands into fists, digging them into the sides of her thighs, trying to keep her temper in check. He held the fate of her ranch in his hands, and he couldn't be bothered to give her an answer? *How could he be so selfish? How could he not say yes?*

"I'm sorry, Lori. I promise I'll look the numbers over this week and get back to you." Wade stood up a little straighter, as if letting them know the conversation was over.

There had to be a way to make him see reason. "Wade, if this is about the other day…"

"Hang on, Lori." Jim set a warning hand on her arm. "We appreciate it, Wade. We really do. We'll look forward to hearing from you." Jim reached out and shook Wade's hand and then took Lori firmly by the elbow, steering her to the truck.

Fury seethed inside. She hated this. Hated that Wade had only been on Marker Ranch for a few weeks and he was already causing her trouble. Once again he showed up in her life and destroyed it in one cool, detached move. She turned, ignoring Jim's murmured warning.

"I take back that apology."

"I figured you might." Wade's jaw was set and stubborn. "Just say your piece, Lori. Then we can both get on with our day."

She'd heard the term *seeing red* before. Now

she knew what it meant. Anger colored everything. Her, Wade and his damn ranch were all on fire. "What you're doing is wrong. *Wrong!* You took our water!"

"I didn't…"

She didn't want to hear his excuses. About anything. "There's a right way to ranch and a wrong way to ranch. And you don't seem to know the difference. You should listen to people who do know right from wrong. Like Jim here!"

Jim put up a hand in protest, as if telling her to leave him out of her tirade. She was beyond caring.

"You know what, Wade? You can pretend you're different from your family. That you are back here trying to turn this place into a legal business. But right now you're acting like just one more Hoffman thief. Just like your brothers! Just like your dad!"

Wade froze as if she'd struck him. If she'd had any kind of large, heavy object, she might have. She was that furious.

Jim's grip tightened on her elbow, and he tugged.

"Let go of me," she spat out, still glaring at Wade.

"Lori, that is enough!" Jim barked and all but dragged her the rest of the way to the truck.

As soon as they were inside and she had the engine roaring, he turned to her. "You want to tell me what was going on back there?"

"He's wrong." She jerked the wheel, trying to get them turned around and away from Wade as fast as possible.

"Yeah, and he probably would have figured that out if you'd given him the time he was asking for. Instead you just drove him into a corner. I'm pretty sure you can say goodbye to that water."

"Well, he was already making it pretty clear he wouldn't share it."

"He was asking for time to think! Don't you remember how that kid struggled in school? He probably just needs some time to work out the math and make sure it's all going to be okay. It was a reasonable request."

Every word Jim said was true. But there was more to it than he knew. And there was no way she could tell him. "I'm sorry I wasted your time today, Jim," she said stiffly. "I'll order some water to tide us over until we get this figured out."

"That's an expensive choice."

His words stung with their truth. "Well, right now it's my only choice, so I'll just have to make it work."

"You say you want to lead this ranch. But your dad wouldn't have…"

She cut him off before he could go further down that road. "My dad isn't here anymore. I think we *both* wish he was sometimes. I'll figure this out, Jim. I promise. And I'm sorry I messed up today."

He didn't answer, and they drove the rest of the way back to the ranch in a clouded silence. Lori just hoped Jim didn't mention any of this to the rest of the staff. The last thing she wanted was for her already skeptical ranch hands to know that she'd totally lost it and called their neighbor a thief. It wouldn't help earn their respect. She knew that for certain, because right now she was having trouble respecting herself.

CHAPTER SIX

WADE HANDED HIS sister the sheet of numbers he'd worked out. Units of water required. Current output from the well. Just like it said in his ranching books. "Thanks for coming by to take a look at this."

But Nora just set his spreadsheet facedown on the dining room table between them. "You don't get it. It's not about the numbers."

He stared at her in shock. "How can you say that? You're a scientist. You're all about the numbers!"

"Mostly, yes." Nora nodded. "But in this case they don't matter. You just need to do what's right. You can't quantify that."

He'd asked his sister over to look at the facts, not dish out morality. "So you're saying I should just give her half of my well water?"

"Yes." She gave him the calm smile he'd relied on for so much of his life. "I think it's that simple."

Nerves twisted in his stomach. "But I can't afford to. It says it right there on that paper."

Wade picked it up again. He'd done his homework last night—almost all night. "Look, I can't afford to make a big mistake. We don't have much capital left."

"Then find a way to make it work *despite* the numbers. This isn't just about the water. It's about being a good neighbor. It's about being a part of the community."

"Those things won't mean much if I fail and lose the ranch."

"So don't fail."

"How?" He stood up, pacing the floor by the table. "How do I not fail if I make decisions based on being nice? This is water we're talking about. A key ingredient for a ranch."

Nora gave him a long look. She'd given him the same look many times when he was a teenager and she wasn't much older than that, and she was trying to raise him right. "Ranches here are failing left and right. Do you really want Lori to lose hers? After how hard she and her family have worked to keep it going all these years? Even after their mom died?"

He remembered how devastated Lori had been. How she'd drifted, sad and empty, through her sophomore year of high school. How she'd grown up after that, become an adult way before the rest of them had, trying to take care of her father and her sister. He'd watched her back then, wishing he knew how to offer comfort. "Of course I don't want them to lose their ranch. But it's a business, right? Everything I've read about ranching says it's a business. And we need that water to make our business a success."

"Any good book on business should also mention that out of hardship can come innovation. You need to let go of some of that water and then innovate. Figure out a way to get by with less."

"But…"

Nora cut him off. "Your books won't help with this issue because they're not written for people experiencing the worst drought in California's long history of droughts! But you and Lori are smart. And you've got me—how many people can say they have an expert on range management in the family? I'll go though her pastures as well as ours if you want, and see if I can help."

"I guess." Wade set the paper aside, trying to put aside his anxiety with it. He was overly cautious. He knew that. Partly because he'd come back here to prove that he could make this a success.

But also because growing up, ranching was his dream. He'd watched the other families in the area with their cattle and horses and their nice clothes and pickups. He'd seen their barbecues and barn raisings and the way they high-fived and slapped backs at local events. And he'd wanted that life. A normal, hardworking life. He'd wanted it badly, and now he had a small chance at making it happen.

He shook his head, trying to loosen the anxious buzzing there. The voice whispering that no matter what he did about the water, he'd find a way to mess this up because failure was in his DNA. He tried to shush it, to see it for what it really was—the aftereffects of months in combat. The whispers of doubt over the smallest decisions. The intense irritation when things didn't go his way. It was making him rigid. It had him digging his heels in with Lori and Jim the other day. Had him grimly clinging on to what he felt might be the quickest path to security and survival—no matter what the consequences to others.

Nora stood up and reached for his hand, guiding him back down to his seat at the table. "Little bro, take a breath. It's going to be okay."

He raised his brows at her. "Really?"

"I think so. You're just in survival mode right now. And it's making you a little frantic."

"What do you mean?" He'd been in survival mode before. With bullets hitting the dirt around him as he scrabbled for shelter. This wasn't that.

"I mean how we grew up. Everyday survival. How to get food, how to get clothes, how to make it without a mom, how to stay out of Dad's way. I think it's easy to slip back into that way of thinking, where it's all about trying to get the next meal."

Wade traced an old water stain on the table. He hated talking about the past. Hated remembering the searing of his dad's belt on his back and the ache of hunger in his stomach.

"Sometimes I wonder if all that surviving made us a little hard," Nora said quietly. "Because we had to look out for ourselves, and focus all our energy on just getting by."

"That's a good thing," Wade countered. "We're not dependent. We take care of ourselves. It's made us successful." It had brought him through some scary battles.

"It *can* be a good thing," Nora said gently. "But lately I've been thinking about how all the independence that saved us when we were kids may not be quite so helpful now that we're adults. I mean, we can *survive* on our own, but don't you want more than survival? Don't you want friends and neighbors and… I don't know…love?"

"Love?" He had to tease her. It was his brotherly duty. "I don't know about that, seeing as you've gone all soft on me since you got together with Todd. Where's the Nora who taught me to look out for myself and make sure I succeeded?"

"All that's still important. But if that's *all* we do, life's not going to be very rich, is it? I don't know. Maybe I'm wrong. But you asked for my opinion. And my opinion is to ignore the numbers and share the water."

"It's not what I expected you'd say." He crumpled up the paper in disgust. And because he was still her little brother, he threw it at her.

Nora caught it in one hand and grinned. "Glad I can still surprise you, bro. Trust me on this one, okay?"

"Sure. But if that well runs out of water, you'll help me figure out what to do next, right?"

"I'll buy you your first water delivery."

"Ah...so consoling." He delivered the sarcasm with a smile. "You always were good to me."

Nora laughed. "Back atcha. And one more piece of advice?"

"Do I have a choice?"

She shook her head. "Nope."

"Fine. Shoot." He sat back, waiting for the lecture. He dreaded it mostly because she was probably right. She always had been. Five years older than him and many, many years wiser.

"Look, if you really want to get rid of the legacy of Dad and our brothers, and make the Hoffman name mean something more than larceny and drug deals, you need to get off this ranch. Don't hide out here. You need to spend some time in town, meet some people. Let everyone see you've changed."

He let out a bark of a laugh. "This from the world's biggest introvert."

"Yes, and even *I'm* trying."

She was. He'd seen it and admired her for it. Todd was friends with most of the town, and Nora gamely stepped out by his side, quietly facing down anyone who despised her for her family history. "I hate it when you're right all the time.'

"It's my job as your older sister."

"Ha!"

"But seriously, Wade, you *need* to get out more."

It was clear she wasn't going to let him off without a promise. "Okay. Fine. I'll go out for a beer or something. As long as you let Todd off the leash for a night so he can go with me."

"I don't have him on a leash!" she protested, flushing.

Now he was in full-on little brother mode. It

was far more comfortable than hearing about his mistakes. "Really? And when's the last time you two spent more than a couple of hours apart?"

"We like each other!" Nora was beet red now. She'd always blushed easily.

"He's leashed. Arf arf!"

"Okay, twelve-year-old. You can borrow my fiancé for a night out this weekend. Now, do you need anything else? Because I told Todd I'd meet him for dinner."

"I rest my case."

She grinned. "Glad you're feeling better. Now go fix things with Lori, you big dork."

WADE WATCHED NORA'S Jeep disappear down the driveway before he sat down on the couch and put his head in his hands. He had no idea how he was going to handle the night out he'd just gotten himself into.

And Lori. He'd have to find a way to face her as well. She'd looked like an angry angel on his ranch yesterday, with her hair swirling around her shoulders and her eyes dark with hurt. So different from the way she'd looked at him, full of longing and acceptance and desire, all those years ago, just before they'd made love. Her first time, and the first time it ever mattered for him.

And damn, it had mattered. He'd loved her from a distance through high school. She'd been smart and strong and good at everything she turned her hand to. He'd leaned on the fence down at the arena, watching her win junior rodeo ribbons right alongside the boys her age. He'd seen her name semester after semester on the school honor roll posted in the fancy glass case by the office. He'd listened to her up at the podium delivering student council speeches and stole glances after school when she headed off to cheerleading practice in her cute uniform.

He'd watched her and wanted her and never felt worthy of her. He was the kid from so far down the wrong side of the tracks he might as well have been living in another country. Most days he was lucky to figure out where his meals were coming from, let alone what his homework was. And he covered his misery in the couldn't-care-less attitude and cigarette-smoking armor of the kids like him. The ones who couldn't go home until their angry-drunk dads had passed out. The ones who had nowhere to study, or who didn't have what it took to succeed in school. The almost-dropouts, the almost-failing, the lost kids.

Until that one day when he'd finally gotten himself kicked out of school for good, and she'd offered him comfort and so much more. And he'd taken everything she'd given. And then pushed her away for both their sakes.

And now, when he'd come home a combat veteran, and possibly, finally, worthy of all that she was, he'd blown it. Because of the anxiety that had him grabbing at the things he could touch and see, like gallons of water and spreadsheets of numbers. Anxiety that had him tongue-tied in front of her, unable to give her the water she wanted or the apology she deserved.

He had to do something different. Had to figure out a way around the throttlehold the PTSD had on him. Because it wasn't just affecting him. It was hurting Lori, the girl he'd loved, who'd given him memories he'd held on to like a talisman during all the dark and fear-filled nights in Afghanistan, when he wasn't sure he'd make it back alive.

DR. HERNANDEZ KNELT over the heifer lying in the dry grass. The young cow was breathing heavily in the soft evening air. Wade could feel his breathing catch right along with hers.

"Did you check the papers carefully when you bought these gals?" the vet asked.

Wade racked his stressed-out brain, trying to picture what the seller had given him. It had been a hectic day. He'd injured his shoulder and Nora had handled the delivery. "Well, I know I got papers. And the seller said they'd had all their shots."

"Yes, but did he hand you a certificate from a veterinarian? Did you have a vet look them over before you accepted them?"

"No." He watched the doctor's brows draw together as he surveyed the rest of the herd. About a quarter of the heifers were standing around listlessly. "I guess I should have."

"Yup." The vet sighed. "It's okay, Wade. It's a pretty common mistake."

Dr. Hernandez wasn't much older than him, and Wade appreciated his blunt honesty. It was what he was used to after the army. "So I messed up. What can I do to fix it?"

"It's a respiratory illness. They probably never got their booster shots. It's treatable. You need to separate out the sick ones and give them antibiotics. And they're all going to need to be vaccinated. Come on over to my van and I'll get everything ready for you." He paused. "You know how to give them shots, don't you?"

He'd *read* about how to give them shots. He knew he should confess his ignorance, but he couldn't stand to have the doctor think he was an even bigger fool. "Yeah," he said casually. "That's not a problem." But then he remembered Lori's harsh words of advice. A rancher needed to face mistakes and fix them fast. These cattle depended on him. There was no room for pride here. "Actually, no, not really."

"Look," Dr. Hernandez said as he opened a box in his van. "I can show you really quick, but do you have anyone who can help you out? Maybe someone who can mentor you a bit? Cattle ranching is complicated—a lot can go wrong. And if too much goes wrong, it can be dangerous for you, for the animals and even for the consumer."

Wade watched the doctor measure out liquid into a glass bottle. He didn't relish folks around here knowing how little experience he had running a ranch. There was only one person he could possibly confess that to. And she'd called him a thief yesterday.

His sister had been right. He might need water, but he needed his neighbor even more. Lori was the smartest person he knew, and one of the most capable ranchers in the area as well. If he shared the water, she'd help him. She had to. He was desperate, and underneath her frustration with him, she was a generous person.

And maybe desperation was just what he needed to push him through the anxiety. To get him to finally say the things he should have already. Things like *I'm sorry*. And *I wish I'd acted differently.* "Yeah, I know someone," he told the vet.

"Great. Have him get over here as soon as possible. You'll need an extra hand."

Funny how the vet immediately assumed that Wade was talking about a guy. Lori probably had to be extra tough, trying to make it in a profession so dominated by men. Which would help explain why she'd been so tough with him over the water. Though he'd also been an insensitive, scared jerk. That would probably explain it better.

He remembered, suddenly, being a kid at school. How he'd almost never had a lunch with him. How Lori had always offered to share hers. She'd fed him just about every day for years. And then he'd turned his back on her when she came to him about the water? What the hell was wrong with him? How had he started making all of his decisions out of fear?

He turned to the doctor with a new resolve. "I've got someone I need to apologize to. And if I do it right, I hope she'll give me a hand around here. *She's* the best rancher I know."

CHAPTER SEVEN

JIM WALKED OUT of the barn with a cardboard shipping box and dropped it in the dirt at Lori's feet. She stepped back as a small dust cloud rose up.

"What *are* these contraptions?" Jim reached down and pulled out a yellow plastic crescent, holding it gingerly between two fingers.

Lori grinned at the ranch manager. "They're the calf weaners I was telling you about." She grabbed one and held it up for him to see. "This part hooks into the calf's nostrils. Then it can't nurse."

"Do you really think we need 'em?" Jim flexed the plastic between his gnarled fingers. "When your dad was here, we kept it simple. Cows in one pasture, calves in another. Split 'em up fast and got it over with. We didn't need these crazy-looking nose flaps."

Was it worth arguing? The last thing she wanted was Jim feeling like he'd been wrong all those years. "Ah, come on, Jim, they'll look cute!"

Jim shook his head and tossed the weaner back into the box. Lori studied his weathered face. Beneath his resistance she saw all his old kindness there. He wasn't trying to undermine her. He was just having trouble with change.

"The way you and Dad did it worked fine," she reassured him. "But there've been some studies lately, proving that stress during weaning is bad for cattle. They lose weight. Calves get sick."

Jim shuffled the heel of his boot in the dust. "I don't know what scientists have to do with ranching."

"With a weaner in place, a calf can't nurse, so it can stay with its mom while it weans. That keeps it calm when it suddenly can't drink milk. And since we won't separate the calves from their moms until *after* they're weaned, they don't fuss nearly as much once they're apart."

"They've always gotten over it pretty quick." He gave her a stubborn glare.

"Have they?" Lori tamped down her frustration and walked with Jim over to the fence where Dakota was tied. She pulled the strap on the mare's cinch tight, looping the extra leather into a knot.

"The calves do a lot of bawling and pacing during weaning," she reminded Jim gently. She untied Dakota and reached for the reins, slipping her boot into the stirrup. She was heading out to take a look at some of the weeds coming up in one of their eastern pastures. With the drought, more unwelcome plants were taking root.

Jim nodded slightly. "Well, sure, there was some of that."

From up on her mare's back, Lori tried one more time. "Last year Dad and I went to Reno for that seminar on calm cattle management, remember? This is the kind of stuff we learned. By making a less stressful environment for the cows and calves, we improve their well-being. And lower our workload and raise our profits."

A snide voice interrupted their conversation. "Why don't you just light them some nice candles and give 'em a massage?"

F off. Lori bit her lip to keep from saying it out loud. Seth Garner was such a jerk. She hadn't realized he'd been listening in.

The ranch hand sauntered over from where he'd been loading hay into a truck. He was smiling, but his face didn't hold the same kindness as Jim's. She'd never liked him much, but ever since she'd taken over the ranch, Seth had been grumbling about taking orders from a woman. Lori wondered if he lay awake nights, thinking of new ways to undermine her. He certainly was inventive about it.

He glanced at his watch as if noting the lost time between his quip and her answer. Lori swallowed. Why should she be nervous? This was *her* ranch. She saw Jim wink at her and remembered his advice from the other day. Dish it right back.

"Don't you have work to do?" She drew herself up extra tall in the saddle.

"I was just doing some work." Seth leaned against the rail, folding his arms over his chest and crossing his legs casually. "Following my boss lady's orders and loading that truck over there with hay."

Boss lady. The words dripped with sarcasm and puddled like murky water. Lori backed Dakota up a few paces so she could see Seth's face under his hat. She met the challenge in his eyes, but forced her voice into a tone way sweeter than she felt right now. "Well, thanks for getting that done. Now, I'm pretty sure they could use an extra hand cleaning up the floor over at the white barn. Since you're taking the hay down there anyway, why don't you take a shovel with you? You can stay and help them out."

Seth's cheeks paled except for some flecks of red on his cheekbones. "That's not my job."

"It's fall, Seth. We have a lot to get done this time of year and we've all got to do our part. Plus, I *am* your boss lady. So you'd best get started."

Seth's eyes bugged, and he stared at her, stuck without a snide comeback for once.

She turned Dakota to go, but Jim's soft voice had her pausing.

"Well done, there, Lori."

"Thanks," she murmured.

Jim picked up the box of calf weaners. "I'll just get started putting these on," he told her, his voice louder than usual, so Seth could hear. "Seems like weaning is gonna go a lot easier with you at the helm." He shot her a wink that Seth couldn't see.

Bless Jim. He might grumble and question the decisions she made in private, but he'd support her 100 percent in front of the others.

"I appreciate that, Jim," she said. "I'll be back to help out in a few minutes." She didn't have to look at Seth to know he was scowling. And that she'd scored her first real win in her struggle to take the reins of Lone Mountain Ranch.

She turned to go and spotted Wade leaning on the fence near the white barn, watching her intently. The last time they'd seen each other, she'd been yelling. Now he'd seen her go head-to-head with Seth. Well, at least he wouldn't have any illusions that she was the sweet young girl he'd left behind. She walked Dakota over to him, bracing herself for whatever their next confrontation would be.

He was wearing that old straw cowboy hat that made his dark eyes even more impenetrable in the shadows beneath the brim.

"Looks like you showed him."

She glanced at Seth, slouching back to his truck, radiating a bad attitude that she could feel from here. "I hope I didn't upset him *too* badly. He's just been giving me such a hard time. But now he looks angrier than ever."

"Hey, it's your ranch. Run it how you want. If he hates it, he'll leave and go work somewhere else, and you'll both be better off."

"That would be awesome. He hates having a *boss lady*, as he calls me."

Wade grimaced. "Well, keep an eye on him. If he doesn't come on board soon, fire him."

He seemed to come in peace, at least. So she teased him a little. "Listen to you, all managerial."

"I learned a thing or two leading a platoon." He sobered, took off his hat and looked right into her eyes. "But evidently I don't know much about being a good neighbor. I'm sorry I couldn't give you the answer you wanted about the water. I just needed time. And honestly, I was scared."

"Scared?" He'd always seemed so tough. It had never occurred to her that he was even familiar with that emotion. "What are you scared of?"

"Failing. I don't know what I'm doing with the ranch, and it makes me too careful about certain things and not careful enough about others. So with the water, I just balked. I didn't want to make a mistake that could cost me the ranch."

"Well, I know *that* feeling. Too well."

His mouth softened into a brief smile. "But I've realized that you were right. We should share the water."

Relief relaxed muscles she hadn't even realized she was tensing. She wanted to raise a fist and shout *hooray*, but she kept herself calm. "That's great news. Thank you."

"And I brought you something." He pulled a carrot out of his back pocket, the greens still on it, and held it up like a bouquet. "I would have brought apology flowers, but I knew you'd be working and there wouldn't be any place for them. This seemed better."

"It's perfect." He understood her, and it warmed her a little inside. She turned Dakota sideways and reached for the carrot, shoving it in the back pocket of her jeans. "I'll share it with Dakota later on, if that's okay."

"That's the idea."

It was her turn to apologize. Her horrible words had been eating at her ever since she'd stormed off his ranch. "I'm sorry I said so many rude things."

"I reckon I deserved it."

"Maybe a little…" She couldn't resist.

He acknowledged the teasing with a brief smile and rushed on. "But I hope you can help me with something."

"What do you need?"

He flushed a little. Swallowed hard. "Look, I'm new at this ranching thing. I mean, growing up, we had animals pass through, but mainly my dad was stealing them from one person and selling them to another, so they never stayed around long. I have no idea what I'm doing. Seeing your ranch running so smoothly… How do you do it?"

Wade asking her for ranching tips? Not what she'd expected when she'd seen him standing there. "Well, part of it is that I've been doing it forever and I studied it in school, and part of it is that I've been trying out some new management practices. As you can see—" she inclined her head slightly to where a group of men were standing around Jim with bemused expressions on their faces "—it's going over *really* well with the staff." Sarcasm couldn't mask her frustration.

"They may give you grief about it, but I'd bet deep down most of them are pretty impressed."

She swung down from Dakota, since evidently Wade was here for a long chat, and tossed the reins over the mare's neck so she could go get a drink at the trough. "I hope you're right. Those are calf weaners they're holding. Calves weaned with this method retain thirty percent more body weight because they're not panicked and pacing everywhere." Wade was staring at her, mouth slightly open, looking stunned. She flushed, realizing she'd probably stupefied him with her love of data. "I'm sorry. I can go on about this kind of thing for hours."

To her surprise, he smiled. A first since she'd seen him again. Dimples cutting into his stubbled cheeks, lines crinkling his dark eyes—it was all as knee weakening as she remembered.

"That's exactly why I need your help," he said.

She studied his eyes, trying to understand his meaning. Bad idea. They were too much for her—all dark and potent like strong coffee. Only they made her a lot more jittery than coffee did. "*My* help?"

"I know you've been angry at me. And for good reason. I shouldn't have dug my heels in about the water. And now here I am, asking for..." He paused, turning his hat in his hand. When he spoke again, his voice was quiet, but she could hear the edge in it. "Honestly, I'm desperate. I need to learn about ranching. When I got my first bunch of heifers a few months ago, I didn't know they'd need a booster vaccine..."

"...and they've got respiratory illness," she finished for him.

His eyes went wider. "You know your stuff. But I don't. The vet showed me how to give them shots, but it's just not going that smoothly. I was hoping you'd consider coming by and giving me a hand."

He was in trouble if he didn't know how to do such a basic task. But *help* him? As in, spend time with him? Lori turned to retrieve Dakota, who'd finished drinking and was starting to wander off, gathering her thoughts as she gathered the horse's reins. She wanted to be someone who helped her neighbors, but working with Wade wasn't a good idea.

"Look, if you can help me, I'll give you first pick when we make our irrigation schedule. I'll hire Bill Cooper, and you can set everything up with him so it suits your needs. But in exchange, I'm asking for your help. Teach me how to give the shots. How to handle the cattle well. I'm reading books all the time, but I have so many questions, so many gaps in what I know. I need a mentor, Lori. I need you."

Damn him, he made begging look noble—and sexy. And when he added first priority on irrigation to the mix...well, how was she supposed to resist? But mentoring meant *a lot* more time together. "I don't know, Wade. I'm happy to help out with the injections, but I'm new at running my own ranch. I honestly don't have much time. Isn't there someone else you can ask?"

"Who's going to want to mentor a Hoffman?"

There was pain and truth behind his words. She looked at him for a long moment. What he was proposing was dangerous. To her heart, to the regrets she tried hard to lock away so they wouldn't overwhelm her. But he was trying to make something of himself. Trying to prove himself. She understood that. She was *living* that.

"All right. We'll try it."

"Thank you," he breathed, relief written stark across his face. "I promise I'll take as little of your time as possible."

He reached over the fence and put a light hand on her shoulder. "I'm truly grateful, Lori."

He was looking at her like she was his guardian angel. His salvation. And then the reality of this, of *them*, tensed every muscle. How would he look at her if he knew what she'd done? With hatred? Disgust? Pity? Certainly not like this. "No problem," she muttered through clenched teeth. Ducking out from under his hand, she turned, put her foot into Dakota's stirrup and swung onto the mare's back. "I'd better get going. I'll come by later today."

He was studying her face, obviously puzzled by her sudden change in mood. Well, let him wonder. When you slept with someone and then disappeared, you lost your right to explanations.

"See you this afternoon, then." His voice was quiet, his reserve back.

"Yup" was all she could get out. She turned Dakota away, trying to breathe through the whirlpool of feelings. Regret, shame, old anger and the newest, unwelcome addition to the general chaos of her emotional life: excitement. This partnership meant they'd be spending more time together. And against all common sense, a part of her was happy about that.

CHAPTER EIGHT

CANCELING THE WATER truck was a huge relief. But driving onto Wade's ranch to help with the injections brought on a whole other kind of stress. How was she going to handle seeing him regularly? The rutted driveway jolted some sense into her. *You're a mentor. So just treat him the way you'd treat any other rancher in the area who needed some help.*

Ha. Maybe she could pull it off on the outside. She could talk cattle and keep it professional. But that wouldn't stop her insides from churning with nerves. Or keep her traitorous heart from noticing his beauty and remembering all the things she'd loved about him when they were young.

She parked her truck and grabbed her tool belt from the back, buckling it tight around her hips. Shoving her hat on her head to block the afternoon sun, she headed toward the dilapidated barn. Wade was around the side of it, leaning on the fence, staring at his cattle. They were a sorry lot. Listless.

He turned when he heard her footsteps, giving her a weak smile. "Thanks for coming. Here are my sick girls." He frowned and turned back toward the heifers. "I hate that my ignorance did this."

His ignorance. She had a lot of experience with the damage that could wreak. But he looked grateful, which put a pathetic sweetness onto his usually severe face. *No. No noticing sweetness.* "It's no problem."

He looked down at her waist. "You brought your tool belt? For injections?"

"We're not injecting yet. We're taking a look at your cattle chute first."

"What's wrong with my chute?"

"I don't know." She glanced around the run-down property. "Probably a lot. Trust me?"

"Sure. But I worked on the chute already. Take a look." He walked her over. She could see where he'd replaced boards and pounded in loose nails that could tear hide. Maybe a year ago she'd have said it was fine. Now she knew better. "Do you have any plywood?"

"Sure." He looked at her suspiciously. "Why?"

"If you want them to go in for injections calmly, we should board up the sides of your chute so they can't see out. Want to try it?"

"Lori Allen, Cow Whisperer. Is that what it says on your business card?"

Her own laugh surprised her. She had no idea he could be funny. "I don't have a business card. I just took a few classes."

"I'll get the wood." He headed off around the side of the barn, whistling. She tried to remember if he'd ever teased her like this, or whistled like this, when she'd known him years before. He'd been serious, hard and mysterious. That was probably why she'd been crazy about him. He'd been different. Opposite. A better kid than his brothers, but always teetering just on the edge of the dangerous cliff they'd plummeted down years before.

She'd been drawn to him, recognizing his softness and intelligence under that tough veneer during the rare opportunities they'd had to talk. And that wildness—that edge he walked—had been so compelling. Maybe because sometimes she wished *she* could do something a little wild.

Stop it. She wasn't here to think about Wade, or the past. She was here to look at his cattle chute. And she could see a few problems already. An old wire dangled from the barn eaves, right before the chute ended in the stanchion. A piece of corrugated metal had been nailed to a post for some reason. She jumped up onto the rail and pulled out her hammer, using the claw end to pry it off.

Wade leaned a few sheets of plywood against the chute. "Why are you worrying about that?"

"The sun is hitting it." The last nail popped out. "The glare can scare the cattle when they come into the chute. You have to remember that they're prey. Anything out of place frightens them."

Lori showed him how to nail the plywood sheets along the sides of the chute, and he got to work. She listened to the rhythm of Wade pounding nails as she made her way to the wire. Climbing up the side of the chute, she pulled wire cutters out of her belt to remove the dangling ends. A simple fix for a potentially big problem. She wished all her difficulties could be solved with a quick snip of her wire cutters. One small cut and Wade and his ranch would disappear. But the thought made her sad—she didn't want him to disappear again, which was why this was all way too complicated.

Shaking her head at her own foolishness, she went to help Wade, holding the boards steady while he nailed. It was the first time in years she'd been so close to him, their bodies almost touching. She could almost feel his muscles flexing under his flannel shirt as he drove the nails in. It wasn't possible. They weren't touching. But the strength of him seemed to emanate with a tangible force. Maybe this was why she'd never dated much. What guy had she ever met could match Wade in sheer masculinity?

She shifted position so she was still holding the board but standing as far away from him as she could. He must have noticed, because he glanced her way with a wry smile curling his full lower lip. "I won't bite."

Heat crept across her face. "I hope not," she retorted. "But just in case, maybe I should work on the next board." She turned away, grabbing a new piece of plywood and a handful of nails. It was better to work on her own section of the chute. Preferably one far away from Wade.

She positioned the wood and slammed the first nail in. She needed to be careful. Her heart had been trampled by this man, and here she was, ogling him the first moment they were alone together. She had to remember that all of the attraction she felt for him belonged to the stupid girl she'd been long ago. The woman she was now knew trouble when she saw it, and had the sense to keep her distance. Sure, she could notice he was good-looking. Who wouldn't? But she had to remember that it was like noticing a pretty desert wildflower or a nice view. It was easy on the eyes, but had no other significance whatsoever.

HE'D FORGOTTEN HOW sassy she could be. He liked it. He'd never met anyone like Lori—who could dish out smart comments and run a ranch and refurbish a cattle chute in half an hour. She had sweat on her face and dirt streaked across one cheek, and she was still gorgeous. And there was something about her in that tool belt. The old, worn leather, slung low on her hips, emphasized her curves there, her tiny waist above and the faded, fitted jeans below. But he didn't just admire how she looked. The sexiest part about Lori in a tool belt was the way she handled the tools with the confidence of someone who'd been using them all her life

He had to keep in mind that she was here because she was kind. The type of person who'd always try to help out a neighbor. And she was here because she needed the water in his well. Whatever he felt were just his feelings and had nothing to do with hers. It was a shame, but reality often was.

He walked over to where Lori was hammering in the last board. He held it steady for her, making sure to give her the space she obviously wanted.

"Ready to bring one through?" she asked, shoving the hammer back into her belt.

"Ready if you say we are." No way was he even going to pretend he was in charge. She was here to work her magic, and his job was to stand back and learn from the master. And that was okay. He had a lot to learn.

It was ridiculously easy to get the cattle through now that the chute had solid sides. Lori showed him how to walk just outside a heifer's flight zone, using small motions to guide her. Just enough to keep her moving, not enough to frighten her.

Once a heifer was in the chute, Lori demonstrated how to slide the needle below the skin to deliver the medication. She made it look easy. Her comfort with it, and her calm, clear explanations, soon had him relaxed enough to do it on his own.

The setting sun lit the paddock in a rosy glow, but they kept working. By the time they sent the last heifer back to the pasture and threw out piles of alfalfa in hopes of tempting their appetites, it was deep dusk. Wade walked Lori back to her truck. He didn't want her to go. Ever since he'd left the army he'd sought solitude, but it was easy to be in her company. She was so confident, making all the ranch chores that were new to him seem commonplace. For the first time he felt like he might have a real chance to make Marker Ranch a success. With her help, at least he wouldn't totally mess it up.

Plus, there was the total miracle that she was actually here with him. Beautiful, perfect Lori Allen. She was like a clear, crisp spring day. The kind you wanted to go on forever.

She'd always been that for him. An oasis where he could escape from his Dad's anger and conniving, cowardly way of life. When they were young she'd been the only person, besides Nora, who'd seen the good in him. Nothing much, just small gestures when their paths crossed at school. He'd kept her as his oasis—or maybe his haven—when he'd been in Afghanistan. When he'd seen so much bad that it seemed there wasn't anything good left in the world, he'd think of Lori. Remembering her smile, with her pink lips parting over teeth like pearls. Or the way she'd squared her shoulders and lifted her chin a little higher when something needed to be done. He'd picture her tenderness toward her little sister. Mostly he'd think about how she looked at him with dark blue eyes that seemed to hold a bit of the dusky mountain sky inside. And the way it had felt to spend a night in her arms.

Living with the prospect of death around

every corner put things in perspective. In long nights lying in his bunk, or on the ground when he was out on a mission, he'd had time to think about what he wanted in life. And he'd narrowed it down to three things. His family's ranch, time with his sister, Nora, and a chance to show Lori Allen the man he'd become. And for some reason, he was lucky enough that all three of those things might be coming true.

"Do you want to have dinner with me tonight?" The words were out before he'd realized he was going to say them.

"No."

He shouldn't be surprised. But her answer was so quick, so definite, that it stung. She didn't even need a moment to consider.

"I mean, no thanks, Wade." He could hear the apology and something else in her rushed tone. "Mandy's cooking. I wouldn't want to be rude and make another plan."

"It's no problem," Wade assured her, glad the deepening night hid the flush he was sure was on his cheeks. He wished there was a way to take the question back, because now it hung there, making things awkward when they'd been so good just a moment ago. "Thanks again for your help tonight."

"You're welcome." She shrugged. "Hey, I need that water."

"Right." He had to remember that this was a business arrangement for her. Not a friendship. That she didn't see him the way he saw her. She'd never needed him for an oasis or a haven or anything.

"So is it okay to have Bill start working on the well?" she asked. "I'll have his guys start laying the pipe down."

"Sure." Her eagerness to get started was one more reminder that her help today had been a simple trade.

She climbed lightly up into her pickup, and he closed the door behind her. The window was down. She leaned her forearm on the frame, gazing up at him. "Look, Wade. I'm glad things are a little better between us. I'm fine helping you out with your ranch, and I'm glad that we're solving the water issue."

She paused and he filled in the silence. "I'm glad, too."

"When you left Benson, you said some really hurtful things."

He winced at the memory. "I have wanted to apologize for them ever since."

She held up a palm to stop him. "Look, it was years ago. I don't need that. But I got hurt then. It was hard for me. And I don't want to go back there. I mean, I guess what I'm trying to say is that going to dinner…well, it would be too much."

"I understand." And he did. He'd hurt her. How could he blame her for wanting to keep that door closed between them? "I just appreciate you being willing to help me out like this."

She sat up a little straighter, reached for the ignition. "All right, then."

"All right." He wished she didn't look so relieved about this little chat. He wished he didn't feel so disappointed "Good night, Lori."

She smiled briefly. A little sadly, he thought. "Good night, Wade."

He stood there in the dark, watching her taillights rock back and forth as she navigated the pockmarked drive. Watched them until she rounded the corner and disappeared, taking the light with her.

CHAPTER NINE

LORI TUGGED AWKWARDLY at the dress her sister had insisted she borrow. The cool night air tingled on her skin as she and Mandy crossed the gravel parking lot behind the High Country Sports Bar. She was so used to her jeans, boots and a T-shirt that anything else just felt odd. Especially this dress, which was short, and pale blue and very fitted. Every time she looked down, she was a little shocked by all the cleavage it revealed.

Mandy had also blown out Lori's hair and styled it in relaxed curls, put makeup on her and added a nice bracelet. Lori's only contribution to her outfit was a pair of cowboy boots with pink roses up the sides that she rarely got to wear. No way was she going to put on the high-heeled sandals Mandy had pulled out.

She felt kind of silly, but Mandy had promised her that she looked gorgeous. And the stranger she saw when she looked in the mirror earlier *was* pretty. Lori could admit that.

But she so rarely dressed up, all that pretty seemed like it belonged to someone else.

Mandy gave her a nervous smile and pulled open the door of the bar. Music flooded around them. "Well, here we go!" she said in a bright voice. The kind of voice you'd use with children on their first day of school. Or when you were trying to talk yourself into the idea that something would be fun.

They made their way across the room. The dance floor was packed, and the bar was crowded at least two deep. "Why don't you go find Sunny and everyone and I'll get the beers?" Lori offered.

Mandy nodded and drifted off toward the tables. Lori made her way to the bar, getting jostled by people who were leaving with drinks, and jostled again as people who were taller than her pushed past. Even in her boots she barely made five foot four, and she was just about to resort to using her elbows on the ribs of the people pushing past her when a large hand closed over her shoulder. She started and looked up at a whole new version of Wade—his dark brown hair combed out, a black T-shirt stretched tight over his broad chest. He looked a lot different than the hot and dusty cowboy she'd helped out yesterday. He cleaned up well. Very well.

"You need some help?"

His words cut low through the music and rolled over her skin. It was a little hard to find her voice. "I can't get a drink. I'm too short."

"You're perfect." He looked startled at his own words. "I mean, you look great…the dress…" His eyes strayed momentarily down her body, then back. "You look amazing," he finished, and she realized he was flustered.

That was kind of nice. The unflappable Wade Hoffman was tongue-tied. Maybe Mandy *had* known what she was doing when she put together this outfit.

"Let me help you out here," he said and reached for her hand. His was warm and wrapped firmly around hers as he walked them past the people who had just cut in front of her. With his military stature and stern expression, they all moved aside for him without question. She followed in his wake, taking in his strong back, the way his jeans fit so perfectly over his…

"What are you drinking?" Wade's question pulled her eyes up to his face, and she saw the flash of amusement there. He'd caught her checking him out. Her skin felt warm, but she tried to play it cool. "Two pilsners, please."

Wade met the bartender's eyes over the heads of others and before Lori knew it, she had a bottle in each hand. "Anything else I can do?" His gaze fixed intently on her face as if her answer was all that mattered. Or maybe he was just trying really hard not to notice her cleavage again. It didn't matter. It was impossible to look away when his dark eyes were locked on hers, and she was grateful for the beers filling her hands. If they'd been free, she would have traced her finger along the sculpted line of his lip.

Enough. This was her being stupid around Wade Hoffman. That was just what she did. An old bad habit. "Can you see my sister from up there?" Lori had to stand on tiptoes and shout it into his ear—someone had turned the music up. The spice of his aftershave filled her senses. She stepped backward, bumping into someone behind her and almost spilled the beers.

"Steady there," Wade's hands were on her arms, making sure she had her balance. He kept them there while he scanned the room, and it felt good. Grounding. What would it feel like if he pulled her close? If she could just lean on him and let his strength hold her up. It had been forever since she'd had that luxury. "She's over there." He pointed to the back corner of the bar. "With a bunch of other women."

"Thanks, Wade." She stepped out from under his hand reluctantly.

"You're welcome."

It was her cue to walk away. But she didn't, because he was watching her as if he wanted to say more. And she was rooted to the ground because, deep down, she wanted to hear it. She had to remember that this moment was nothing. A quick little fantasy that had nothing to do with the reality of them. That no matter how nice this was, he was the guy who'd hurt her. Her worst mistake. The reason she'd tried so hard to avoid mistakes ever since. "Well, thanks," she said, raising the beer bottles vaguely in his direction.

"Anytime."

"Oh, good. Have fun tonight."

"You, too." He raised his beer in a small salute. "Come find me if you need someone tall."

"Thanks. It's always useful to have a tall friend." *Ugh.* Why couldn't she think of something better to say? She took a swallow of one of the beers. If she was going to be that socially inept, at least she should have some alcohol in her system to blame it on.

She made her way carefully through the crowd, trying not to spill any beer on Mandy's dress. Trying to get used to the idea that from now on she'd run into Wade in the local bar. Or in the grocery store. Or at town events. Thank goodness she didn't get out much, because she didn't *want* to run into him. She'd worked so hard, for so long, to put everything that had happened between them behind her. But the way her heart was pounding right now showed her just how unsuccessful she'd been.

LORI WAS THE most beautiful woman in the bar. The most beautiful woman he'd seen anywhere. Wade tried to focus on his game of pool and what Todd was telling him about the horse he was training. But his eyes kept drifting back to Lori over at her table, chatting with her girlfriends. What did she talk about when she wasn't talking about cattle?

She was a magnet for him. He'd noticed her the moment she'd followed her sister into the bar, and when he'd gotten over his initial jaw-on-the-floor reaction to the way she looked in that dress, he'd realized she'd needed some help at the bar.

And he'd practically sprinted across the room to be the one to offer.

But what had surprised him was how easy it felt. He'd always felt kind of awkward out at bars. He was too honest and blunt to be good at pickup lines, and he'd never mastered small talk. But with Lori's hand in his, her voice sweet in his ear with her drink order, he'd felt like he was right where he was supposed to be.

When he finished bungling his shot, he glanced up again and saw Lori out on the floor, laughing with her sister in a line dance. Everyone always said that Mandy was the pretty one, but to Wade she looked like Goldilocks—pale, simple and sweet. It was Lori who radiated beauty. She always had. There was so much life glowing from within her. With her wide, friendly smile, her deep blue eyes, her hair streaked with sunlight, she outshone any other woman on the dance floor.

He was used to Lori in jeans and a T-shirt. Tonight her cheeks were flushed, and that blue dress set off the gold of her skin. It showcased a lot more, too. And he wasn't the only guy in the bar who'd noticed. Not by a long shot. Envy coiled in his gut every time someone looked her way, which was pretty much every thirty seconds. All night she'd had attention—a few men stopped by her table, asking her to dance. He'd been happy she'd refused them all, but not surprised. That was Lori. If she was on a girls' night out, than it was all about her girlfriends. She wasn't the type to desert them just because some guy was checking her out.

"You know you haven't stopped staring at her all night." His future brother-in-law, Todd, elbowed him and handed him a new beer. "Why don't you just go talk to her?"

Wade took a pull from the bottle. "I already did. That's Lori, the one I told you about who helped me with the heifers."

Todd raised an eyebrow. "The one whose water you swiped?"

"I didn't swipe it. Not intentionally."

"You also didn't mention that she was gorgeous."

"No, I didn't. Because she's just a friend." She'd made that abundantly clear the other evening. Though maybe, just maybe, she'd felt something more between them over by the bar tonight. It seemed like she'd been checking him out a little. He hoped so.

"I don't get it," Todd said. "If you like her, just tell her."

Tell her what? That he'd always been crazy about her? Or that he was damaged? That war had turned him into a weakling who could barely hold it together in a noisy bar? "I screwed it up a long time ago. I don't think she's interested." Wade took another drink and then turned back to the pool table. "Come on, it's your turn."

Playing pool was simple. Better to stick with that than to stare at Lori. Sometimes he felt as if he'd been watching her like this, with this intense longing, his entire life. And as always, he had no idea what he needed to do to be worthy of her regard.

But he couldn't concentrate on the game. Lori was dancing again. Then he bumped into a few guys he used to hang out with in high school, so there were some back slaps and *hey, how you been*s. It was kind of nice to know that a few people seemed happy to have him back in town. When he glanced up, Lori was back at her table. Some guy was trying to talk to her, so Wade forgot his turn and then missed every ball, and Todd finally got fed up. "I'm finishing this table out solo," he said, removing the cue from Wade's hand. "And you're going to go ask her to dance."

"She's not dancing with guys. She's here with her friends."

"I'd bet she'd dance with you."

Wade took a swallow of his beer. Todd was so in love with Nora that he'd taken up matchmaking. "Nope. Not doing it."

"Yes, you are, because I'm sick of playing with someone who's so pathetic. You've been shot at. In a war. Surely compared to that, asking Lori to dance is easy."

Wade shook his head and downed the rest of his beer. "I've never asked a girl to dance."

Todd stared at him in disbelief. "Not even in high school?"

"Definitely not in high school. Didn't go to dances."

"Let me guess. You were the guy leaning on the truck outside the dance, a beer in one hand and some girl under your arm?"

"Sometimes. When I was trying to be cool." But he sure didn't feel cool now. In fact, just the thought of going up to Lori's table made him feel like the most gangly school kid ever.

"I've got two words for you," Todd said, leaning against the pool table and eyeing him speculatively. "Man up."

Todd was right. How had he turned into the guy hiding in the corner, too scared to talk to a girl? Wade set his beer down on a shelf along the wall and wiped his palms on his jeans. He squared his shoulders and turned to cross the room. And froze. Something was wrong. The guy was gone and Lori's friends were chatting and laughing, but Lori looked pale. Miserable. She drank the rest of her beer in one gulp, said something to her friends and all but ran out the side door of the bar.

Every instinct Wade had went into protective mode. Without a single conscious thought, he was on his way across the bar, pushing past others to get out the door and into the night. He had to find her. Had to make sure she was okay. Only then could he breathe again.

CHAPTER TEN

LORI GASPED, WELCOMING the night air into her body, trying to cool the burning behind her eyes, in her lungs, deep in her heart. She stumbled down the slope alongside the bar, desperate to get away from the chatter inside. Glancing around, she spotted a group of picnic tables under a shadowy stand of pines. The tears came before she made it to their sheltering darkness. And with them, a sense of bewilderment. How could something that happened so long ago still hurt so much?

"Oh God," she whispered, the weight of regret pushing her down onto one of the wooden benches. "Why did I..." The sobs didn't give her a chance to finish.

Her friends had been talking about babies. Sunny had two. Heather and Tina each had one. They were great moms, showing photos and trading sweet stories about their little ones.

She should have been happy for them. But all she could think about was the baby she didn't have. The baby whose tiny, barely there life she'd ended.

Seeing Wade again had cracked the walls she'd built around this pain. And all the innocent excitement of those new mothers had completed the demolition. It was there, glowing like plutonium in her mind, as poisonous as ever despite her efforts to contain it. She hugged her knees as the sorrow suffocated and the regret lashed, so merciless, so cutting. There was nothing she could do but huddle under the agonizing storm and gasp useless apologies—to herself, to God, to that tiny person who never got to *be* because she'd been too damned frightened to face what she'd done.

"Lori? What the hell? Are you sick?" Wade knelt before her, trying to get her to lift her head with strong hands that she pushed away, not willing to show him the wreck of her face. The chaos of her soul.

"Lori, *please*, talk to me. Are you okay?"

"Go away," she gasped, trying to stop the sobs, her whole torso heaving with the effort. He was the last person on earth she wanted here.

"Are you hurt?"

Always. She always hurt. Because this pain had lived inside her, corroding her heart, for years now.

"Lori?" He took her hands and pried them gently from her face.

"No. Don't look at me," she whispered, utterly broken, and now totally humiliated. "Leave me alone."

"Shh…" He handed her a bandana. "I can't leave you until I know you're okay."

She dabbed at the streaming tears, but there was no point. They weren't stopping any time soon. She buried her face in the fabric. "I don't want you to see me like this."

"Hey," he whispered, stroking her hair. "Trust me, I've seen a hell of a lot worse."

War. He'd seen war. He'd gone to serve his country. So brave, while she'd been the biggest coward. She sat and shook with grief and guilt.

He stayed, his hand in her hair slowly soothing until the worst of the shaking stopped. Then he moved quietly to sit down next to her. "I need you to tell me—did anybody hurt you tonight?"

She could hear the fear in his voice. And the fierce, protective note beneath it.

"No one." She pulled in a jagged breath. *Just me. I hurt me. And our baby.* "Oh God," she said again as the pain returned, throwing wild punches to her middle. She folded underneath it, collapsing on his shoulder, wracked by silent sobs.

"Lori… Honey…" She'd never heard Wade sound helpless before. Or so kind. He pulled her in with strong arms, cradling her to his huge chest and holding her tight, as if he realized that he was the only thing keeping her together. "Lori…" He murmured her name over and over, into her hair, into her neck, a plea for her to stop.

But how to stop, when there was no way for this pain to end? No matter how much she cried, or wished she could go back in time and make a different choice, she couldn't. What she'd done could never be undone. At the clinic the counselor had assured her that she'd feel better as time went on. But she never did.

Her tears had soaked his shirt. In a moment he'd ask again what was wrong. The thought sobered her and slowed her sobs just when she'd rather have kept crying and prolonged the inevitable.

He sensed the pause in the pathetic torrent he held in his arms. "Lori, please. There has to be a way for me to help."

"You can't help." All the tears had diluted her voice to a watery whisper.

"Can you at least talk about it? Tell me what's wrong?"

The dilemma she'd been facing ever since he'd come home was on her now. He'd tried to comfort her—how could she repay him with lies? But if she told him, this pain would be his, too. That wasn't fair. It had been her choice. He shouldn't have to live with the consequences.

She unballed the sodden bandana and dabbed at her face. Drew in a shaky breath of the cold, clean mountain air. Then another. "There's no point talking about it. It's something I have to live with. Something I did a long time ago."

"I might know something about that," he said, stroking her hair softly. "Living with ghosts."

Living with ghosts. A ghost. "It's not something you'll want to know." And then it occurred to her. What if she told him and he thought it was no big deal? Many people seemed to feel that way. But for her, that might be even worse than him getting upset.

He shifted, trying to see her face in the darkness. "What do you mean? Lori, we grew up together. You couldn't tell me anything that would change how I think of you."

Ha. "This will." She felt like she was about to jump off a cliff. And she had no idea what it would be like at the bottom. But he deserved to know.

"There was a baby," she said, forcing her voice out a little louder. Still not looking up.

Still taking the coward's way, huddled against his chest. So she felt it when he stilled.

"In the bar tonight?"

He was still innocent, thinking this was all about something simple in a bar. She was about to shatter that. "No... When I was inside the bar, my friends were talking about their kids. I couldn't stand it—couldn't deal with it. Because I got pregnant. Right at the beginning of college. And I...and I..."

How could she say it? How did you spit out something that felt unspeakable? "I ended it."

"Oh, Lori," he whispered, pulling her in closer. "Oh no." His hand in her hair started moving again, trying to soothe the unsootheable.

She waited. He'd struggled with math, but this calculation didn't take many skills. The deep breath, the harder thud of his heart against her ear, told her that he'd realized. "It was from us, wasn't it? From that night?"

She nodded, relieved that he'd guessed. But she knew that a nod wasn't what was owed here. "I'm sorry, Wade." Tears. How could she have any left? They slid down her cheeks in quiet rivers now. "I'm so, so sorry."

He didn't answer. Just held her. Breathing long, slow breaths that she could feel. He was trying to absorb it. The dawning realization she knew too well, as all the different things that her decision meant for him, for his beliefs, for his conscience, hit one by one.

But after realization would come reaction.

"I had no idea." He sounded stunned. "All these years, I had no idea."

"I called. No one ever answered. I couldn't find an email address for you. I had to make a decision." She pulled away from the warmth of his chest and scrubbed the soggy bandana over her face again. It was easy to remember her frantic search for him. The panic.

"Did you tell your dad? Or Mandy?"

"I didn't tell anyone. Until now."

"You went through it all alone."

A bitter laugh hiccupped out of her throat. "You made it very clear that you regretted what happened between us. After a while, when I couldn't find you, I just figured you didn't want to be found."

"I was such a jerk to you. It's a piece of my life that I wish I could undo."

Lori stared ahead of her in the dark. So weary she wanted to curl up and sleep right there on the picnic table. She'd always thought that telling someone, especially Wade, would help ease the pain. But the hurt was still there. Dulled from crying, but still there.

"I wish I knew what to say." Wade's voice

sounded hollow in the quiet night. "I wish there was some way I could help you. You're sad. And I—" he paused and cleared his throat "—I don't really know what to do. I'm just so sorry."

"That's why I didn't want to tell you." The words felt rusty and hoarse. "It was a long time ago, and there's nothing to do about it now."

"I'd rather know." He sounded more definite, at least about that. "I'd rather know than have you walking around alone with it. Thinking about it every time you saw me. And me not knowing."

But now it was all reversed. He knew, and he'd think of it when he looked at *her*. And she'd know he was thinking about it. The flicker of hope she'd had for them earlier tonight fizzled out, leaving a quiet desolation. "I think I need to go home."

"Let me drive you." Wade slid off the bench and stood, holding out his hand.

"I can have Mandy take me."

"I don't want to send you back in there to pretend that everything is fine. Let me take you. Send Mandy a text."

She'd never be able to pretend with her puffy, postcrying face, anyway. She pulled her phone out of her dress pocket and sent a message.

Wade helped her stand and kept an arm around her as he walked her gently to his truck.

On the way out of town he turned to her, his face lit up by the last streetlight. "I can listen, if you ever want to talk."

She couldn't face it—the pity she saw in his eyes now, or whatever other emotion might be there once he'd had time to let it all sink in. He might think less of her, and she couldn't blame him. "I doubt there's much to say." She stared out the window as the streetlights of town disappeared behind them and all she could see was a blur of black countryside. "But thank you for listening tonight."

She watched the darkness until the lights of her ranch came into view. He stopped his truck in front of her porch, and she slid out quickly, meeting up with him at the porch steps.

He took her hand in his and walked her to the front door, turning her there under the light so he could see her face. "I have regretted, every day, the way I treated you, way back then." His eyes were black and brimful of pain.

"And now you have something else to regret." It seemed impossible that she could feel more guilt than she already carried with her. But there it was.

"I do. And more to atone for. I abandoned you. I left you to deal with our consequences alone. I want to try to make it up to you. I'll help you in any way I can. Around your ranch…

with the water. Hell, you can *have* the water. All of it."

Payback wasn't what she wanted. "Don't do this. Don't let this change everything."

"But how can it not?" He looked at her helplessly. "I hurt you beyond what I can even imagine."

"Don't you see?" She could feel the tears starting again and willed them away. But they broke in her voice. "If you let it change things, you undo everything. All the effort I've put into moving on and trying to be okay with it. All the ways I've tried to prove to myself that something positive came out of that decision— that some grain of rightness came out of all that wrong."

He stared at her, and she felt sorry for him. He'd had a few minutes to take this in while she'd had years to wrestle with all the impossible dilemmas and what-ifs the abortion had created in her mind. She could see those questions in the light from the porch, clouding his eyes. Suddenly she couldn't stand seeing him like this.

Going on tiptoe, she reached up and put her hands behind his neck. Pulling him down, she kissed him hard on his startled mouth. All her need to ease the pain she'd caused and the moral burden she'd just added to his life was in the kiss.

He pulled back, his hands coming up to cradle her head, to weave into her hair. He studied her face with hooded eyes, and she saw what she was desperate to see. He was looking at her with passion. With desire. Which was much better than the pity and regret that had been there before.

He brought his mouth down on hers, seeking her with an intensity that resonated—as if there was some kind of solution for all of this sadness in the heat between them. Or maybe, hopefully, some kind of salvation.

And then he pulled back.

"Lori," he whispered and tilted his head to kiss her softly, on the mouth, on the cheek, on her forehead and back to her lips again. And it was still there, the heavy-lidded wanting in his eyes, the intent in the way he sought her mouth with single focus.

She'd been afraid that if he knew, he'd turn away from her, in fury or sorrow or disgust. But he was here. And even if he was sad, he wanted her with him. The knowledge was more healing than anything she'd imagined.

But this was Wade, and he'd desired her before. And then changed his mind. Once he'd had some time to think about what she'd done, he'd likely change his mind again. She couldn't go through that rejection twice.

She stepped back, putting cold air and porch light reality between them. "Thank you for helping me tonight. And I'm truly sorry to tell you such a horrible thing."

"I'm glad I know." He closed the distance she'd created and kissed her forehead gently. "I'm here for you now. I promise."

"You don't have to be. I'm okay. You don't owe me anything. Please don't let this change things for us."

He looked at her somberly, ran a soft knuckle down her cheek. "I don't know if I can promise that. I want to support you however I can. If that's a change, then I'm sorry."

She'd always handled her pain privately. She had no idea how to go forward sharing it with someone else. Especially not with the man who'd left her to face it all alone.

"Good night," she told him. And ducked into her house and shut the door, thankful for the barrier between them. She leaned on the old wood until she heard his soft good-night, his footsteps on the steps and the sound of his truck driving away into the night. She touched her fingers to her lips, conjuring the memory of his mouth on hers—an unexpected bolt of passion in a devastating night. She wanted to feel it again. Wanted to feel more. Wanted to go after him in her truck and beg him to stay the night.

But that would mean facing the fear that drove her. Tuning out the haunting whisper reminding her that she'd made a mistake with Wade once before, with dire consequences. How could she possibly be foolish enough to want to sleep with him again?

But she wanted to. She wouldn't, because she'd learned her lesson. But she really did want to.

CHAPTER ELEVEN

WADE TRIED TO focus on what Todd was saying. Something about the grant he was applying for. He was opening a sanctuary for wild mustangs and trying to secure funding for veterinary care. It was important stuff, and normally Wade would have been interested.

But normally he wouldn't have just found out about Lori's pregnancy. And the dilemma she'd faced alone, and the decision she regretted. He'd thought about her all week, in the same way he thought about battles, or guys he'd seen wounded. His mind went there for a moment and then skittered away. Because you could only absorb stuff that life altering in tiny doses.

He'd never thought much about abortion before now. He'd assumed that if he ever got someone pregnant, they'd raise the kid together. *And* he'd been really careful to make sure he never got anyone pregnant. Or so he'd thought.

Did he regret her choice? He sure as hell

hadn't been ready to be a father back then. But what she'd done didn't sit easily with him, either.

Guilt had colored everything this past week. Old guilt for being a careless kid who'd gotten her pregnant. For abandoning her back then—for shutting her out and leaving town. For making her go through it all alone.

And then there was the new guilt. Because he couldn't stop thinking about the way that night had ended. Their kiss. And how badly he wanted to kiss her again. He tried to remind himself that it hadn't been real. That they'd been seeking some kind of comfort after all that heartache.

The problem was that the taste of her, that intense connection, had felt pretty damn real, and it made him want more. But now wasn't the time to be thinking like that. Now was the time to figure out how to be a friend and support her, the way he should have in all the years between then and now.

It was a lot to take in and he was a mess. His brain was misfiring, and he couldn't focus on anything for long. It was the reason he and Todd were out riding this morning. A few days ago, when it looked like his heifers were feeling better, Wade had brought them up to his highest pastures to graze. He'd never thought to check the weather report.

A couple of days later, temperatures had started dropping drastically at night. And early this morning, rain on the ranch had meant snow sugarcoating the highest of the Sierra peaks. So here he was, collecting his small herd and bringing his heifers back down to the same pastures he'd taken them from just a few days ago. It was one more mistake in a growing list. His own inexperience was the most frustrating thing about resurrecting Marker Ranch.

He'd forgotten how fast the weather could turn here on the stark east side of the mountains. And he'd learned how a woman you cared about could swipe your decision-making abilities with a devastating confession and one mind-blowing kiss.

When he'd mentioned his idiocy with the heifers to Todd, his friend and future brother-in-law had offered his help. Because that's the kind of guy Todd was.

A guy who deserved to have his friend listen to him instead of wondering about Lori. She'd dropped a note in his mailbox, apologizing for crying all over him and saying she'd like to have some space for a few days. So he'd given her that. But a few days had turned into more than a week, and the truth was, he missed her.

Because alongside all the mixed-up feelings of kissing and sorrow and regret was the fact that they'd become closer since she helped him with the heifers. And he wanted more of what it felt like when she was nearby.

"You still with me?" Todd had turned in the saddle and was watching him with a huge grin on his face. "Man, you've got it bad... You disappeared into la-la land for a minute there. Or should I say, Lori-land?"

Wade felt himself flush. "Sorry, I guess I've got a lot on my mind today."

"Have you asked her out yet?"

"Who said anything about asking her out?"

Todd shrugged. "Well, from the way you couldn't stop staring at her in the bar, and the way you disappeared outside with her for the rest of the night, I just figured there'd be dating."

"Well, you figured wrong."

"But you *were* thinking about her just now."

"Nope." Wade didn't lie much. Almost never. For a split second he was tempted to confide in his friend. To ask him what he thought, or how *he'd* handle it. But it wasn't his secret to tell. So he'd have to get his head around this on his own. "Nah, I haven't asked her out. She was kind of upset about something that night in the bar. We ended up talking. And I said the wrong things, so I think she's kind of pissed at me."

Todd laughed. "Of course you did. We all say the wrong things. It's part of being a guy. Doesn't mean you shouldn't ask her out."

"Really? That's your dating advice? Ask someone out who's mad at me?"

"It worked with your sister."

"Not right away," Wade reminded him. "Believe me. I was there. I saw the whole damn thing."

Todd sighed. "Yeah, you're right."

"So what should I do, Romeo?" Wade asked. "What's your sage advice?"

"Don't give up," Todd answered. "Just be patient and be her friend for a while. She'll see what a stand-up guy you are."

Wade shook his head. He was pretty sure *stand-up* wasn't the adjective Lori would pick to describe him. "I wasn't great to her when we were young. I think that puts me permanently in the friend category. I doubt she'll change her mind."

"But I messed up with Nora when we were young. And we got through all that."

"You didn't mess up like I did," Wade admitted. He focused on their surroundings, the old fence line and the muted colors of the pasture beyond. Beige, gray, smoky green. Colors of plants tough enough to survive the unforgiving drought. Colors that suited his mood, because there'd been days lately when all he'd been doing was surviving. His mind was so damn unpredictable. And as a result, life was all about getting by. Taking the antianxiety meds, avoiding too much alcohol, trying not to overreact to loud noises or unexpected events, anything that might trigger the craziness that lurked inside his damaged mind.

Even if Lori could forgive him, she deserved someone better. Someone whole. "We're friends. And it's for the best," he said firmly. "We're sharing water. She's helping me on the ranch. We've got a business relationship, and I don't want to mess that up."

A sadness settled on him like low-lying mist. A sadness teetering on the depression he'd been fighting off every day since he left the army. He shoved it back—it reeked of self-pity. He'd screwed up with Lori and he had to face that like a man...and live with the consequences.

"How's JM doing?" Todd asked.

Wade gave the mustang a pat on his sleek neck, grateful for the subject change. "He's a good guy. Pretty steady. Hard to believe he was born in the wild."

"Born and raised," Todd assured him. "Glad he's working out for you."

"Well, I've had him about three weeks now, right? But it's like he's been on the ranch forever. He seems pretty content."

Todd nodded. "JM here is a pretty tough guy. He survived a lot of abuse at the hands of the Department of Range Management after they rounded him up. It took me a long time to get him to trust me."

"Well, he's good now," Wade said. "In fact, he's so relaxed these days, I can barely get him to go faster than a trot."

Todd laughed. "Sometimes you don't know what the horses are really like until they've been in a good home and have some time to realize that they're safe."

"Well, don't get me wrong. I like JM's personality just fine. But if I need him to do something quickly, I may be in trouble."

"Which leads me to something I wanted to ask you," Todd said.

"Fire away. Though if my sister wants me to wear a tux to that wedding of yours, the answer is no."

Todd laughed. "I'm pretty sure we're getting married on my deck. In jeans."

"Hallelujah." Wade grinned at his friend. "Bet you're relieved about that."

"One more reason your sister is the woman of my dreams. But getting back to my question…

I have more horses than I can handle right now, and I've got one that I think would be great for you. You could have him at no cost as long as you'll work with him."

"Work with him?" Wade echoed.

"He isn't trained yet. He's somewhat tame. He'll let me touch him, put a halter on and lead him a little, but he's never been ridden."

Wade tried to think of a polite way to say *hell no*. "I wouldn't know what to do with him."

"I'll help you."

"Why do you want *me* to do it?" Wade didn't know the first thing about training a horse, and when added to the long list of all the stuff he didn't know about ranching, it felt a little overwhelming.

"Desperation. We haven't secured the new land for the sanctuary yet, and my property is getting really full. I have more horses than I have time to work with. And I have a feeling about this one. He's skittish, but he's smart. Above-average smart. I think he could be great at working cattle someday."

"With the right trainer," Wade countered, feeling the anxiety spiraling in his chest. "Not with someone like me, who has no idea what he's doing."

"But you're great with JM. And I'll advise

you every step of the way. Will you take him? Just try it?"

It was crazy to say yes. Here they were, paying the price right now for his ignorance with cattle. It didn't seem fair to put a half-wild horse at his mercy as well. But Todd was family, almost his brother by marriage. And ever since they'd met, Todd had been there for him.

Plus, Wade had seen the wild mustangs captured by the Department of Range Management. The conditions the animals lived in were horrifying. Training a mustang, helping it fit into its new life, was a small way to help. It would feel good to do his part, and he could use all the good feelings he could get.

And he had time for it. Especially now that Lori was avoiding him. "Okay, I'll try it," he said.

Todd's grin was infectious. "I know you'll be great with him."

Now he was embarrassed. Todd was a heart-on-his-sleeve kind of guy, and Wade was ex-military. "Does he have a name yet?"

"Nope. I thought maybe you'd like to name him."

Wade looked at him, startled. "How did you know I'd agree to take him?"

"Because underneath all your thick army-ranger skin, I know you're a total softy. I watched your face the day you saw the mustang holding pen."

"I think that was just sweat, bro." Maybe he'd teared up a little. But that didn't mean he had to admit it.

"Well, whatever it was, you'll need another horse around here, anyway."

And then it hit Wade what his friend was really up to. "You're trying to fix things for me aren't you?"

"What are you talking about?" Todd pretended to look surprised, but Wade saw the spark of humor there. Todd was always trying to save the world and everyone in it.

Wade was onto him. "You've read one of those articles, haven't you? About how ex-soldiers get a dog and suddenly their PTSD clears up and they're all happy again."

"It works with dogs," Todd countered. "Why not mustangs? And by the way, you should get a dog, too."

Wade shook his head in admiration. "You just don't give up, do you?"

"Nope!" Todd's wink was completely unapologetic. "Not when I have a good idea. We might rescue these animals, but in the end, *they* rescue *us*."

"Or trample us because we have no idea what we're doing."

"Not gonna happen. Put me on speed dial. How about I bring him by on the weekend. Maybe Saturday morning? Do you have time?"

It was a courtesy ask. They both knew Wade had no social life. The ranch was the only thing on his agenda. "That would be fine," he answered.

They rode in silence for a moment while Wade tried to picture himself training a wild horse. He couldn't. He'd just have to trust that Todd would show him the way.

"Hang on." Todd pulled his horse, Edward, to a halt, and JM stopped, too. "Look at your fence." He sidestepped Edward off the trail, and Wade saw it. A post, the wood gray and mottled with lichen, had been pushed over. The wire had snapped out of the rusted staples that used to hold it. Tufts of beige hair were caught on the barbs.

"I've got cattle out, don't I?" Wade stared at the trail ahead, but the soil was too dry and compacted to show hoofprints.

"Looks that way." Todd carefully guided Edward to the other side of the tangled mess. "The grass isn't too trampled around here. I'd guess you have one, maybe two out, is all. Let's head for the gate. We'll get the remaining cattle down to the ranch first. Seems like it's most important to get as many as possible sheltered from the cold before you go after your strays."

It was a relief when they caught sight of the heifers grazing in the pasture near the gate. A quick head count proved that Todd had been right. Only one of his girls had gone missing. At least she hadn't taken the rest of the herd with her. "Let's go ahead and bring them down," he told Todd.

"I've got to get going once we get them back on the ranch. I'm expecting a big delivery at the repair shop this afternoon. Gotta keep my day job going."

Wade felt his hopes sink a little. "No problem. I'll head back up on my own."

That knowing grin was back on Todd's face. "Lori's supposed to be helping you out, right? Isn't that your deal? Give her a call. A nice ride through the woods, looking for missing cattle…it'll be downright romantic."

"Dude, stick to rescuing horses. Matchmaking doesn't suit you."

Todd laughed as he turned Edward downhill to start collecting the heifers. The guy was downright giddy now that he was engaged to Nora. Wanting everyone else to overcome their troubles and waltz off into the same happily-ever-after that he was living in.

Wade thought again of Lori crying the other

night. They were miles away from happily-ever-after. But as a friend, he could offer her a ride in the mountains. It would give him a chance to make sure she was okay and maybe help them find a way forward now that this strange, sad connection was out in the open between them. And no, he wouldn't think about that kiss. Not at all.

CHAPTER TWELVE

MOST OF THE TIME, Lori figured it was best to face a problem head-on and get it over with. But when her phone screen lit up with Wade's name, she touched Decline in a moment of pure cowardice.

Ever since her confession that night at the bar, she'd been doing all she could to avoid him. There were just too many layers of misery there. Embarrassment for sobbing her heart out all over him. Regret because telling him had been a bad decision. The information would always be there now, lurking between them. He would see her differently—a living reminder of a horrible mistake.

And then there was the kissing. Another bad idea. Because those kisses wouldn't go away. They kept popping up from her memory at random times, bringing heat and longing with them. The past she shared with Wade was already so complicated. Why did she have to kiss him and make the present complicated, too?

So she'd stayed on her ranch and kept herself

busy for over a week now. It was easier than trying to figure out how they were going to navigate the strange and uncomfortable connection between them.

In her more panicky moments, she wondered if perhaps there was a way to never see each other again. Maybe they could coexist on neighboring ranches and share water, but never actually come into contact. She pictured herself sneaking up to the well in the middle of the night to switch the irrigation line. Ridiculous. She had to grow up and face the consequences of *all* her choices. Whether it was the pregnancy years ago, or a kiss a week ago.

So she'd called him back, and said yes when he asked for help. Which meant that at the end of a long day, with her emotions tied in knots, she was climbing a mountain with Wade, looking for his lost heifer.

The path Lori and Dakota followed meandered through stands of pine on the edge of an enormous open meadow. Wade was riding JM somewhere along the other side. Just as the trail turned back into the meadow again, Lori saw tracks in the soil. She jumped down from Dakota's back to examine them more closely. Cloven and way too big for a deer. Wade had been right. The heifer *had* come this way.

A rustling in nearby shrubs had her turning in relief. She'd grab the heifer and bring her down, and get home in time to knock a few more chores off her list before dark. She reached for the coil of rope hanging from her saddle horn and headed toward the noise. A loud snuffle stopped her in her tracks. That wasn't a sound she'd ever heard from a heifer.

Turning quickly, she grabbed Dakota's reins so she wouldn't run off. With a snap of breaking branches, a black bear lumbered from the bushes just a few yards away from them.

Oh no. She'd forgotten how big they could get. Dakota snorted and danced at the end of the reins. Lori went with the mare's instincts, backing them both away along the trail into the meadow.

The bear eyed them, swinging its head to catch their scent. It took a step closer, and Lori's heart slammed into her chest. The bear was too interested. She moved closer to Dakota.

The bear went up on its hind legs, sniffing, trying to get a read on whether or not she and Dakota were dinner. Suddenly she remembered what to do. "Bad bear!" she yelled, still moving slowly backward with Dakota. But now the mare had decided she'd better run and was hauling on the reins, stomping, doing her best to leave Lori in the lurch. Lori clung to the reins. "Get out of here, bear!"

Dakota was frantic and circling when the bear went down on all fours. Was it getting ready to charge? Lori made a snap decision not to stick around and find out. Throwing the reins over Dakota's neck, she tightened them, shoved her foot into the stirrup and vaulted onto Dakota's back. Miraculously the mare stayed still long enough for Lori to reach the saddle. The bear watched them with what seemed like a bemused expression. "Go on, bear!" she screamed at it.

The bear didn't budge, so she gave Dakota her head, leaning low over the saddle horn as the mare spun around and charged up the path. They covered a few twists and turns of the trail in moments. Glancing back over her shoulder, she was relieved that there was no sign of the bear. Still, she wouldn't slow the horse until she was sure there was more distance between them.

After a few minutes, Dakota seemed satisfied that they'd escaped the threat. She slowed easily to a walk at Lori's signal, blowing hard, catching her breath. Lori caught her breath, too. She'd seen bears before, but never that close, never where she could look right into those beady dark eyes and see a life so different from hers.

Over the thud of her own heart, another

sound penetrated. A plaintive moo coming from the meadow. She turned Dakota toward the sound and let her pick her way carefully out of the pines and into the dry grass. Down the hill she saw Wade and JM riding behind the wayward heifer. Wade was driving it across the meadow toward the trail Lori had ridden up on. The trail with the bear.

Lori urged Dakota into a jog to close the distance between them. It wasn't that difficult, since the heifer seemed intent on grabbing as much grass as she could before she was marched back down to the confines of the ranch. "Wade!" she called, relieved when he looked up.

"I found her," he called. Then, as she came closer, "What are you doing so far uphill from me? I figured I'd catch you on the way back down the trail."

"There's a bear!" She pointed to the woods, at a fallen tree she recognized. "Over there, back under the pines, on the path. We ran!"

"You met a bear?" He brought JM closer, and she could see the deep line of worry between his brows. "Are you okay?"

"A little shaken up, but we're fine." Now that it was over, she felt a little silly. People met bears all the time around here. It wasn't a big deal.

"Why didn't you call for me? Why didn't you ask for my help?"

She looked at him sharply, surprised by the anger spiking his voice. "Because I didn't need it. I just yelled, waved my arms, the usual."

Wade took a deep breath as if trying to steady himself. "You could have been hurt. And I would have been just across the meadow, and I wouldn't have known."

"I was okay."

"*This time* you were." He scowled at her, his fingers tapping restlessly on the reins. "I just don't get it. I know you're trying to prove to the world that you're tough. But this is *me*. You can ask for help. I *want* to help. I would have helped with that bear."

"You wouldn't have heard me if I had called. Did you hear me yelling at it?"

"No." His glare was sullen.

"So back off. I scared the bear away by myself. You should be proud that you know such a bear-savvy person."

He looked away, in the direction of the bear, the strong line of his jaw set at a stubborn angle. "You can turn to me when you need help."

And then it hit her. "Oh." She let what they were *really* talking about sink in. "You're talking about my decision. Back then." Disappointment settled leaden hands on her shoulders. "You're angry about what I did."

"No," he said quickly. The late afternoon sun gilded his face, and she could see the depth of emotion in his eyes. "I'm not angry. But I can't stop thinking about how you did it alone. I just keep wishing that I'd been there for you. So yeah." He smiled faintly. "Maybe this isn't really about the bear."

Here it was. The judgment, the admonition that she should have done things differently. She didn't need it from him. She'd had plenty of it from herself, on a daily basis, for years now. "I did it alone because I had to." Her voice was rising but she didn't care. "Let me see if I can recall your exact words that morning after we'd had sex. There was the part where you told me it was all a mistake. That was uplifting. And then the bit where you said you could never care about me the way I cared about you. That was especially nice to hear, by the way…"

"I was a total jerk," he said quietly. "I'm not denying it. But for what it's worth, I said those things because I *did* care about you. Too much. I always had. But the way I felt, and the way I could see that *you* felt—it scared me. We were so young. I'd been kicked out of school and I was moving away. I knew I wasn't good enough for you. I thought if I pushed you away, made you hate me, it would set us both free."

"And what gave you the right to decide that for me?"

He grimaced. "I know it was wrong. But I never understood it—why you were always so good to me. I was a loser Hoffman with a bad attitude and a hundred-pound chip on my shoulder. You were class president, cheerleader, 4-H champion… Hell, Lori, you were *everything*, and you just got smarter and better every year of high school. It was crazy that you liked me the way you did. How could I let those feelings slow you down? I knew that you could do better than me. That you'd move on to some good, wholesome guy if you thought I didn't care."

"But that didn't happen."

"I was wrong about a lot of stuff." He was quiet for a moment, watching the heifer graze. "I just wish I'd known. I feel so horrible, so guilty, that I wasn't there for you."

She didn't know how to talk about this. It was one thing to have her own regrets and to have wrestled with them for almost a decade. It was another to listen to his. They sat on their horses in silence, watching the heifer eating.

Finally Wade spoke. "I keep thinking about

it. What I would have done if you'd called me. I like to believe… I have to believe that I would have been on the next bus to you. That I would have done anything I could for you."

Her voice shook a little, but she managed to steady it. "There was no good answer for what to do."

"But maybe I could have helped you find the best answer for you. For us."

"Maybe." She shook her head doubtfully.

"I could at least have held your hand."

"And what if I'd decided to keep it? Would you have raised the baby with me? Become a teenage parent? If we'd done that, you would never have joined the army and done what you did for our country."

He looked ill for a moment. "I'm not sure that would have been such a bad thing. The army didn't get me very far."

"How can you say that?" She stared at him in shock, seeing the soldier in every part of him. "You're different. You're grown. You're a man." She stopped before she embarrassed herself with adjectives she'd regret.

"You don't think having a baby would have grown me into a man?"

"Ha. No. I think there are about a billion examples out in the world that prove that having a baby is not an experience that magically grows men up."

He smiled ruefully at that. "I guess you're right there. My own father being one of those examples."

"You can't fix this for me," she told him softly. "*I* made my decision and *I* live with the consequences. Maybe your decision would have been different. Maybe you being with me would have made my decision different. But it's all just useless wondering now. And it gets you nowhere. Believe me, I know that firsthand."

He was silent, running his fingers through JM's messy mane, obviously thinking about her words. Then he looked up, his expression soft with worry. "Are you okay?"

"I don't know," she told him truthfully. "Sometimes, sure. But other times, like sitting with all those new moms in the bar last weekend?" She put her hands to her flushed cheeks. "You saw me. Definitely not okay."

"You wish you'd done something different."

"Yeah," she said, feeling the old knots wind again in her stomach. "I regretted it the moment it was over. The moment it was too late." It was the first time she'd said the words out loud. They hung there in the still, clear autumn air. She could almost see them, and she stared in wonder at their stark sadness.

"I'm so sorry, Lori."

She straightened in the saddle, forced her shoulders square. "Look, it's done. I don't want you feeling sorry for me. I don't want your guilt or pity. I'm sad sometimes. I have regrets. But everyone has stuff they're sad about, right?"

He nodded slowly, still watching her intently. "I don't pity you, not like you're thinking. You're strong, Lori. So strong. You always have been. I saw how you carried your family after your mom died. You became the heart and soul of your family."

She stared at him. How had he seen so much? She'd walked around pretending everything was okay, but she'd been terrified. She'd never felt so lonely. It had been one of the reasons she'd run straight into Wade's arms when he'd finally opened them. A chance for connection, for emotion, for a living, breathing body to reassure her that she was still alive.

"And you're right," he continued. "Most of us have some kind of sadness in us. My family might not have died, but I lost my parents and my older brothers to all their poor choices. And there are other kinds of sadness, too..." He looked away. The heifer had moved several yards off while they spoke, and he nudged JM to walk around to the other side of her. With a gentle wave of an arm, he brought her closer to Lori again. "I just want you to know that I get it. That I might not know *exactly* what you went through, but I know loss."

Tears were starting at his unexpected kindness, and she didn't want them.

"We'd better get back." She urged Dakota closer to the stray heifer, who took a few reluctant steps, then stopped to glare at her with doe eyes and about a pound of dry grass sticking out of her mouth.

Wade had the sense to let the topic go. He swung his rope gently at the heifer's hindquarters to get her started. They rode in silence back to Marker Ranch, picking their way down the steep slope. By the time Lori had Dakota wiped down and loaded into her horse trailer, the heifer was back in the pasture munching on its evening hay, totally oblivious to the havoc it had wreaked upon Lori's afternoon.

Wade was leaning on the fence, watching his cattle. Lori walked over to say goodbye, but it was so peaceful—the heifers home safe, the sound of their chewing, the quiet light at the end of the day. So she leaned her arms on the rail next to him and pillowed her chin on her forearms, mirroring his posture.

She meant to watch quietly, but the words came tumbling out. "Maybe I should have tried harder to find you. I was lost. Confused. I felt this pressure to get through school fast. To do well there. My dad wanted to leave the ranch and start again somewhere else. But Mandy... well, it seemed like she was going to need to stay on the ranch. And I knew—I'd always known—I wanted to be a rancher. So Dad and I, we made a plan for him to work maybe ten more years. Just long enough that I'd be ready to take over."

"That's a lot of pressure," he said. "To have your life all planned out so young."

"Maybe it was. When I found out about being pregnant... I panicked. All I could think was, how could I have a baby on my own? During college? I just couldn't figure out how to make it all work. I was scared, and I think I was trying to fix things for my dad, for Mandy. Maybe even for my mom, in some weird way."

"You made the best decision you could. Maybe it's not the one you'd make now, but your choice makes sense to me."

"Then why does it feel awful?"

He swallowed, and she recognized his expression for what it was. He was holding back tears. "There was no good choice. Maybe that's why it's hard to find peace with it."

"I was doing okay with that, you know, until you came home. But seeing you again... it brought it all back for me, I guess."

"I understand how that would happen," Wade studied her carefully. "I hope, going forward, I can be a help to you and not such a burden."

"You're not a burden," Lori answered quickly. "I don't know what you are, but you're not a burden."

"Then let me know how I can help."

It was harder when he was sweet. She'd never have imagined she'd see Wade like this, swallowing tears. It made her own well up. They were always too damn near the surface, anyway. And then it dawned on her: she did need help with something. A job that had been sending waves of panic through her every time she thought about it. "Are you serious about helping me?"

He nodded, looking more hopeful. "I am. What do you need?"

"The Harvest Festival is coming up. In town. And I volunteered to organize the rummage-sale booth for our church. Yesterday I got a call that someone donated five huge boxes of baby clothes and a bunch of nursery furniture. I'm dreading it. But it's my responsibility to deal with it."

"You want me to do it?" The look of discomfort on his face would have been comical except she knew she was asking a lot, given what he'd so recently learned about her pregnancy.

"Not on your own. Come with me? Help me sort it and price it?"

"Sure." He swallowed hard. "Of course I will."

"Can we do it tomorrow night? It's at the Lutheran church up on the hill above town."

"Yeah." He looked worried.

"You don't have to. No point in both of us being upset."

"No, I'll do it. I'm happy to," he assured her.

"I'll be in the parish hall around seven. Everything is being stored in there."

"Can I bring beer or something? Or is that bad at a church thing?"

"It's just you and me. I was thinking whiskey. And loud music. Everything is better with loud music. I don't think there's anything else going on at the church on a weeknight."

Why did his smile still have the power to warm her? Even when they'd been dealing with so much sadness. Maybe all this talking had actually done them good. Maybe they were becoming friends.

"Okay, then," he said quietly. "I'll see you there. Don't worry. We'll get it done."

CHAPTER THIRTEEN

"THE NEXT TIME someone asks for a volunteer, I will run the other way," Lori told the heavy cardboard box as she shoved it away from the wall where it had been stacked. She heaved it into her arms and staggered over to one of the folding tables she'd set up, her footsteps echoing in the empty parish hall.

Pressing the button on her iPod, she let the music rip. Miranda Lambert might not be Wade's brand of country, but he wouldn't be here for a few minutes. She'd come early, needing a little time to gather her thoughts before he arrived. She felt guilty for asking him to do the job she'd signed up for. But it had been such a relief when he'd said he'd deal with the baby things.

Her plan tonight was to sort out all the clothes by gender and size so she would know where everything was on the morning of the sale. She pulled a faded men's flannel shirt out of the box and fastened the buttons, trying to ignore the strange fluttering in her stomach.

There was no place for flutters here. She and Wade were friends. They'd talked about all the old hurt, and they could finally move on. Except now Lori had a new problem. Leaning on the fence with Wade, talking so intimately, seeing him so emotional and intent on making things right, had stirred that part of her heart he'd always held, reminding her that maybe she didn't want to be just friends.

"Hey."

Lori dropped the shirt, whirling around to see Wade at the door. He was wearing a clean pair of jeans and a faded black army sweatshirt. Her pulse kicked up another notch. "You startled me."

"You looked like you were lost in thought."

She flushed. What would he do if he knew what she'd been thinking about? Probably run away fast. He was here to help her because she'd asked. Because he felt obligated to say yes after finding out what she'd been through. She had to keep that in mind when her thoughts ran toward things like kissing him. Which they did when he was leaning on the door frame, looking as good as he did.

He held up a six-pack of beer. "Want one?"

"Sure."

He came toward her, and she tried to remind herself that it was just Wade. She'd known him for almost her entire life. But her nerves weren't getting the message. He set the beer on the table by the iPod. "Nice music," he said, and she saw the glint of humor in his eyes.

"Too girly for you?"

"Hey, I was raised by my sister. I can take it."

It was strange how she knew the big stuff about him. His family history, his attempts to get the ranch going, their shared trauma. But she didn't know much about his everyday life. "What would we be listening to if this was your iPod?"

He grinned. "Not Miranda. Classic rock and classic country, mainly."

"Old school, huh? Let me guess. Johnny Cash? Willie and Waylon?"

"You got it." He twisted the cap off and handed her a bottle.

"Pilsner," she said, recognizing the familiar label. "Thanks."

"It's what you ordered at the bar, right?"

It was a small thing, but she liked that he'd remembered. "Yup. I don't like my beer any darker than this."

"No Guinness?" he teased.

"Bleah." And then she realized what she'd said. "Oh, wait, do you like it?"

"Occasionally."

"To each their own," she said, flushing a little. "I guess I don't know much about you."

"Strange, isn't it? But we've got all night to learn." He pointed to the boxes stacked in a far corner. "I take it the baby stuff is over there?"

"Yup."

He went over to grab a box, and she couldn't help but admire the ease with which he lifted a huge carton that she would have had to drag across the floor. The guy was strong.

He set the carton on another table and pulled out a baby blanket. "Well, here goes nothing. What do you want me to do with it all?"

"Sort it by size? And by boy or girl or stuff that could go either way like yellow or green? And maybe make separate piles for the blankets and bedding."

"Will do." Wade took a gulp from his beer and set it down next to him. She watched him fold the baby blanket with exacting care.

"It doesn't have to be perfect," she advised, while he smoothed out the corners and admired his handiwork.

He grinned and held the meticulously folded blanket out for her perusal. "Army, remember? They drill this kind of stuff into you."

"Were you in any particular part of the

army?" She glanced his way in time to see him flinch a little.

"I was a ranger."

"That's a ton of training, isn't it?"

"A fair amount, yes."

It explained so much. His composure, his strength. "And you fought in Afghanistan? Doesn't that mean you were going into really scary places?"

"Sometimes." He wasn't looking at her anymore. All his focus was on the blankets he was folding so carefully.

"I'm sorry. We don't have to talk about it if you don't want to."

He glanced up then, looking relieved. "Thanks. Maybe some other time. Weren't we going to learn all the little stuff about each other?"

"Sure." She pulled out a big pile of clothes to hide her nervousness. This felt like a date all of a sudden.

"Okay, so, my turn to ask. Beer or wine?"

"I have to choose?"

She must have looked as dismayed as she felt, because he burst out laughing. "Okay, she likes her booze."

"Sure. You?"

"Beer. In moderation."

They folded for a few moments in silence. Then Wade asked, "Read or watch TV?"

"I feel like I should say read. But honestly, Mandy and I are addicted to a bunch of shows. You?"

"Lately I've been reading a lot. Westerns, mysteries, stuff like that."

She thought about him reading. Lying in a hammock under a pine tree with a book. It suited him. "Vacation in the mountains or at the beach?" she asked.

Wade shook his head. "Haven't taken too many vacations. Once when I was on leave, I went home to South Carolina with a friend. It was pretty nice. So I might say beach."

That's right. His childhood hadn't included perks like vacations. Or food. Or love. "I haven't been to the beach much, either," she said. "But my dad's living by the ocean in Florida. I hope I can get down there and see him sometime soon."

"Is he happy? Giving up ranching?"

"He likes Florida. And I think he might be in love." Wade looked at her in surprise, and she went on. "Mandy and I sent him on a cruise to kick off his retirement and get him to do something fun for once. And he met this woman and they had some kind of shipboard romance. She owns a couple of gift shops on Sanibel Island in

Florida, and he'd been dreaming of a life there. So he moved to Sanibel and they're dating."

Wade shook his head in disbelief. "Your dad was a rancher through and through. I don't think I ever saw him without a truck or a horse. It's hard to imagine him under a palm tree in some Bermuda shorts, selling trinkets to tourists."

Lori giggled. "I know! But that's what he wears now. And he loves it. Says he did the right thing, getting a new start." She reached into her purse and pulled out her phone, scrolling through until she found the photo she was looking for. Her dad holding some fruity drink, ocean and palm trees in the background. She handed it to Wade. "See? Proof that it's real."

He studied the photo. "Well I guess people really can change." He handed it back to her. "He looks happy, Lori. That's good news."

She set her phone back in her purse and grabbed some jeans to fold.

"Coffee or tea?" Wade asked.

"Coffee, of course."

"One of those latte things or real coffee?"

She grinned. "I'll take one of those latte things when I can get it. But we don't have espresso on the ranch. And I'll bet I don't even have to ask you what you like." She stepped back and crossed her arms, pretending to scrutinize him. "Coffee. Black," she announced.

"And you're psychic, too." He grinned. "Skiing or snowboarding?"

"Skiing. You won't see me strapping into one of those ankle-breaking boards."

"It's fun! I'll teach you if you want."

She pretended to think about it for a moment. "No, thanks."

He laughed. "Noted. Dating?"

Lori froze. Did he want to ask her out? *Don't read into it. He's making small talk to take your mind off all this baby stuff.*

"Single," she said. "Very single. You?"

"Single," he said, regarding her solemnly. "Very single."

"Right," she said. "Great." Cheeks burning, she grabbed a new heap of clothing from her carton and sorted it into piles. For a moment she'd hoped that he'd ask her out. Which was stupid, because it wasn't even what she wanted. Wade represented everything that could go wrong with dating.

She was getting caught up in the emotion of telling him about the pregnancy. He was the only person she'd ever told, and it was creating an artificial closeness. It wasn't real. He wasn't the guy she should want.

She set the clothing down and took a gulp of

her beer. Then went to the iPod and changed the music. Waylon Jennings.

Wade glanced up, and she smiled at him. "For you," she said. "Figured you'd had just about enough of Miranda."

"She was growing on me," he teased. "But this is good."

Music he liked meant music he'd listen to—she turned up the volume so they wouldn't have to keep chatting. She had to keep her distance. At least until this strange closeness between them passed and things were more normal. Whatever *normal* meant now that Wade lived next door. She forced herself to concentrate on the clothing, taking satisfaction in the organized piles growing around her.

She'd gone through three of the big boxes of clothes when she set down the sweatshirt she was labeling and glanced across the hall. Wade had made piles of neatly folded baby clothes on a big blanket on the floor. Baby furniture that he'd already priced was stacked along the wall. He'd insisted he work on the furniture far away from her so she wouldn't have to face any of it.

He brought her a fresh beer, and she took a sip. "How are you doing over there?" she asked.

He reached into a box and held up a tiny T-shirt with a picture of a tractor on it. "This stuff is pretty cute," he said. "They should make it in my size."

Okay, he was not only rescuing her from having to sort baby stuff, but also being adorable about it. She didn't need Wade to be adorable. "Is it weird, going through it all?" she asked.

"Not as bad as I'd thought. It's really not horrible."

He looked so at ease with it that Lori took the T-shirt from him. It *was* cute. "See?" he said. "It's just a shirt. And that's *all* it is."

Lori held it up, marveling at how tiny it was. It didn't make her want to cry, but maybe that was also because Wade was here and Waylon was singing and the beer was warming her up inside.

"Here's what I've been thinking." Wade motioned toward the furniture leaning on the wall. "All of this stuff, it's just things. Pieces of wood. Furniture. There's no special meaning to it unless we give it meaning. It's not a sign that you should have done something different, or that you should feel terrible forever. It's furniture some nice folks bought for their kid, and now they're done and another family will buy it. End of story."

She stared at the furniture. It was nice stuff. And it wasn't scary. It wasn't making her feel the loss. "Who knew?" she breathed, walking over to touch the rail on a crib. It had been painted kind of an odd gray brown. "It's just wood. And I don't even like the color."

He laughed. "That's the spirit."

She looked around in wonder at the piles of baby clothes. "It's okay, isn't it? I mean, what I feel sad about, it's more of a spiritual thing. It's intangible. This is just stuff."

"Yup," he said. "And when the time is right for you, you'll buy some furniture that you love for the child you are going to love. And that stuff will have meaning because your child will use it."

"I don't know if I'll have a child," she told him.

"You don't want kids?" He looked at her, surprised.

"No... I do. I mean, it's just..." Why did she have to open her mouth? What was she doing giving him so much information? "I haven't dated much. Kids, if they happen, are a long way off. All that dating stuff has to come first."

"The dating stuff?"

She was beet red, and she could only hope that the shadowy room hid some of it. "Yeah."

He took a long swallow of beer and regarded her steadily. "Have you ever thought of doing some of that dating stuff with me?"

She froze. Tried to answer but it came out

as a cough. "With you? Um…no. I mean, you and me, we have so much history. We barely even get along. But…"

"…but we're getting along okay tonight," he finished for her.

"Well, yeah. We've been on opposite sides of the room all evening," she countered.

"True."

He was watching her intently, and she forced herself to return his look. "Have you thought of dating? I mean, dating me?"

His slow smile answered for him. "I have. A lot. But now I'm not sure… I want to be there for you. To support you. And I know, logically, the best way to do that is to be your friend."

Disappointment and relief were all mixed up. She nodded. It was safest to agree.

"But that kiss. I can't stop thinking about it."

Her heart sped up, pounding so hard against her chest that she could hear it. "I think that was just a one-time thing. You know, because we were both upset that night."

"So you're saying we don't have that kind of chemistry?"

"Yeah. It's like you said. We're friends." It hurt to say it. It was a lie. But she had to do the right thing. And getting involved with Wade again couldn't be right.

Wade drained his beer, then set the bottle

down purposefully on the table. He held out his hand. "Dance with me."

Her body warmed at the thought of being in his arms. "Why?"

He shook his head. "Damn, you are stubborn. Just dance with me. If you hate it, we'll stop."

He walked over until they were inches apart. She could feel him there, this energy, restless and edgy, but now she knew the kindness that held him steady underneath. There were a lot of reasons not to, but she ignored them and stepped into his arms.

His big hand behind her back held her up when she felt her knees go wobbly. Being this close to him now, after they'd shared so much, was just *a lot*. She drew a shaky breath and put her hand on his shoulder. He wrapped the other in his, and they swayed to the music.

His strength was magnetic. She'd prided herself on being strong, on keeping everything going on the ranch, on being the person everyone could count on. His thick muscles under her hands, the way he held her up so easily, were sheer relief. She closed her eyes. Her body relaxed into his. He pulled her closer, moving her with him. She laid her head on his chest and inhaled his scent: soap, spice, Wade. She took breaths of him.

She nestled closer, and he tilted his head to bring his cheek down next to hers. She could feel his end-of-the-day stubble against her temple, and her breathing went bumpy and troubled. There was so much heat inside her, as if muscle and bone long frozen were coming alive. She looked up, and he caught the movement and looked down, and his eyes... God, his eyes...serious and deep, dark brown with thick black lashes and then a tiny spark of humor when he whispered, "Do you hate it?"

"No," she whispered back. "I don't hate it."

"Is there chemistry?" he whispered.

She let a few beats go by before she admitted it. "There's chemistry."

He didn't answer, but she caught his smile, just a little triumphant, before he pulled her close again and danced her around in a circle.

When the song ended, he held her tight for an extra moment. She slid her arms around his neck and hugged him.

"Lori," he whispered against her ear. "I want this with you, so much."

She buried her face in his chest. Every particle of her was yearning toward him, wanting him closer, wanting him with her. Wanting to find a way to take this heat and sear away all the pain they'd caused. Wishing there was a way to quiet her fears that he'd walk away from her again. "I don't know," she whispered into his shirt. "I just don't know."

His hand came over her hair, sheltering, soothing, as he stroked it back from her face. He stepped back so he could see her. "I get it," he told her. "I get why you don't know. I'll wait. I'll be here. And I'm going to prove to you that you can count on me."

Tears stung. Frustration that the choices of their past squatted ugly and solid between them, blocking something that felt like it could be so beautiful. "Okay," she told him. What else could she say? She wouldn't make promises she couldn't keep.

"Hey, let's turn up the music and get to work," he said, squeezing her shoulders gently and letting her off the hook. "Only this time, I get to choose."

He walked over to the iPod and grabbed his beer again. Scrolled through her music and tapped. Miranda came back on. It was a sweet gesture, and she smiled her thanks for his choice. But she wished he'd stop being so damn sweet. It was hard to build walls when he kept tumbling them back down.

He gave her a thumbs-up and headed back to the piles of baby clothes. Her rummage sale savior. The man she'd loved, then hated and now, possibly, forgiven.

Dammit. She wished so much that it wasn't true. She glanced over at him, smiling despite herself as he shook out a pair of miniature overalls. He was right. There was chemistry. But this was a whole lot more than chemicals. And that was what scared her.

CHAPTER FOURTEEN

WADE WOKE UP when he hit the floor. Guns blazed around him and he cowered against the bed frame, his mind stuck between the nighttime shadows of his bedroom and the dark cave in Afghanistan, the rock walls shaky protection from the machine-gun fire strafing the outside.

A white flash lit up the room, the shabby furniture pure relief to his wild eyes. The flash was followed by a rolling boom. Thunder. It was nothing but thunder over the mountains. No guns. No fragmenting desert rock, no platoon, no danger.

He was home.

He sucked in air, trying to slow his heartbeat, trying to get a grip on his shaking hands, his racing pulse. Sitting back against the bed frame, he ran sweaty palms over his face.

The thunder rolled again and he winced.

He was such a coward. Couldn't handle a simple thunderstorm. Couldn't handle a bad dream. Even the pills he was relying on to get him through the day were no match for his nighttime fears.

He pushed himself up on shaking limbs, bracing himself as white light flickered. He held his breath, then let it out in relief at the long pause, the thunder distant and low now as the storm passed. He staggered down the hall to the bathroom, flipped the bare bulb on and welcomed the icy water from the tap as he sluiced it over his heated face. He filled a cup and drank it down. "Get a grip," he muttered at his shadowed face in the mirror.

Such a coward. Here he was, shaking in the face of a thundercloud and a bad dream.

The other day, after they'd brought the stray heifer down, he'd vowed to Lori to be a man who'd stand by her. In the church hall, he'd held her and told her he wanted to be with her. To be there for her. *Ha.* He couldn't even sleep at night. How the hell was he going to be there for her?

He closed his eyes and pictured her. That was where his mind went automatically, for comfort, for some small piece of grace. Her hair tumbling down over her shoulders the other night in the parish hall. Her funny answers when they'd asked each other questions. The way she'd reached out to touch that ugly crib.

She was brave. All alone at college, she'd

done what she felt she had to and then moved forward, learning what she needed to make her dream of taking over her family ranch a reality.

He thought of all she knew about cattle, about managing them in a positive, healthy way. Every time he was around her, he learned something new.

He opened his eyes and stared at the gaunt lines in his face, stark under the bare bulb. His fist came up, wanting so badly to smash the weak reflection. No. It was almost painful to stop his hand, but he did. *No.* No more smashing walls, no breaking stuff like a toddler in a tantrum. If he really wanted to be there for Lori, he had to get himself under control.

He was kidding himself. What did he have to offer? He was a grown man who couldn't get over a war he'd been lucky enough to survive. He hadn't even been wounded. So why was he here, with anxiety running havoc through his system, setting every nerve ending buzzing on hyperalert? Why did *he* have PTSD?

Some kind of flaw in his system. A weakness in his wiring. It must be.

Lori had been through terrible stuff and she was okay. Why the hell was he like this?

He had to get it together. It was that simple. Just tell his mind to calm down and stay in the present. Take all that nervous energy and use it for becoming the man Lori deserved. That should be his focus. That *would* be his focus for now on.

He turned out the light and went back to bed, closing his eyes and willing his mind to stay in the present. He thought about the repairs he was making inside the barn to make it as warm as possible for winter. He thought about the hay he'd ordered today, and how the guy on the phone had been so friendly. He thought about cutting firewood so he could use the fireplace in the living room as the weather got colder.

And then he fell asleep, and dreamed of war again.

TURNING INTO LONE MOUNTAIN RANCH was always like driving onto a movie set. Wade was pretty sure he'd never visited anyplace where everything was so well maintained. There was a green-and-white-painted sign over the drive, just as you'd expect on a ranch. Old wagon wheels were nailed to the fence near the sign, and after them came rambling roses that some Allen ancestor had planted. The fields on either side of the drive were irrigated and weed free, and dotted with cattle grazing in the morning sun.

He parked his truck, but when he opened the

door, his old anxiety hit. He was a Hoffman. He didn't belong at a nice ranch like this.

He shook his head. He was a ranch owner now, and he was here on business. *Stay in reality.*

Wade glanced at the envelope on the seat next to him. A draft of the water sharing agreement Bill had helped him draw up, just to make everything official. He decided to leave it in the cab for now. He'd go look for Lori and then he'd get it for her.

Okay, if he was honest, he was hoping if he left the plan here, she'd walk him back to his truck to get it. And he'd have a little time alone with her. Because it had been a few days since they'd folded all those clothes and danced in the parish hall, and he'd thought about her nonstop since. She'd said she didn't know if she wanted to date him. He got that. But he wanted to see her.

He came around the corner of the barn and slowed his steps, amazed by all the activity taking place. They were separating out the cows from the calves. But it was quiet. No one was talking or whooping or waving anything around in the air. It was just Lori out there in the corral, looking dusty and beautiful in her straw hat and tight jeans, leaning against the entrance to a chute that led out to a pasture.

Cows were walking toward her and heading obediently down the chute. The calves were avoiding her by ducking under a rail too low for the cows to go under, into a separate corral. All Lori was doing to separate them was occasionally lifting her hand in the direction of a calf, to guide it toward the rail.

And the animals were calm. The calves weren't bawling for their mothers, and from the cows there was only an occasional slightly anxious moo. He'd never seen weaning time look like this. Usually it was noise and hysteria.

"What the heck did she put in the water here?" he asked, joining a group of ranch hands watching from the corral fence.

"Crazy, isn't it?" a stocky, sandy-haired man said. "She calls it calm cattle management. She went to some seminar on it last year."

"She's bringing all kinds of fancy ideas onto the ranch these days," a tall, dark-haired, lanky guy added with a grimace. "Seems like every other minute she's telling us we've been doing it all wrong."

Wade studied him for a minute. He recognized him. He was Seth, the guy who'd been challenging Lori last time he'd come here. "New ideas don't mean you've been wrong," he told him.

"Who the hell are you?"

"My name's Wade Hoffman. I've got the property down the road."

"Seth Garner," the bitter man said. "And this is Terry Evans."

"Nice to meet you both."

"Hey, Wade." Lori was close enough to make them all jump. Wade looked past her and realized the cows and calves were separated, the gates closed. Every animal was nibbling on alfalfa hay, looking extremely content.

"Nice work," he said, keeping his expression neutral. It was hard not to smile, or pull her in for a hug, or tell her how damn beautiful she was.

"The calf weaners really do make a difference." She sounded relieved, and Wade realized how stressful it must be to take this kind of innovative approach in front of such a skeptical audience.

"But it's a big old pain because you have to put them in the chute an extra time to get the paddle on," Seth told him.

"Which took you, what, a couple of hours?" Lori countered. "I think it's well worth it."

Wade noticed a few other ranch hands drifting toward them to witness the exchange. This power struggle happening between Lori and Seth was probably becoming their daily entertainment. He almost pitied Seth. He'd put his money on Lori coming out on top any day.

"Lori here has us jumping through all kinds of hoops to make sure our cattle are happy and content," Seth told him, evidently hoping to enlist Wade in his scorn for his boss. "We do everything but cuddle them and sing them to sleep at night."

"Oh, you hadn't heard, Seth?" Lori's voice was all earnest sweetness. "Now that the calves are separated, I do need you guys to read to them at night. You're on the first shift. Eight p.m. to midnight. I've put a stack of storybooks and a flashlight in a box in the barn. They're going to need a calm tone, but put some animation into your reading as well. We don't want them to get bored."

"But, I..." Seth stared at Lori, his mouth gaping open. The rest of the men waited, eyes shifting from one to the other. Wade looked away, trying to hide the grin that wanted to take over his face.

"Eight p.m. to midnight. Okay?" Lori repeated.

"But..." Seth sputtered.

"And I like your idea of singing to them. Maybe an hour of songs after the stories, and then you can knock off for the night?" Lori's smile was innocent and bright enough to melt a glacier.

Wade knew her well enough to see the sparkle of humor in those deep blue eyes and the dimple quivering in her sweetly freckled cheek. But Seth didn't know her. He just stared open-mouthed until a broad laugh came from the back of the group.

Jim stepped up, guffaws so loud he sounded like a mule. He clapped Seth on the back. "Son, you've been had by the best of them." He held his hand up to Lori, who gave him a high five as the other men burst into laughter.

Seth shut his mouth and scowled as the other men high-fived Lori and swatted each other on the shoulder as if they'd made the joke. It looked to Wade like they'd been ready to see Seth get what was coming to him.

The ranch hand went red, then pale, then stalked off toward the barn. Wade noted the clenched fists, the anger that had Seth in its grip. Suddenly he feared for Lori. It was one thing to put people in their place if they were normal. But Seth's rage seemed out of proportion.

"Excuse me," Wade said and went after him. He found him sitting on a hay bale, elbows on knees, fuming.

"What the hell do you want?" Seth asked.

"I want to know why you're working here when you hate it so much."

"I've worked here a long time." Seth scowled at him. "Why do you want to know?"

"I've known Lori a long time," Wade said. "And I don't like the way you speak to her."

Seth's eyes shifted, and Wade glanced behind him. A few of the other hands had followed them in. Great. An audience. And clearly Seth felt like he had to perform when there were onlookers.

Seth stood leisurely, but Wade was trained for combat. He could see the other man's muscles tensing.

"And why the hell should I care what you say?" Seth was barely done speaking when he launched himself at Wade.

Don't fight. It defied every instinct he had, but Wade sidestepped at the last minute, letting Seth's own momentum send him down sprawling on the cement floor. Forcing himself to take the high road, he walked over and offered the other man a hand up. "You should care, because I'm right. And because with your attitude, I'm sure you'll get yourself fired soon. So why don't you just spare yourself the trouble and leave?"

"*I'll* say when it's time for me to quit," Seth grunted as he grasped Wade's outstretched hand and yanked hard, trying to bring him to the floor with him. Wade brought a foot to Seth's chest and shoved him back to the ground, freeing his hand. It was all he could do not to follow through with the kick to the gut that the guy deserved. *Stay in control*, he ordered himself, trying to breathe, to calm the adrenaline that surged. *You're a trained soldier. You stay in control. Even in combat.*

Seth staggered up and launched himself at Wade again, anticipating his side step this time. He made contact, hands grasping Wade's shoulders, clawing for his neck. Wade ducked low, the surprise of the move loosening Seth's grip. From there it was easy. Wade grabbed the other man by the waist and flipped him, taking the time to aim him toward a pile of hay. The least he could do for Lori's ranch hand was provide a little cushioning before he slammed him down on his back.

Seth lay in his hay bed, gasping for the breath that Wade must have knocked out of him. *Oops.*

"That's enough!" Lori shoved a path between her men and planted herself in front of Seth, her hands on her hips. "Seth, you're fired. Please go pack your things and leave immediately."

Jim arrived, hastening to her side. He offered

Seth a hand up, but Seth shoved it away. He stood on his own and looked at Wade, his lip curling in a sneer. "Look at you, coming here all badass, trying to tell me how to do my job."

"Seth, mind your words," Jim cautioned.

Seth spat a gelatinous gob that landed just a few inches from Wade's boot. "If you know so much about ranching, why do you need Lori to come to your rescue all the time?"

Shame was a good weapon. Shocked by Seth's words, Wade didn't see the punch in the stomach coming. Seth hit him hard and Wade staggered backward, doubled over with the pain. Then he started forward, fists curled. His mind seemed to have gone somewhere else. Somewhere disconnected, as if he was watching himself from a distance as he grabbed Seth by the collar and twisted, brought his fist up and hauled it back, ready and eager to crush Seth's face.

"Wade, no!"

It was Lori. Her small hands were clinging to his upraised arm, and her voice was in his ear. "You stop it! Now!" Talking to him sternly as if he were a bad dog. He started to shake her off, doglike, but strong arms were around his waist, pulling him back. Some huge ranch hand had a grip on him. Then Lori's voice went low in his ear. "You wish you'd helped me back then? Help me now, dammit. You hit him and I could have a lawsuit that will end me. So could you. You stop now, do you hear me? You stop!"

He stepped back, his arm lowering, his mind coming back to to the reality in front of him. His hand, unclenched from Seth's collar, felt numb, and he shook it out. He glanced around, taking in the circle of men all watching him warily.

The huge guy who'd pulled him back was now standing cautiously at his side. "You all right, man?" he asked quietly.

Wade gave him an abrupt nod, shame draining his adrenaline as it washed through. "Thanks," he mumbled.

Jim led Seth away, and the other ranch hands wandered back to work now that the show was over. Then it was just the two of them, he and Lori, standing there at opposite ends of the barn.

"What the hell was that?" Lori stalked toward him, her own hands balled into fists.

Wade wondered if she was going to hit him. He was so tired, he didn't really care if she did or not. "The last time I came by here he was hassling you, too. This time he looked so furious, he had me worried for your safety. I didn't mean to start a fight. I just suggested that if he was so miserable, there were other jobs out there for him."

"That wasn't your place!"

"You weren't doing anything. You let him stay on here, even with him heckling you like that."

"I wasn't *letting* him heckle me. I'd already won the battle with that bedtime story joke. He lost face in front of the men. He would have come into line or left on his own. I *was* handling it."

"I just couldn't stand seeing you treated that way."

Her face was pale in the dim barn light, but her eyes went dark with rage. "It is not your job to determine how I am treated. *I* run this ranch. *I* decide how to handle the guys who work here. *You* have absolutely no say over it!"

"But you deserve better." He was being stubborn, but he wouldn't allow her to accept mistreatment as the norm.

"And I will get better. For myself. In my own way." She threw up her hands in disgust. "Don't you see it? How you undermined me just now? I've been working for months to assert my authority here. And that's exactly what I was doing, with humor, when you showed up today. And you know what? Now the guys who work here won't see me as the funny, tough boss who put their ringleader in his place. They'll see me as the weak boss who needed some man to step in and fight my battles for me!"

She turned on her heel and stalked away, heading out of the barn. At the door she stopped. "I don't know why the hell you came here today, but please don't come here anymore. If you need me? Call me. Or send an email. But don't show up here and get involved with my staff again."

He wondered if he was going to puke. A few staggered steps took him to a hay bale where he sat down, head in his hands, and let the world spin around him. A world he didn't seem to belong to, where none of the rules made sense anymore. He'd been trying to help and instead he'd ruined everything.

His head hurt. A low, aching throb of stress and adrenaline dregs. Had he taken his meds this morning? He couldn't actually remember. He hated them. Hated the need for them. It felt wrong to rely on a pill to regulate his mood. Plus, it was disorienting. How did he even know if what he felt was real or not when his mind was swimming in antidepressants?

A big hand covered his shoulder. Wade jumped up and away, fists up, combat ready.

"Well, shit," drawled the big cowboy who'd pulled him off Seth before. "You got it bad."

Wade straightened, red faced, trying to act like he hadn't just jumped out of his skin. "Got what bad?" he asked.

"That was a hell of a startle," the man said. He stuck out a hand. "My name's Ethan."

Mystified, Wade shook the man's hand. "Wade Hoffman."

"I know who you are." Ethan was studying him like he might study a horse he was considering buying. Measuring his qualities with his almost eerie light blue eyes. So Wade studied him back.

The guy was a little scary looking when you looked past the cowboy attire. There was an eagle tattooed on his beefy neck. A dagger dripping blood etched on his forearm. Wade was almost six feet, but Ethan was a good three inches taller. And built like a linebacker.

"I knew your older brothers. Arch and Blake. Went to school with them," Ethan said. "They were a couple of mean-ass dudes. I got in a few fights with them over the years."

"Why?" Wade was intrigued. Everything he knew about his older brothers was from being their little brother. The kid they beat up on, picked on or just ignored.

"They were bullies. And big. Not too many

kids could take them on at school, so I had to do it."

"Oh." What else could he say? That he wished Ethan had shown up to fight *his* battles a few times?

"After high school I joined the army," Ethan went on. "Fought a few tours in Iraq. Ended up front and center in the fight for Falluja. When I got back home, I was messed up. PTSD. Seeing things that weren't there. No idea how to be normal again."

Wade shifted uncomfortably. Ethan's words hit too close to home.

"I could see it, just now. You have PTSD, and it was taking you over in that fight. I saw it because I used to be the same way." Ethan reached into his back pocket and handed Wade a scrap of paper with "Monday 8 p.m., Benson Grange Hall" scrawled across it. And a phone number.

"We have a support group. Just local guys who've been through war. Some older vets and a bunch of us younger ones. It doesn't solve everything, but it helps."

"I wasn't in battles like Falluja. I was in Afghanistan."

"It doesn't matter where the bullets are flying. We all came home messed up, and we're all trying to figure out how to get over it. I think you should join us."

Wade hesitated. The idea of walking into that room… Who would be there?

"You need me to show up on your doorstep and pick you up like a date? 'Cause I'll do that if you're too scared to show."

It needled him just the way Ethan meant it to. "Why do you care if I show?"

Ethan shook his head in disgust. "Maybe you weren't in my platoon, or hell, not even in my war, but you're my brother in arms. We're like family. Isn't that what the recruiters told us before we signed our lives away? Well, fuck them. They don't look after us now. But I look after my brothers. So show up at the grange on Monday night. Afterward a bunch of us grab a beer or two at the High Country. Play some pool."

Wade stared at the paper, then back at Ethan. "I'll think about it."

Ethan grinned and delivered a punch to the shoulder that almost took Wade down. "Trust me, you'll be glad you did." He turned to leave the barn, then stopped, looked back and grinned conspiratorially. "Don't tell Lori I said this, but great job with Seth. I was thinking about doing the same thing. You just beat me to it."

It was nice to feel this kind of brotherhood again. But he still didn't think he had what it took to go share all his troubles with a group. "Glad there's someone here who has Lori's back."

"You've got a thing for her?" Ethan laughed when Wade shook his head to deny it. "Damn. Maybe we need a second support group for all the guys in this town hoping Lori Allen will give them the time of day. Good luck with that, Wade. See you Monday." And Ethan strolled, still laughing, out of the barn.

Wade stared after him and then glanced down at the paper in his hand. Holy hell, life was strange. Was his PTSD really that obvious? He thought he'd kept it somewhat under control today. He'd stopped when Lori asked him to. He was making progress.

The memory of the disappointment in Lori's eyes mocked him. He'd been a millisecond away from losing it, and he knew it. It didn't matter how much he wanted to pretend he was doing okay. Whatever demon was inside him was just biding its time. It had almost found its way out today.

Wade shoved the paper into his pocket. He'd think about the support group. But he had a whole history of keeping his personal troubles private. So it was hard to imagine sharing his problems with a bunch of guys from Benson, a town that had gossiped about the Hoffmans for generations. A town that had never felt like home.

CHAPTER FIFTEEN

How could he do that to her? Lori stalked toward the house, anger fueling her pace. She'd finally put Seth in his place. And in his misguided attempt to support her, Wade had ruined everything.

Now she was glad she'd pulled back at the parish hall the other night. She'd been wondering just about every five minutes since then what would have happened if she'd leaned in. If they'd kissed. If she'd told him she wanted to date him. She'd been wishing that she'd had the courage to go for it. But now she was grateful she hadn't.

A twinge of guilt flickered. She'd been hard on Wade just now, telling him never to come back here. But she needed things to run smoothly on the ranch. When Mom died, Lori's life had been turned upside down. Getting pregnant had thrown everything into chaos again. Dad retiring had been difficult as well. But now she had her life organized. She had her ranch, and she was starting to earn respect from most of her staff. The last thing she needed was some unpredictable guy coming around and messing all that up.

She picked her way over the cats sleeping in the sun on the back porch steps. The motley group was Mandy's collection of strays that were too damaged or odd looking to adopt out. If people kept dumping these animals on their property, it was going to get expensive to feed them all. They made Mandy happy, though, so in that way, they earned their keep.

One old tomcat raised a lazy paw and batted her boot as she went by. She bent down to scratch the white patch between his black ears. They both jumped at the sound of a sharp bark behind her.

She turned around. In the dry grass at the foot of the steps was a small dog. It was peach colored and blond streaked, with fur sprouting every which way off its body. It looked like a dust mop had a close encounter with a light socket. Or a porcupine had gotten a perm.

"Who are you?" she asked.

Its hairy tail swung back and forth in a blur of excitement. Two dark brown eyes never left her face. Lori stepped back over the cats and knelt down next to—she took a peek underneath—*him*. He looked to be somewhere under fifteen pounds. His nails were long and his coat was full of burrs.

He put his front paws up on her leg and looked up at her with eyes that brimmed with intelligence. "Arrowf," he said.

"Hey, little guy." Lori scratched him gently between the eyes where his fur sprouted like eyebrows gone wrong. He had long golden lashes, and his eyes were rimmed in startling black. "Have you been getting into the eyeliner?"

His ears came forward at her words. Oversized triangles with plumes of hair streaming off. When Lori stopped scratching, he stood on tiptoes and nuzzled her hand with his black nose, demanding more of her attention. "You look like you just got dumped off here today. Someone decide they'd had enough of you? Did you stop being a cute puppy and become a real dog?"

He cocked his head, listening intently, nuzzling her hand each time she stopped petting him. "You have a big attitude, buddy, but out here you gotta be careful, okay? You're just a coyote snack in this part of the world."

She sat down on the lowest porch step, and the dog climbed onto her lap as if he'd always belonged there. He stuck his nose into her cheek, and his snuffling noises made her laugh. She pulled a few burrs off his chin and a couple more off his paws. Then he lay down on her legs and prepared for a snooze.

"Hang on, little guy. I gotta work. I'm heading to the office to cut a paycheck for the man we just fired." She ran her hands over the little dog's rough coat. His sun-warmed fur was soothing. But she didn't have time for this.

She put her hands along the dog's sides to move him off her lap. He thwarted her efforts by going noodle limp, flopping around in passive resistance when she nudged him. She picked him up, meaning to set him down again, but he curled up in her arms with a sigh of blissed-out contentment.

With her own sigh of resignation, she carried the coyote snack with her into the old parlor that served as an office and set him on her lap while she wrote out a check to cover Seth's final wages. Biting back all the rude things she'd have liked to say, she wrote "Thank you for your work at Lone Mountain Ranch" on an envelope, slipped the check in and sealed it.

Sinking back in her chair, she rubbed the little dog's velvet-soft ears. They were the only soft part of his coat, thanks to what was probably some kind of terrier heritage. She could feel his ribs. Mandy was going to want to fatten him up. The dog grunted in appreciation and nosed her hand, giving her a polite lick. "Why, thank you," she told him.

He looked at her searchingly as if trying to figure out what she meant, and a part of her heart went squishy. He really was a cute little guy.

She should have gotten back to work, but there were incredible smells wafting out of the kitchen. Whatever Mandy was concocting wouldn't solve her frustration with Wade or make her feel better about firing Seth, but it would taste awfully good. And she could really use Mandy's company right now.

She scooped up the little dog and headed for the kitchen.

Mandy was up to her elbows in flour. "Wait!" she cried when Lori reached for a cupcake decorated with pink and yellow daisies. "Those are for Patty Tompkins. She's throwing her daughter a baby shower."

Lori was going to protest when she saw the tray of chocolate chip cookies. "May I please, please have a cookie? I deserve chocolate after my day so far."

"One," Mandy said. "That batch is for the city council meeting tonight."

"Two and I'll deliver them for you," Lori bargained.

"It's a deal."

Lori reached for the cookies.

"What are you holding?" her sister demanded.

Pulling her hand away from the cookies, Lori looked down at the little dog. "You haven't met him? He was by the back porch."

Mandy sighed. "Must've been dumped off on the driveway. He's gorgeous. But you can't bring him into the kitchen. What if his scruffy little terrier hairs end up in the cupcakes?"

Lori glanced down at the dog, who looked up at her in mute appeal.

"Oh, look at that!" Mandy's smile was ear to ear. "He loves you! I think you found yourself a new dog."

"He's *not* my dog," Lori protested. "He just hitched a ride in from the porch."

"Uh-huh," Mandy said, putting all of her lack of conviction into the words. "And never, in your entire life, have I seen you cuddle a lap dog."

"Yeah, I'm not sure how that happened. He seems kind of sneaky that way." Lori took the dog back to the porch and set him down in the sun. Then she opened the bin where Mandy kept the pet food. She poured a cup of kibble into a dish and looked down at the stray, who was sitting bolt upright, watching her expectantly. "You can stay here," she told him. "Eat your food. And don't go out into the woods."

She set the dish down and the coyote snack dove for it, crunching the kibble like he couldn't remember his last meal. Which made Lori angry at whoever had dropped him off here. He deserved better.

But she was tired of being angry, so she closed the porch door behind her and returned to the kitchen, stopping at the sink to scrub her hands. She put two cookies on a plate and poured herself a glass of milk. Sinking her teeth into a still-warm cookie, she let the melted chocolate chips transport her to a happier place.

"So, what's going on?" Mandy asked, stirring milk and eggs into her batter.

"What makes you think something's going on?"

"You're in the kitchen in the middle of the day. Cuddling a small dog and eating cookies."

"I was just in the office writing out a check for Seth. I fired him today."

"Good." Mandy stirred her batter emphatically. "He was creepy."

Lori jolted abruptly out of her cookie reverie. "Did he hassle you? You should have told me."

"He never said anything. Or did anything. He just looked. But it was the kind of look that made you want to take a shower afterward."

"You should have told Dad when he hired him. Or me."

"I just figured I'd stay out of his way. It's hard to get reliable help, and it's not like I'm contributing much to the ranch."

"What?" Lori stared at her sister. "What part of your poultry business, keeping the garden, cooking everything, cleaning everything, helping me with the books, scheduling all the repairs for the house and running a baking business on the side qualifies as not contributing?"

"You know what I mean. I'm not out *there*—" she lifted her chin toward the window "—doing ranch stuff."

"Do you want to be?"

"No," Mandy said quickly.

"So we're good. Because I sure as heck don't want to be in here making dinner."

"What happened with Seth?" Mandy asked.

Lori filled her in on the morning's events while Mandy poured the batter into the waiting cake pans.

"It's kind of sweet that Wade was trying to help you with Seth."

"Sweet? No! He undermined me in front of the whole staff! It was humiliating."

"Oh, Lori, only you would find a hot guy rushing to your rescue humiliating."

"No self-respecting rancher would want someone else stepping in to solve problems with her staff."

"Really?" Mandy was smiling mischievously, but Lori chose to ignore it.

"Really. I swear. Wade coming back here has caused so much trouble. I mean, I know he's not trouble like everyone in town thinks of when they hear the name Hoffman, but between the well and having to help him with his ranch, and now this, it's just too complicated."

"You think he's trouble because you care about him. When you talk about him, you light up."

Lori stared at her sister in disbelief. "Light up in anger, maybe. Or frustration. No, I'm done with him. I'm thinking about asking Jim to go over there and help him out from now on. And handle the water sharing deal. I just don't need this headache."

She looked up when Mandy snorted. Her sister had abandoned her batter and had her wrist over her mouth, laughing so hard she'd *snorted*.

"What? Why are you laughing?"

"Because you *like* him. It's so obvious. Rushing over there to track down his cow for him. Getting so mad today when he was trying to help."

"He's my neighbor and he has our water. I don't like him. I'm *stuck* with him."

"Hmm...stuck, huh?" Mandy looked at her thoughtfully. "What if you did hand everything to do with Marker Ranch over to Jim? You'd almost never see Wade. Would that really make you happy?"

"Sure it would," Lori said, taking a long swallow of her milk to hide the blush she could feel traveling across her cheeks. Why did her sister have to be so perceptive?

"Well, I guess you have your answer, then." A small smile played over Mandy's face, making it clear she didn't believe Lori's words *were* the answer.

But how could she explain how she felt to Mandy when she didn't understand it herself? Yes, she'd be sad if she never saw Wade. But Wade worried her. And how he made her feel flat out scared her. It was so much easier to be angry with him, and today had given her the perfect excuse. "Life was just so much simpler before he came back here."

"Sure," Mandy agreed. "Simple, safe and boring. All you did was work."

"Well, I have a lot of work to do. And I don't need some guy who can't control his temper messing things up."

Mandy studied her for a moment. "Is that

what happened? He got in a fight because he couldn't control his temper?"

Lori shrugged. "Not exactly," she admitted. "He got in a fight because Seth tried to spit on him and then hit him in the stomach really hard."

Her sister smiled. "You want to hear my theory about why you're upset?"

"No, but I'm sure you'll tell me."

"I think you're upset because you want everything to be in control."

Lori stopped chewing. "I'm some kind of control freak?"

"Well, I think ever since Mom died, you've been focused almost completely on the ranch. On making sure nothing else unexpected or bad happens to any of us. And don't get me wrong. I appreciate that. You have worked really hard to make me feel safe. But I can see how Wade coming along and making you feel things you can't control would upset you."

"Doesn't all my work simply mean I'm a good rancher?" Lori decided to ignore the second part of her sister's little speech.

"Yes, you're a great rancher. But you are also a perfectionist."

"I'm not a perfectionist," Lori protested. Then she thought for a moment. "I just like it when everything goes perfectly."

Mandy giggled. "Exactly. So when Wade got into it with Seth today, and it wasn't ideal, it worried you. You want everything to work out...like some ranch you read about in one of your college textbooks. And you take it personally when it doesn't. But real life *isn't* perfect like that."

"Dad always made everything work out perfectly around here."

"No, he didn't. He just didn't stress much about the messy stuff. Think about it," Mandy demanded. "Remember the fight those two hands got into? When they trashed the south bunkhouse?"

"Yes, of course."

"Did that make Dad some terrible rancher? Because a fight happened on his ranch?"

"No." Sometimes Mandy's logic made her nuts. Because it was usually correct.

"You weren't *in* the fight today. It wasn't in your control. Why take it personally?"

"I don't know. It feels like it reflects on me. And what if Wade gets in a fight again? Because, yes, maybe I do have some feelings for him. But it's so complicated, Mandy. More than I can explain."

"Maybe I don't know the whole story," Mandy said. "But are you expecting Wade to be perfect, too? I think you're holding both of you to a pretty high standard. You are allowed to make mistakes, Lori, and so is Wade."

Lori considered her sister's words. She *did* try to do everything the best possible way. Maybe that was part of why she couldn't forgive herself for ending her pregnancy. She'd gone for the fastest, most obvious solution but not, in hindsight, the best one for her.

"Am I right?" Mandy asked.

"Maybe..." Lori grumbled.

"I'm not making excuses for Wade. I don't want you to be with someone who has a terrible temper or anything like that. I'm only saying that if you hold out for people to act perfectly before you let them in, you could be on your own for a mighty long time."

"I've been on my own so far and done all right."

"Sure. But are you happy? After you see Wade, you come back all sparkly. And I saw his face when he looked at you in the bar that night. He couldn't keep his eyes off you. It was pretty romantic."

"Sparkly?" Lori stood up from the table. "I've never been sparkly a day in my life. I'm just dust and cattle."

"And I'm just saying that if you asked Wade, he'd tell you he likes dust and cattle. A lot. And that he sees way more than that in you."

"Well, I'm not asking." Suddenly the kitchen felt hot and stifling. Lori wanted wide-open space and a good gallop on Dakota. And to be far away from Mandy's insights that hit way too close to home. "I have a cattle drive to plan. I'm gonna get going."

"Why don't you ask Wade to go with you?" Mandy asked, a wicked smile on her face. "I'm sure he could use the experience."

She couldn't take any more. Lori covered her ears with her hands. "What was that, sis? I can't seem to hear you."

"Oh my gosh, you're ten years old again? You *like* him, you *like* him…" Mandy crowed, regressing right along with her.

"Can't hear you, la la la la…" Lori sang, and then they were both giggling hysterically. Lori uncovered her ears and came around the table to give Mandy a quick hug. Then she clapped her hat on her head and headed out to find Dakota. She still wanted that gallop, but thanks to Mandy and her cookies, she was feeling a few years younger, a few pounds heavier and a whole lot better.

CHAPTER SIXTEEN

THE NEW HORSE came down the trailer ramp in a riot of hoofbeats as if he had a few extra legs. He danced and snorted at the end of the lead while Todd spoke to him in a low voice, reassuring him that this new place was safe. Todd's friend Jack, a professional trainer who helped work with the rescued mustangs, stood to one side, quiet and ready in case he was needed.

Poor horse. Wade understood the fear in its wide eyes. Born wild, brutalized in a helicopter roundup, then confined to a packed corral in the blistering summer heat. Then, just when he thought he had a safe haven with Todd, he'd endured a trailer ride to an unfamiliar ranch. No wonder he looked so miserable.

A certainty settled in Wade's heart. This horse needed him and needed a home. So he *would* make this work. He'd make this ranch into a great home for him, no matter how hard it was. Strange to think of Marker Ranch, with all of its bad history, as a place that could help anyone feel safe. But he'd find a way to make it happen. He knew too well what terror felt like.

Wade hung back, figuring it was best to let Todd comfort the frightened animal. He was a strange-looking horse. His coat was a mish-mash of reddish hair and white, the combination almost pink in the sunlight. There were random white splotches all over his body. His eyes were brown but encircled in pale pinkish skin. His thin, red-brown mane hung in tangles down the side of his neck.

Jack said the color was called red roan. Which meant a color so mixed up it made you a little dizzy to stare at it too long.

The new horse raised his head high and whinnied, and JM, munching on some morning hay over in the next paddock, answered. They'd made sure the two horses would have a common fence so they could keep each other company without getting into any scuffles.

Todd got the new horse calm enough to walk him over to the gate Wade had left open. The roan tossed his head up as he walked past Wade and regarded him with his strange pink-rimmed eyes. Wade swallowed hard. What the hell had he got himself into?

In the paddock, Todd removed the halter and came quickly back through the gate as the horse trotted off. Latching it carefully, he climbed the rail and watched as the pink horse trotted the high fences of his new home, tail up, snorting and huffing as he took in all the possible dangers of this new place.

Wade and Jack walked over to join him.

"That is a fine-looking horse," Jack said. "Todd's right. He's gonna be good working cattle, I bet. No way that's a pure mustang with those big round hindquarters."

"Seems like he's part Appaloosa to me," Todd said. "But whatever he is, I'm glad he's in a good home."

"I'll do my best," Wade assured them. "But what the hell do I do first?"

"I'll email you a training schedule," Jack said. "With stuff you can do every day. And I'm happy to stop by and help out anytime. Well, anytime when I'm not on daddy duty."

"That would be great," Wade said. "What should I do today?"

"Nothing," both men said together and then grinned.

"He's got what he needs," Todd explained. "Hay, water and his new buddy JM next door. Just hang out near the fence some. You can even bring a chair and a book out and read close by. Let him get used to your smell and your presence. But don't even talk to him today."

"That I can do," Wade said. "Kind of nice to have an excuse to kick back with a book."

"And tomorrow just feed him, and then do the same thing," Jack said. "On Monday you can start on the schedule. The first step is sitting on the fence, then going into the pen but kind of ignoring him."

So far it all sounded like stuff he could do. "All right, then."

"You thought of a name yet?" Todd asked.

"Jackson," Jack said.

"I was asking Wade." Todd elbowed his friend. "You want us to name the horse after you?"

"No!" Jack laughed. "Look at all those white splatters. It's like Jackson Pollock decided to paint his coat."

Wade laughed. "You're right. Plus, I did my training in South Carolina at Fort Jackson. It's perfect."

"All right." Todd walked along the fence until he was a little closer to the horse. "Jackson, welcome to your new home. This is Wade Hoffman. He's gonna take good care of you."

Jack rolled his eyes at Wade. "The dude's crazy."

Wade rolled his eyes back. "Just be glad he's not gonna be your brother-in-law." But he grinned. He was lucky his sister had picked such a good guy.

"Hey Doctor Dolittle," Jack called. "Are you done talking to the animals? I gotta get back."

"All right. Wade, want to come over for dinner tonight? I think your sister is cooking."

Wade winced.

Jack laughed. "That good, huh?"

"Hey, careful, that's my fiancée you're talking about." But Todd's grin revealed that he got the joke.

"I'll come. Can I bring something? A pizza, maybe?"

Todd laughed. "Maybe I can talk her into a pizza night. I'll call you later and let you know."

Jack headed for the truck and trailer, but Todd lingered behind. "What's up with the fighting?" he asked quietly.

Wade stared at his friend in shock. "How did you hear about that already?"

"One of the Lone Mountain Ranch hands dropped equipment off at my repair shop yesterday."

"Does Nora know?"

"Nope."

"I appreciate that." Wade paused, trying to gather his thoughts "I was trying *not* to fight. I even sidestepped the guy a couple of times.

But then he got a good punch in and I kind of lost it. Luckily Lori grabbed me before I actually hit him."

Todd nodded. "It's good you stopped."

"What can I bribe you with so you don't tell Nora?"

Todd grinned. "I won't tell her. Though if you bring some beer with that pizza tonight, I wouldn't mind."

"Deal," Wade said with genuine gratitude.

"See you later, then." Todd went to the truck where Jack was waiting, and the two men climbed in. Then it was just Wade, JM and the newest addition to Marker Ranch—a wild horse named after a wild artist. And what was even wilder was that somehow Wade was supposed to figure out how to train him.

He glanced over at Jackson. The speckled horse was still wandering along the fence, looking like he was plotting his escape. JM stood by their shared fence, nickering at the newcomer as if trying to tell him to calm down because there was good food here and not too much expected of you. But Jackson wasn't listening. He'd spotted Wade. He threw his head up and glared at him defiantly, raised his tail and trotted further away from him. "It'll be okay, big guy," Wade murmured. It would be.

It had to be. At least, he sure as hell hoped it would be.

The sound of a vehicle clattering down his driveway had him turning to look. An unfamiliar silver SUV was bumping along toward him, slowing down to pass Todd's truck on the drive. Strange to see that, since he rarely had visitors.

Wade left the horses and headed down the dirt lane that led to the house. A woman got out of the vehicle and waved, waiting for him to arrive.

As he got closer he recognized her. It was Mandy. Lori's sister. Was something wrong with Lori? He quickened his pace.

She must have seen some of the panic he felt on his face, because she burst out laughing. "It's okay, Wade. Lori's fine."

He tipped his hat to hide his confusion. "Hey, Mandy...just trying not to keep you waiting. What's up?"

She was gracious enough not to comment on his lame excuse. "I'm here to ask you to come to church tomorrow."

If she'd asked him to board a rocket to the moon, he would have been less surprised. "I wasn't really raised to go to church. Kind of the opposite." His dad had laughed at all those "straights and squares wasting perfectly good

Sundays." Wade could still hear the words perfectly, complete with the bitter, alcohol-slurred tone that accompanied them.

"All the more reason to give it a try," Mandy said placidly.

Had Mandy become a missionary? He didn't think the Lutheran church had them. "Hey, that's nice of you, Mandy. But I've got a lot on my plate right now…" He gestured to his dilapidated ranch. The run-down buildings explained it all better than he could.

"Lori will be there," she said, and he noticed a sparkle in her eye.

"I think I'm just about the last person Lori wants to see at her church tomorrow."

"I know my sister better than you."

"Did she send you?"

Mandy bit her lip. "Um…not exactly. She doesn't know I'm here."

He had to laugh at the guilty look on her sweet face. "Why exactly *are* you here?"

Mandy stood up a little taller. "Because you two are being silly, staying mad at each other. You've known each other too long for that. What better place than church to make your peace?"

"A bar?" he asked hopefully. "I could meet you and Lori for a drink afterward, and you could broker your treaty then."

"Wade Hoffman!" She looked shocked. And then she laughed. "Think of it this way. She can't yell at you in the middle of a sermon."

"True," he admitted.

"She's upset. And confused. But she's got so much pride, she'll never let you know that. I want her to be happy. I owe her so much. That's why I'm here."

He didn't know what to say.

"Look," Mandy went on. "Lori hasn't told me much, but I know it's been hard for you, coming back to this town. Not everybody's as welcoming as they should be. But what better way to show folks you've changed than by coming to church?"

She had a point. "Is there a lot of kneeling and getting up and all that? Because I won't know what to do." He wasn't going to show up in church just to make a fool of himself. He could do that fine in plenty of other places.

She grinned. "Sit with us and I'll give you the elbow when it's time."

She was funny. And spunky. Pretty much what he would have expected from Lori's sister. "I still think a bar would be better."

Mandy's brows furrowed together in what must have been her stern look, though it was too sweet to frighten. "I know you got in a fight yesterday on our property. And I know you were at war for a few years. I'm not saying church will make everything better, or even give you any sense of peace, but don't you think it's worth trying? And then you can see Lori and ask her out. It's pretty darn clear that you like her, and she likes you and you're both too stubborn to do a thing about it!"

"Go back to the part where you said Lori likes me? Because it sure didn't seem like that when she tossed me off your ranch yesterday."

"I love my sister, but she doesn't always know what she wants unless it has horns and hooves. Trust me? Come to church tomorrow?"

It was just about the last place he wanted to go, but he wanted to see Lori. He needed to apologize, to let her know that he'd heard her and he understood why she was mad. And it just might take some divine intervention to get her to listen to all of that. "Okay."

"It's the Lutheran church above town," Mandy said with a satisfied nod.

"I know it. I was there helping Lori out the other night."

She looked at him in astonishment. "I had no idea. Well, that's good. So be there at 9:45 and we'll meet you out front. Your nicest jeans and a good shirt will be fine," she added, anticipating his question.

He'd underestimated her. She might have

looked like a blonde Barbie doll, but she was a powerhouse of determination.

"Can I leave at halftime if I hate it?"

She laughed. "We don't really have a half-time. But it usually only lasts about an hour. You can handle it."

He must have somehow gotten the word *pushover* tattooed across his forehead when he wasn't looking. First he'd agreed to take on a wild horse and now he was going to church, all against his better judgment. But... *Lori*. He wanted to see her. He wanted the anger between them gone. It had sat like a scratchy sweater on his spirit all day.

"Tomorrow, then," he said on the exhalation.

Satisfied, she turned to get back into her SUV. "Oh, and when you see Lori? Be sure to ask her about her new dog."

"She got a dog?" Wade could picture Lori with a border collie trotting at her heels. Super smart and ready for work.

"She sure did. A really special one." She gave him a wink.

Wade watched the SUV get smaller and finally drive onto the main road. He turned toward the house, wanting to grab a glass of ice water before feeding time. But the water didn't do much to soothe his unease about going to church. *What had he just gotten himself into?*

CHAPTER SEVENTEEN

LORI STOOD NEAR the entrance of the church, waiting for Mandy, who was moving in slow motion today. If her sister didn't hurry they'd be stuck way in the back, where people always whispered to each other. She liked to sit up front, where she could see and hear everything. Mandy teased that she was still the straight-A, front-row student she'd been in school. Maybe it was true.

She passed the time looking at the view. The church was in a beautiful spot, on a hill above Benson. From here Lori could see all the way out across the high desert east of town. And if she turned to face the other way, the peaks of the Sierra rose sharply behind the church, as if lifting their fingers up to God. At least, that's what the pastor always said.

She fixed her eyes on Mandy, trying to will her away from her conversation with Marybeth Bradford, a widow who ran the senior bingo games and was always hitting Mandy up for cookie donations. And of course her sister always obliged.

Just then, a man walking up the rise from the parking lot caught her eye. He wore dark jeans, and his black cowboy boots were clean and polished. Her eyes traveled up past his slim hips to the simple pale blue dress shirt. Broad shoulders. Dark eyes. Dark hair. Seriously handsome. Then it registered. *Wade.*

She took a step back and bumped into the pillar behind her. What was *he* doing here? He came straight for her, eyes locking on to hers. He didn't stop for a greeting—typical Wade— just went right into what he wanted to say. "I'm sorry if I messed things up with Seth last week. I never meant to undermine your authority—I was being protective and I didn't have the right. I don't know how to make this better, but I'm here because I want to."

His words raced over her skin, igniting nerves. He was danger. Making her want so much. Reminding her of that kiss. That dance in the parish hall. Both had left an impression of softness and heat that she kept tasting on her lips. "Why here? You don't go to church."

He glanced over at her sister and then back. "I do now. Your sister has some pretty strong opinions about what a little religion might do for me."

"My sister?" Lori looked over at Mandy and caught her watching them. She narrowed her eyes, and her sister glanced away, biting a smile off her lip. "She invited you here today?"

"She did. But I'm the one who said yes. I wanted to see you."

He was braver than she was, just putting his thoughts right out there. His words were tempting her to give in. To admit how much she'd missed him this past week. To acknowledge how sad she'd felt when Mandy made her imagine life without Wade.

But seeing him wasn't easy, either. Because she liked things organized and orderly, and he had her emotions in chaos.

"Lori, who is this fine young man you're chatting with?"

The voice was unmistakable and unwelcome. Tabitha Lawrence, former head cheerleader and homecoming queen, who tried to relive her mean-girl glory days at every opportunity.

"Tabitha, do you remember Wade Hoffman?"

Tabitha gave the smile a cat gives to the bird under its paw. "Why, of course I do! I wondered if it was you when I spotted you talking with rancher Lori here. I had to come see it with my own eyes." She glanced at Lori conspiratorially. "I heard they were letting a lot of folks out of prison these days to save the government money."

Wade paled, and Lori almost gasped out loud. But she wouldn't give Tabitha the satisfaction. "Huh… I hadn't followed that piece of news. But I did hear that we had a new military hero in town, so I was happy when my sister invited him to worship with us today. It's quite an honor."

It was a blow, but when it came to verbal combat, Tabitha was ruthless. "Oh my, I didn't realize!" She batted her eyes at Wade. "I'm surprised I didn't see anything about your homecoming in the local paper. I know when Lewis Quinn came back, they threw him a parade. But isn't that just like a Hoffman, to sneak back into town with none of us knowing?"

Lori had wondered, in her more charitable moments, what had happened to Tabitha to make her so mean. But right now she didn't care. "It's funny, Tabitha; but not everyone needs to have an audience all the time. I wouldn't call Wade moving back here 'sneaking.' I'd call it living his life and minding his own business. You should try it sometime."

Tabitha stared at her in shocked fury. "Lori, I don't know what you're hinting at."

Lori stepped up, right up, into Tabitha's face, which she was sure was in there somewhere beneath the thick layers of makeup. "Well, luckily there is some time for quiet contemplation in church every Sunday. Maybe you could try making use of it. Now, if you'll excuse us, Wade and I are going to head on inside. There are a few good people who I know will want to welcome him before the service starts."

She grabbed Wade's arm, momentarily disconcerted by the warm, strong feeling of him under her hand, and hauled him into the church, straight down the center aisle and into an available pew just two rows back from the altar.

She sat down on the bench with a thump and pulled Wade down next to her. "Sorry about that. She can be truly awful…well, pretty much all the time."

Smile lines crinkled the corners of his eyes. "You came to my rescue."

"I just don't have any patience for people who make a habit of insulting others. Mandy would remind me that she's probably unhappy. Disappointed with the way her life worked out. But I'm sorry. If you're disappointed, take a class, get a degree, move away, do *something*!"

"You defended me," he said again. "It was awesome. I think you might still like me, despite my idiocy at your ranch."

He was so close, so intent on her, and it was

amazing to see him smiling. Heat rose in her cheeks. "*Sometimes* I like you. Sometimes I honestly don't."

"I get that. But if we spent more time together, you might like me more often."

Heat pooled other places as well. Her heart pounded. Why couldn't she get all fluttery like this for someone else? Someone safe, who she didn't share so much bad history with? "I don't know."

"I heard you got a new dog."

His sudden change of subject surprised her. "A what? No! I didn't get..." Realization dawned. "You mean the coyote snack? What did Mandy tell you? No, I did *not* get a new dog. It's just some stray who showed up at the ranch. Not my kind of animal, trust me."

"Huh. Well, I have a new animal, too. You should come by and check him out sometime."

"A new animal? Please tell me it's not another loco heifer you got for cheap."

He grinned. "Nah. I might have learned my lesson about that. It's a horse. From Nora's fiancé, Todd. Another mustang."

"Oh, great! I'd love to check it out."

"He's not broken to saddle yet. I'm going to train him." He looked almost shy.

"It's a great project," she assured him. "I'm a

little jealous. I've been trying to get the nerve to try it myself."

"I'd welcome your help anytime. I don't know what I'm doing."

He looked worried, and she wanted to lighten his burden a little. "You'll figure it out. Just don't stand behind him." She winked at him. "They kick."

He laughed at her obvious advice, and a few people turned around with disapproving glances. "Oops," he murmured. "Guess this thing is getting started."

"This thing?" She grinned. "Oh, you mean church?"

"Where's Mandy?" He glanced around, looking a little panicked. "She promised to elbow me at all the kneeling parts."

Lori glanced around, too, but Mandy was nowhere in sight. "She's probably setting up cookies for after the service." His words sunk in. "You mean you've *never* been to church before?"

He shook his head.

He'd come here for her. To do something he had no idea how to do. To participate in something that he quite possibly didn't even believe in. For her. Warmth flooded her. Not the heat of attraction she'd felt when they first walked in. Just warmth in her heart that he would take this risk to see her again.

"Never, ever? Not *any* church?"

"It wasn't exactly my family's style."

Their style. That was one way to put it. *Abuse* and *neglect* were other words for it. A long-ago memory surfaced. She'd been about twelve years old and nestled safely next to Mandy in the backseat of the family SUV, on the way back from church. She'd looked out the window and spotted Wade walking along the road between their ranches. Alone. It was January and he'd had no coat. Her father had pulled over at her exclamation and gotten out to talk to him. Then he'd bundled Wade in the car and driven him to their ranch.

They knew each other well. They were childhood friends on the playground. But he wouldn't look at her that day. He just sat next to her in the backseat, staring straight ahead, two crimson spots on his cheeks, answering her father's questions with a stiff "yes, sir" or "no, sir." His hand had brushed against her arm accidentally, and she jolted. His skin was like ice.

Her parents had brought him into their warm kitchen, made him cocoa and fed him lunch. Then her mom had left with him. Lori found out later that she'd taken him into town and bought him a coat, a hat, gloves, warm socks and new boots.

A few weeks later, on another icy morning, Wade had shown up at school with no coat again. The hat, gloves and boots were gone, too. Worried, Lori had cornered him, demanding to know where his winter clothing was. He'd finally confessed that his dad had been furious that he'd accepted charity and had sold the clothing to some thrift shop in another town. Wade begged Lori not to tell her parents. He didn't have to say more. Lori saw the fear in his eyes.

Yeah, church hadn't been a part of Wade's family. That was an understatement.

She stared at the floor for a moment, stunned at the vivid memory. She'd been so intent on hating Wade ever since he'd left town. She'd let her regret about their night together, her resentment of his harsh words, push aside all her earlier memories of the lost boy he'd been. Since he'd returned she'd been caught up in herself, in all the emotions his return brought up for *her*. But what about *his* emotions? He must have a vault of memories like that coat, but so much worse because of the abuse he'd suffered at the hands of his horrible father. No wonder he'd lost his temper when Seth struck him. How many times had he been struck growing up?

Between the way he'd grown up and his time in Afghanistan, he probably had more bad memories than anyone in town. But he was moving on, trying to create a new life for himself. He wasn't letting the past hold him back. She needed to do the same for him. She wanted to. Tentatively she slipped her hand in his, relieved that it was warm and strong and no longer the icy hand of that little boy on that freezing winter day. "Don't worry," she whispered as he looked down at her wonderingly. "I'll get you through the service. I've got an elbow, too."

HOLDING LORI'S HAND, Wade savored her nearness. Her perfume, a little spicy and mysterious, mixed with the old wood of the building, the wax and smoke of the candles, formed a heady cloud around him. Maybe it was her next to him, or the pastor's words, but he felt different, being here in church. The pastor talked about the meaning of fall, of cleaning house for winter, of making ready for darker nights by getting one's house in order. His words resonated.

Wade was suddenly filled with a certainty that he was perched on the edge of something new. Something more meaningful that involved a wild horse and his work on the ranch and this woman by his side. Slowly but surely, he'd get his house in order.

Tears stung behind his eyes, and he was shocked to realize they were of gratitude and joy. Both unfamiliar, both powerful. And maybe that was God or maybe it was just how he felt about Lori, but he said a quick prayer of thanks that Mandy had asked him to come here today.

It had been a morning of strange miracles. Lori sticking up for him with awful Tabitha. Being there for him. Holding on to his hand as if he were her lifeline. As if they were a couple. If all that could happen, was it greedy to ask for just one more miracle that would get his mind back into shape?

After the service, he stumbled through the handshakes and introductions in a happy daze. Lori still held his hand. The pastor looked into his eyes with kindness and asked him to come back next week. Mandy gave him a grin and a thumbs-up as she loaded his plate with sweets at the coffee hour afterward.

When he offered Lori a ride home, she said yes. And when she climbed into his old truck, she slid across the bench seat to sit right next to him.

He put his arm around her shoulders and looked at her questioningly.

"Yes, please," she answered. So he pulled her in close and guided his beat-up Ford out of town.

He didn't want to jinx it, but he had to ask. "So, what's changed?"

Glancing up at him from under her long lashes, she shrugged. "I realized in church that you've always meant a lot to me. Way before things went wrong between us. And I thought about how we can't change what happened. I'm always going to carry that sadness and regret around. But I don't want it to paralyze me or keep me from what I want."

"And what's that?" he asked huskily, forcing himself to keep his eyes on the road when all he wanted to do was pull her into his arms.

"I want you," she said simply, leaning her head on his shoulder.

He kissed her hair softly, glad she was looking at the road ahead and not at the tears that threatened to fall. He turned into her driveway, not wanting this life-changing drive or the peaceful silence between them to end.

When he put the truck in Park, Lori looked up at him, her deep eyes such a contrast to her fair hair. Like ocean and sunlight. She looked beautiful and sophisticated in her dark wool dress and high heels, her hair slicked back into a neat ponytail, but he kind of missed her usual tousled mop busting out from under her old brown cowgirl hat.

He swallowed hard. This was it. He was going to lay it all out there and hope he was reading this crazy day right. "I want to date you, Lori. I want to take you out and spend time with you. I want to get to know you, get to know us, as we are now. I promised I'd be there for you as a friend, and I swear, if you don't want to go out with me I will shut up and be that friend to you. But I want much more."

Her hand came up, small, strong and calloused. She brushed her knuckles along his jaw, and he tried to memorize the look in her pretty eyes. Searching his, wanting something, giving something. "I want that, too."

His heart was leaping but he tried to play it cool. "I haven't asked a girl out for a long time. What would be good? Dinner?"

"Too much pressure." She smiled up at him. "How about something really simple. A movie? And then we can grab a drink after, and if we run out of things to say we can just talk about the film."

He laughed. "Sounds perfect. You want to go tonight?"

"Sure," she said, glancing at him shyly.

"You choose the movie and let me know when to come pick you up."

"Okay," she said and pulled her hands away to reach for her purse.

But he didn't want her gone. "I know it was only a ride home," he said, "but is there any way…" He paused. How did he do this without sounding lame? He gave up. "Can I kiss you? Goodbye?"

She flushed—dusky rose that made her cheeks glow a little.

"It's okay if you don't…"

She cut him off with a hand at his jaw, and her lips over his. It was heaven—better than that—a blast of warmth straight to his iced-over heart, and he threaded his fingers gently through hers and kissed her back, slowly, carefully, finding his way through the emotions that kept his tears from church so close to the surface. He concentrated on the impossible softness of her lips, and on the velvet of her skin when he traced a thumb gently over her cheekbone.

He pulled away, aware suddenly of his breathing and hers, quick and audible in the still world inside the cab of his truck. So much desire, but he wanted to take this slow. No way was he going to mess up and remind her of the callous kid he'd been.

He took all the want and shoved it away somewhere inside. And kissed her lightly on the forehead. "I'll see you tonight."

"Looking forward to it." She kissed him one last time, lightly, lingering with their lips barely touching. He breathed her in, cherishing the gift. Then she gave his hand a light squeeze and slipped out of the truck.

He watched her walk, her quiet confidence apparent even in her pumps and pretty church dress. She gave him a little wave from the porch and then disappeared inside her house. He turned the truck around and headed home, thanking God, and especially Mandy, because when he woke up this morning he hadn't dared to dream that this could happen.

Partway to his house, he pulled over on a side road, dirt and rutted, heading pretty much nowhere, and parked. He hiked a little way out, through the sagebrush, the prickly chollas and the high desert scrub that thrived in the neglected pastures of Marker Ranch. He jumped up onto a big chunk of granite and let out the whoop he'd been holding in ever since those kisses in the truck. His voice was startling, like a big rock plunked into the still pond of desert air, rippling out in circles until it dissipated into the dry silence.

And then he sat down and sunk his head into

his hands, letting the emotion of the morning finally come. Tears of gratitude and brand-new hope streaming down his face, falling onto the parched soil like rain.

CHAPTER EIGHTEEN

DAMN, SHE LOOKED BEAUTIFUL. Even in the neon light under the movie marquee, Lori glowed with irresistible golden health and strength. A surge of pride had Wade squaring his shoulders. She was here with him. She was his date. Which made him the luckiest guy on this planet. He put an arm gently around her and felt another thrill. "Ready?" he asked.

"Next stop, popcorn," she told him. "My treat."

"No way. This is our first official date. Ever. I get to buy." When he saw her jaw set at that familiar stubborn angle, he resorted to pleading. "You can pay another time, I promise. But right now I want to take you on a totally traditional, guy-paying date."

She laughed. "Is that why you brought me flowers?"

"Of course. Isn't that what you do on a first date? Show up on the doorstep with flowers for your girl?"

She laughed and leaned into him. He could

barely keep his grin from going ear to ear, which probably made him look like a total idiot. He didn't care. She felt so good tucked against him, he hoped she'd let him hold her this way through the entire film.

There was a short line for the popcorn, and of course Lori knew pretty much everyone in it. He'd met a few of the people at church this morning, and a few he recognized from high school. Wade braced himself for the dirty looks, the snide comments about his family, but they didn't come. A few handshakes, a back-slap or two, and they had their popcorn and were heading into the dark of the theater to find their seats.

"That wasn't so bad, was it?" Lori asked as they sat down. "Thankfully not everyone in this town is a Tabitha."

Wade grinned. "She's something else. But you know, I was kind of glad she said that stuff. I need to get a thicker skin. People are going to say things sometimes, and I have to be able to deal with it."

Lori set her popcorn down and took his hand, turning a little in her seat to face him. "I'm sorry people are like that."

"I try not to let it bug me, but sometimes it sucks to have spent every day of the past decade so far away from the path my family took, and yet people still judge me like I'm one of them."

"I think they just have old information. Once they realize who you are now, and all that you've done with your life, it will stop."

"Yeah, I guess you're right." A quick epiphany had him smiling. "Maybe I should think of this time as payback for the trouble I caused as a kid. A little justice."

"Can I ask what you did?"

"Mostly stupid stuff. Graffiti. Swiping a beer from the liquor store. I'd stolen a couple of cars. It all came crashing down when I hot-wired the vice principal's car and took it for a joyride. I chained it up to a tree in a stupid prank. I got caught and they kicked me out of school. I don't blame them. I *was* heading down a bad path. It was a good wake-up call."

"That's when Nora showed up to take you to Reno with her."

"And you and I spent that night together. Which was a dream come true, by the way. I'll never understand why you chose to come with me that night. How I got so lucky. And I know it had awful consequences, but I loved being with you. You should know that."

"Thanks," she said softly. "I loved that night, too."

He picked up her hand and brushed his lips

softly over her fingers. "I turned it around when I left. I got into a new school and repeated my senior year because I hadn't passed my classes here. I had Nora watching me like a hawk, and it saved me."

"Your sister has always seemed like such a good person."

"She saved my life more than once."

"I never thought of you as like your older brothers. Or your dad," Lori said quietly. "Not when we were growing up, at least. You were smart and nice to me, and I liked you. I had a crush on you forever. But after you left, I was so mad, and I did lump you in with them. It felt better just to think of you that way." She paused, bit her lower lip. "I just thought you should know."

He put his arm around her shoulders and pulled her in. "I get it. It makes sense after the way I treated you. But I hope I can make you think better of me from now on."

"I know you can." She put her arm across his chest and leaned her head on his shoulder. It was the best answer he could hope for.

He hugged her back. Kissed her hair one more time. And then the lights went down and the previews started, and she pulled away and reached for the popcorn.

Wade took a deep breath and let it out as quietly as he could in the sudden dark. It was the first time he'd been in a movie theater in years. He felt himself becoming slightly more vigilant, his eyes darting, seeking exits, suddenly wanting to know exactly who was around him in the shadowed theater.

It's just a movie. Movies happen in the dark. His heart thudded too quickly and he breathed deep, trying to slow it.

The preview was for a holiday film. Totally innocent, but just the size of the images in front of him, the speed they flickered across the screen, the dialogue booming out of the speakers were assaults to his senses. He shifted uneasily in his seat. His palms were starting to sweat. *Get a grip. They're just pictures on a screen. They mean nothing.*

Lori held the popcorn out to him in a sudden motion, and he started a little. Then took a handful and whispered his thanks. He sat there in the dark, staring at seats in front of him, concentrating on the buttery, salty taste of the popcorn. The crunch of it in his mouth. But it felt dry as dust on his tongue. Furtively he dropped his handful onto the floor and worked on slowing the rapid-fire thud of his heart, forcing each breath to move evenly in and out of his lungs. He dug his fingers into his thigh—the pain was a welcome distraction. He counted backward from a hundred to keep his mind busy. He pressed his feet into the floor to stay grounded.

The previews ended and the movie started. A rookie cop with a crooked boss. They were at the firing range, and the shots had Wade flinching. Sweat, clammy on his forehead, trickled in ominous threads down his back.

Then across the screen a bus crashed and sirens ignited and he was out of his seat, pushing blindly past Lori, past the knees of the people in their row, their protests muffled by the thrumming in his head, the roar of his own breathing in his ears mixing with the screams and chaos of the movie. He lunged through the lobby, shoved through the glass doors and out into the crisp fall night. He was halfway up the block before he remembered where he was and who he was supposed to be with.

He stopped in front of the old courthouse, its granite facade rising ghostly white in the night sky, and put his hands to his knees as he fought for breath. Glancing around, his only comfort was that no one was out for a stroll right now. He sank down on the lonely sidewalk and leaned his back against a lamppost, grateful for the solid ground. How the hell had he come to this? *Pathetic.* Self-hatred ran like thick acid in his veins. This wasn't him. So weak he couldn't even take his girl to the movies.

He closed his eyes and let the night air, iced with coming winter, chill the sweat and cool the burn in his lungs and chest.

Breathe in and out, in and out. Dr. Miller had given him some pills for moments like this. Groping blindly at his side where his pocket should be, he realized he'd left his jacket in the theater.

"Wade?"

He opened his eyes slowly, not wanting to face what had to be faced. Lori was standing a dozen yards away, holding out his jacket.

"Hey." His voice was rough, like he'd been screaming.

She walked up slowly, warily, like she was approaching a stray dog, and held out his jacket from a safe distance. "Why don't you put this on?"

He wanted the cold. Wanted it to freeze the demons in his head. To still the fingernails they ran over his chalkboard spine. He put the jacket down next to him on the pavement.

"These fell out." Lori held up the pill bottle. "I'm sorry, I know it's private, but they landed on the sidewalk when I ran outside the theater."

She'd had to chase him. And now she knew about the pills.

A strange relief settled over him. An acceptance of what had to happen next. Bitterness curled the edges of his tongue. "I'm messed up, Lori."

She moved a little closer and held out the pills again. "Take one." She pulled a small bottle of water from her pocket with her other hand. "I ran back in the theater and got this when I realized."

He didn't take either bottle. "Realized that I'm totally screwed up?"

"No! You're not screwed up. You have medicine you need to take. So take it." Her voice went firm. "Now."

He reached out and took both bottles. He hated popping a pill in front of her but did it anyway. It wouldn't fix much, but if it could take the edge off the clawing anxiety, maybe he'd find the courage to say what needed to be said. The water was tepid, perfect. So neutral sliding down his throat and into the chaos inside.

Lori sat down across from him in the puddle of lamplight, her blond hair haloed. An angel sitting close, but totally out of reach now. Her dark eyes wide with worry that he'd put there. Again.

"I'm sorry," he said finally. "I thought I could handle a movie like that. I kinda wish you'd picked a chick flick."

A smile flitted across her face. "You thought

I'd pick one of those for my first date with you? That doesn't seem like the way to get a second date."

He smiled faintly, loving that she could find a way to add a little humor into the most horrible situations. Then he remembered what he had to say and the smile was gone. "We can't have a second date."

"Excuse me?"

"Lori, I'm messed up. Really messed up. I should have told you a long time ago." There. It was out.

"Tell me what you mean." She leaned in and took his cold hands. Tried to warm them with her small ones.

His throat closed up, so it took sheer will to force the truth out.

"A couple of months ago, when I first came back to the ranch, I lost my mind a little."

Her hands went to her mouth. "Oh no, Wade…"

She didn't finish her sentence, and he didn't blame her. What was there to say to that, really? "I was clearing out a shed on the ranch. A local rancher came by and told me my dad had stolen cattle from him years ago. He demanded that I reimburse him. Told me he was thinking of taking me to court if I didn't. When he left, I lost it. I started drinking and I don't remember much after that. Nora found me, throwing stolen stuff everywhere—bikes, car parts, all flying through the air. I was screaming like a crazy person. I broke a window."

She was watching him solemnly, knees tucked up, arms wrapped around them.

"So she and Todd got me to calm down, and they called Dr. Miller out. He said I have PTSD. From the stress of being in combat." He took the bottle of pills back out of his pocket. "I've been taking medication ever since. Antidepressants, and these for when the anxiety gets really bad."

"That's good," she said softly. "You're dealing with it."

"Just barely. Tonight in the movie was bad. Like the sounds and pictures were coming right through my skin."

"But you're getting help," she insisted. "I'm sure it takes time."

"That's the thing. It does take time. But I don't know how much." He swallowed hard. "And in the meantime, I can't seem to control my behavior. I can't even take you on a goddamn date. You deserve someone who can be there for you, Lori. Not someone like me. Someone broken."

"I don't want anyone else. I want us to be together. To go to church like we did this morning. To ride and work on our ranches. I don't care if we see movies or not. I don't care about that stuff."

She was too kind. Too good. She'd taken care of her dad and her sister for years, and now she was trying to take care of him, too. After all he'd put her through. "The memory of me, and the situation I left you with, was a huge burden for you. I don't want to be a burden now. Again."

She squeezed his hand. "It's *my* choice who I want to be with. Why are you pushing me away? Are you embarrassed?"

"Partly, yeah." His voice broke a little. "I hate that you're seeing me this way."

She bit her lower lip as if looking for the right words. "Remember the night outside the bar? When I cried all over you?"

"Of course," he told her.

"I was embarrassed then. And I still am. No one in the world has seen me like that, sobbing hysterically. Just you. And sometimes it's scary to know that you've seen me that way. It makes me feel vulnerable."

He took her hand. "Knowing what you've overcome, the pain you've had to work through, makes you seem stronger to me."

"Well, knowing what you've been dealing with all this time makes *you* seem stronger to *me*. You've had to overcome so much, even back when we were young. PTSD has nothing to do with being weak. It just means that you experienced a lot of bad stuff in the war, and your brain can't figure out how to process it."

He was silent, considering her words. She elbowed him playfully. "Plus, I refuse to let you break this off because you couldn't see a movie. That's just lame. Especially since I almost never go to the movies."

He couldn't help but smile at that. Maybe it was the medication kicking in, or her understanding working its magic, but he was feeling better. So they wouldn't go to movie theaters. Like her, he'd never gone to them very often, either.

He reached for her hand, brought it to his lips and kissed it. "I have no idea what I did to deserve your loyalty."

"I don't think it's any one thing you did," she told him. "I think it's just who we are. Besides—" she grinned up at him "—you still have all my water, remember? I have to be nice to you."

"That's a side benefit I never even imagined when I drilled that well."

"You look tired," she said, running her fingertips over his jaw. "I think we should finish this date another time."

He was bone weary after all that adrenaline. "I think that would be best."

"I'll drive us to my place. Then you can drive yourself home from there." She reached out and gave him a gentle punch on the shoulder. "Good thing we're neighbors."

They made their way to his truck. She got behind the wheel and drove them home in silence from what might have been one of the most disastrous dates in the history of dating. He was trying to put his faith in what she'd told him. That she understood. That she didn't care he was having such a hard time.

The problem was that he had to find some faith in himself. And how could he do that when his own brain couldn't be trusted?

CHAPTER NINETEEN

"ARE YOU OKAY?" Mandy was in full-blown maternal mode, shoving multiple sandwiches into Lori's saddlebag.

Lori knew she should help, but exhaustion kept her in her chair at the kitchen table, face buried in her third cup of coffee. "Sure," she lied. "Thanks for talking with me about my disastrous date last night."

"Hey, what are sisters for if not to help with disasters?" Mandy came around, put a hand on Lori's shoulder and added another blueberry muffin to her plate. "I'm sorry—I feel like I pushed you guys into that date by inviting him to church."

"No. It was a good idea. It made me realize how I feel about him. And at least now I know what he's going through."

"You'll work it out. You two are connected to each other. I remember you sitting together at lunch in grade school."

"That's because he never had a lunch," Lori said.

"And because he was willing to let *you* know

that. And *you* were willing to help him. Wade never let anyone else in."

"Well, he tried to kick me right back out again last night."

"Because he was embarrassed! And can you blame him? It must be hard for him. He's used to being the big tough strong guy and now he can't even see a movie."

"I'm worried about him," Lori said quietly. "I looked it up on the internet last night. PTSD in veterans is no joke. And there's no one cure. They just have to learn to manage it. I found all these blogs where veterans' girlfriends and wives post what they're going through with their partners. It's scary how bad it can get."

"It seems to me that a lot of the horror stories are from situations where the person is in denial that they have PTSD," Mandy said mildly. "But if Wade knows he has a problem and he wants to deal with it, then it's just a question of him getting the right treatment." She gave Lori a quick wink. "I looked it up, too."

Lori laughed. "Thank you."

"Look, you can't fix it. But you can try to be there for him while *he's* trying to fix it. You can love him anyway." Mandy smiled gently. "Even if the situation isn't perfect."

Lori wanted to be there for him. She remembered Wade standing in the church hall, folding baby clothes for her because she couldn't do it. She of all people should understand his PTSD. Heck, she probably had some form of it herself. And he'd been right there for her, trying to help.

Like she should be helping him. But the stakes were higher now. Something had changed for her. Her heart, locked up for so long, had cracked open. And last night, when he tried to break up with her, it had hurt so much. She didn't know if she could handle it if he tried to push her away again. She set down her coffee cup down abruptly. "Why does this have to be so complicated?"

"The stuff that matters usually is, I think," Mandy said, handing her the saddlebag.

"Well, cattle matter, and rounding them up is usually pretty simple. I'm looking forward to a day of just that. Nothing else. No Wade, no dates going badly, just good old-fashioned normal life."

"I'm not sure there really is such a thing," Mandy said. "But good luck with that. And try to have faith in Wade. In the two of you."

"Thanks, Mandy. For the food, the talk, everything."

"Of course. Be safe out there." She turned away, but not before Lori saw the furrow between her sister's brows. Mandy hadn't ridden up into the mountains since the day their mom died. And every time Lori rode up there, Mandy worried.

"Hey," Lori called as she pushed open the back door. "I'm going to be fine."

"Yes. Of course you will." Mandy gave a little wave and bustled back into the kitchen, where she'd probably bake her fears into heavenly sweets.

Maybe Mandy had some kind of PTSD, too. Lori paused on the porch, stilled by the thought.

She hadn't asked Mandy lately about how she was doing. They'd always been a practical family. Not sharing their deepest thoughts, just working together to get things done. Ever since Mom died, they'd been like that more than ever. Lori knew she'd been so busy just carrying on, trying to make everything as normal as possible on the surface, she hadn't given a lot of time to Mandy. They lived together, but it was only recently, with Wade coming back, that they'd started to talk about much beyond running the ranch.

Maybe trying to understand Wade was helping her see the cracks in her own world. Underneath her success with the ranch, underneath Mandy's animal rescues and baking business, was a whole lot of unspoken pain.

A beam of sunlight made it over the pines and warmed her face. *What time is it?* She'd woken up muffle headed, still stunned by Wade's revelation last night. And here she was, staring into space, lost in her own thoughts when she was supposed to be on the trail already. Jim and the others had probably been waiting almost an hour.

Something brushed against her boot, and Lori glanced down to see the little terrier mutt, one paw up, begging for a morning hello. "Hey, it's the coyote snack!" She knelt down and ran her hand down the dog's short back, used a couple fingers to scratch him between the eyes. He'd taken to following her everywhere he could, and when she woke up this morning she'd found him sleeping at the foot of her bed.

Mandy had cleaned him up, and now that he was getting two square meals a day he looked a little sturdier. He nuzzled her hand with his cold nose. "I think that's your name. Coyote Snack. Snack for short. Do you like it?"

Snack sat down and offered her a paw. "Good. Now, Snack, go lie down." She pointed to his dog bed on the porch. He climbed in reluctantly, flopping down and heaving a doggy sigh of abject depression.

Straightening, Lori slung the saddlebag over her shoulder and left the porch to cross the dry grass that in the predrought era had been a green lawn. *Time to get to work.* All her worries for Wade, for Mandy, for everything would have to wait.

She jogged down to the main barn, pulling her jacket closed and zipping it up. Fall was here for real. This early morning chill would last well into the afternoon now. She and Mandy had pulled out their down comforters last night to drape over their blankets.

Usually she loved fall, when the aspen turned gold and the days cooled off. But now, during the drought, she loved it even more. Because in fall there was a glimmer of hope that something might change. The possibility of winter rain to ease the parched earth.

When she got down to the barn, Jim had Dakota saddled for her. Two other hands, Juan and Robert, were already mounted, ready to go. It was a three-hour ride to where the herd was grazing, and they needed all the daylight they could use. Jim glanced at his watch and then at her. She was never late. She was usually the first one at the barn.

"Rough night?" Jim's kind old eyes were full of concern.

"Something like that," Lori said. She nodded a greeting to Juan and Robert. "I'm really sorry I kept you all waiting."

They were nodding their acknowledgment when she saw their eyebrows rise and their eyes go wide, and then huge grins spread over their faces. Juan pointed at something and started laughing.

"What the..." Jim said, and then he was laughing, too.

Lori turned in time to see Snack bounding joyfully up the dirt track she'd taken to get to the barn. His tail was spinning in wild circles behind him, and his every-which-way hair was practically exploding off his body. His mouth was wide open in his huge black-lipped doggy grin, his long pink tongue lolling to one side. He arrived in a blur, threw himself against Lori, somersaulted off and landed on his feet. Then he looked up at her with his eerily smart eyes and went into a happy dance on his hind legs, batting at her with his front paws. True to form, he didn't bark—he wasn't a barky guy— but he let out one of his loud snorts.

Peals of laughter rang out behind her.

"What the heck *is* that?" Robert asked, barely getting the words out he was laughing so hard.

"Is that a friend of yours, Lori?" Jim asked, pulling out a bandana and wiping tears of laughter from his eyes.

"I don't think I've ever seen this kind of animal before," Juan added. "Is it some kind of endangered species Mandy's trying to save?"

That sent Jim off again, laughing into his bandana, while Snack capered and danced, totally unaware of how ridiculous he looked. But he did stay away from the horses, Lori noticed. At least he had half a brain in that walnut-sized head of his.

She looked around, hoping to see Mandy coming to get him, but there was no sign of her. "It's a dog. Some kind of terrier that got dumped off near our driveway. Mandy rescued him."

"Of course she did," Jim said. "That gal wouldn't turn away a rattlesnake if it batted its eyes at her."

"We have to get going," Lori said, looking at the sun, which was way higher in the sky than she wanted it to be.

"We could put him in a stall for the day," Robert said. "Give him an old blanket and some water."

"I don't know." Snack might be making her a little crazy, but she couldn't stand the idea of him locked up in an old stall. Plus, he was sitting now, looking up hopefully with those big brown eyes, tail wagging a mile a minute. He was ridiculous. He didn't belong out here.

But the men had laughed about him and

the sky hadn't fallen in. It was kind of nice to have a guy, even a twelve-pound fur ball of a guy, wanting more than anything to spend some time with her after Wade's attempt to end things last night. "Let's try something," she said.

She scooped up the dog, who instantly settled down and snuggled into her arms with a happy wiggle. She carried him over to Dakota and let the mare snuffle him. Both animals seemed calm, almost as if they'd already met. Shrugging, Lori tucked Snack under one arm and swung up on Dakota's back.

"What are you doing?" Jim asked.

"I'm going to see if he can come with us." She set the terrier carefully on the saddle between her legs. "Sit," she told him.

He sat right down on the padded leather seat, looking like a miniature scruffy lion king on his throne. She kept one hand on the reins and the other on the dog and asked Dakota for a walk. Snack rode effortlessly, his little black nose high, his big ears up and alert, and his mouth wide open in an enormous doggy smile.

"Look at that!" Robert exclaimed. "He's a natural."

"Well, I'll be." Jim shook his head in disbelief.

The men rode alongside her, staring.

"He's a circus dog," Juan said. "Looks like he's been riding all his life. What's his name?"

"Gentlemen, meet Coyote Snack—Snack for short."

They burst out laughing, and kept on laughing for at least a half mile up the trail. Lori's smile was almost as big as the dog's. Maybe Wade's problems and her worries about Mandy had put everything in perspective. Or maybe she was just desperate for a laugh. Any laugh.

Whatever the reason, for the first time since she'd taken the helm at the ranch, she didn't care that she looked ridiculous. She didn't care that she wasn't acting just like her dad. She had herself a new dog. He sure as hell wasn't perfect. But neither was she. And it was a relief to finally realize that maybe that was okay.

CHAPTER TWENTY

JACKSON'S NECK MUSCLES quivered under Wade's hand. It had taken hours of standing in the corral to get to this point, but his new horse was finally letting Wade touch him. Sure, he looked ready to bolt at any moment, but it was progress. Jackson took a tentative bite of the alfalfa hay Wade offered in his hand. His ears twitched as Wade talked. He had been telling him about Lori all morning. About their date gone wrong. About how beautiful she'd looked. About how he'd messed it all up. How for some crazy reason she still wanted to hang out with him.

Maybe Jackson just felt sorry for him, but he reached over and nuzzled Wade's shoulder for a brief moment. It felt like a blessing. It felt like medicine.

It *was* medicine. Having to be calm for Jackson forced Wade to slow his breathing, move with deliberation and empty his mind of everything but what the horse needed. It was calming Jackson down, but it was soothing Wade, too. When they were together he felt like all the jagged edges inside his brain smoothed over. His hypervigilant nervous system went from red alert to yellow. It was the only time since he'd come home that he'd felt this way. Training the horse was bringing him closer to peace than he'd thought possible.

He had to thank Todd, though it needled him just a little that his future brother-in-law had been right about how much the horse would help him. Todd was thoughtful that way. He had some kind of special insight into the way people and animals and nature interacted.

Jackson snorted, probably sensing that Wade's mind was wandering. "Hey, boy," he murmured, running a slow hand over the horse's withers and resting it on his back. "It's okay. I'm here. And I appreciate the chat." He pulled a piece of carrot out of his back pocket and offered it to the horse, who whuffled it up.

Over by Jackson's pasture, JM whinnied, missing his friend. Jackson threw his head up, listening. "Okay, you can go back now. You did good today." Wade unbuckled Jackson's halter and opened the gate that separated the round corral they'd been using from the pasture. Jackson trotted out, tail up, and headed for JM. There was a little squealing and prancing on both sides of the fence, but then both horses settled down to grazing side by side.

Wade closed up the gates, glancing at the sky. The day was almost over. Somehow he'd gotten through it, just trying to breathe.

Frustration at himself, at his faulty brain, rose every time he remembered how he'd cowered on the sidewalk last night because he couldn't see a simple movie. How pitiful he must have looked to Lori's eyes.

He started toward the house, so lost in thought it wasn't until he got almost to the porch that he saw his sister's Jeep parked next to his truck. She was sitting on the porch steps, a large pizza box next to her.

"Awesome," he breathed, reaching for it.

"There's a price for it," she said shortly, batting his hand away from the box. "Tell me what's going on."

"What do you mean?"

"Todd's friend Jack and his wife Samantha were at the movies last night. They saw you run out. Jack called Todd today. He was worried."

"This town!" Wade crossed his arms over his chest as if that would help keep the prying eyes of Benson away. "What the hell is wrong with this place? Don't people have anything else to talk about?" He could feel the words, all the words people said about him, crawling across his skin, stealing his privacy.

"Not all gossip is bad. There are good people here. People who care and don't judge. Jack is one of them. He just wanted to make sure you were okay."

"I'm okay." Maybe he was being stupid, but it rankled. He admired Jack. The man was taking him step by step through working with his new horse. He didn't want his pity. Didn't want to seem so weak.

"Let's go inside. We'll eat way too much pizza and you can tell me what's up. Come on. Don't make your big sister worry."

He owed her so much. Those words were ones he couldn't refuse. He nodded. She hopped up and grabbed the pizza, leading the way into his house. *Their* house, really, though she'd moved over to Todd's when they got engaged. Wade missed her.

Working in comfortable silence, they got out plates and napkins, and Wade popped the tops off a couple of beers. Plunking herself down at the well-worn kitchen table, Nora fixed him with her big sister glare. She took a gulp of her beer and then commanded, "Shoot."

"What, no small talk? What's new with you?"

"What's new with me is I'm leaving in the morning to consult on a ranch near Bakersfield. And I need to know you're okay before I can go."

"I'm okay."

"No, you're not. You had a hard time at a movie."

"Well, who needs movies? They're over-priced. Predictable."

"Wade Hoffman, stop!" she ordered.

He hated her fussing. But he heard the concern in her voice. "Okay. Here's what happened. I went to the movies with Lori. And all the noise made me feel really weird, so I walked out. Well…ran out."

Nora nodded. "What about Lori? Is she okay?"

"She's amazing. I told her we shouldn't date, and she told me where to go."

"She's a great girl."

Wade sobered. "I don't deserve her, Nora. She should be with someone normal who can handle stress. Who can take her places."

"But over time you'll be able to do more," she assured him.

"I hope so."

"Wade, it's not about hoping. It's about working at it. The medicines will never work by themselves. Dr. Miller told you that. Have you called any of those counselors I wrote down for you?"

"I just don't see how talking to someone who's never been through it is going to help."

"Okay, who *do* you want to talk to? Because keeping it all locked up inside is obviously working real well for you."

"I dunno," Wade mumbled. He was used to her sarcasm, but the truth in it still stung. "Someone who has actually been in the military before, I guess."

"What about Dan Sanders? He told me he asked you to come on by his store in the early mornings sometimes and have coffee with him. Have you gone?"

Wade remembered Dan's kind eyes. His generous offer. "No," he admitted.

"Go see him tomorrow. Tell him what happened at the movies. He's probably been through something similar."

"I don't know…" he started, but Nora cut him off.

"Wade, this is your pride getting in the way! You need help."

"Okay," he said quietly. She was right.

"Isn't there some kind of veterans' group that meets in town?"

Ethan's group. He'd never shown up. "They meet Mondays."

"As in tonight?" Nora glanced at her watch.

"Have you fed the animals? I'll do it for you if you'll go tonight."

"I fed them already. Everything's set for the night. But I dunno, Nor. I've had a long day, and…"

Nora stood up so suddenly her chair fell over behind her with a thud that had Wade on his feet, combat ready, in an instant.

"See? Look at you. A chair falls and you jump a mile."

He glared at his sister until he took in her pale skin, her hands clenched into fists. She was furious. And frightened.

"I won't lose you," she said. "We've lost them all. Mom, Dad, Arch, Blake, and I will *not* lose you."

"You won't lose me. I'm not going to kill myself or something like that. It's not that bad."

"But if you don't deal with it, if you push Lori away and you isolate yourself out here, it *could* get that bad. Please go to this meeting tonight. If you need me to, I will drive you there and wait in the truck until it's over. Just go get help. Now."

He couldn't argue. Not when she was scared like this. They'd only ever had each other, and they'd always had each other's backs. He sighed. "Okay, I'll go. As long as I can eat one piece of this pizza without you giving me a hard time about anything."

He grabbed another slice of the meat combo with enough cheese to clog an artery. But what the hell. He was going to need the extra strength to walk into that meeting tonight and admit the truth. That he had a problem. And he had no idea how to fix it on his own.

THERE WERE LESS than a dozen vehicles parked outside Grange Hall when Wade pulled up. He was glad to see it. He didn't think he could go in if there was a huge crowd.

Taking a few deep breaths as he approached the entrance, he pushed open the door. His limbs were leaden and anxiety was rippling through his chest, but he forced himself forward across the hallway toward the main room.

He froze at the doorway, scanning the scene. A few guys were helping themselves to coffee from an urn set across from the door. There was a plate of cookies that looked homemade. A circle of chairs were set in the center of the room, and a handful of men were already sitting down. He recognized one of them vaguely. Maybe they'd gone to high school together?

"Hey, man, you made it." Ethan's beefy hand grasped his shoulder. "I thought I was going to have to pay you a visit out on that ranch of yours and drag you down here myself." He propelled Wade into the room by the sheer force of his enthusiasm. "Hey, everyone, we have a newbie. This is Wade. He got back from Afghanistan just a couple of months ago."

"Hey, Wade," several people said, and every single one of them came over to shake his hand.

"Coffee?" Ethan asked. "It's decaf. None of us want to be up in the middle of the night with too much caffeine in our systems. Feeds the demons, you know?"

"Sure," Wade answered.

A big black-haired man offered him a seat next to his. "I'm Luis. Welcome. Glad you could make it."

Luis looked like he could bench-press Wade. Here he'd been worried that this support group would be some kind of sissy thing, but these men were all pretty formidable. Luis wasn't even the biggest guy here.

Ethan handed him a cup of coffee and a cookie. Wade accepted them and set them on the floor under his seat, too nervous to eat or drink anything.

Ethan took a seat on the other side of Wade. "It's eight o'clock, guys. Let's get started." When everyone had joined the circle, Ethan bowed his head. "Let's start with a moment of silent prayer."

It was a long moment. Wade prayed he'd get through the meeting without throwing up or making a fool of himself. When he finally looked up, it seemed that everyone was done praying. They were waiting on him. *Great.*

Ethan read from a page in a binder that explained the rules of the meeting. Confidentiality was evidently a big rule, as it came up a few different times. Then Ethan closed the binder. "First order of business. Does anyone here need anything urgent? Urgent means housing, medicine, a referral to a doctor or shrink, or a job. And Wade, just so you know, a need to get laid doesn't count."

Everyone guffawed. Ethan had effectively broken the ice. Luis said he'd been living with his parents since he left the Marines, and he felt like he was ready to get a place of his own. He asked whether anyone knew of a place. A guy named Parker said he'd forgotten to fill his prescription and missed a couple of days of his medicine, and he wasn't sure how much to start taking now. Wade just stared at them all in awe. They were so relaxed, so casual, mentioning their troubles and asking for what they needed like it was no big deal.

Once everyone had finished offering advice to Luis and Parker, Ethan got his binder out again. "We have a speaker tonight. Darren is going to share his story. How he first realized he was having some problems and how he's been dealing with it. You ready, Darren?"

Darren was the guy Wade had recognized. Now he remembered him. He'd been a year behind Wade, a star on the basketball team. Kind of a stud, really. He still carried that prom-king aura, but he was somber, one booted foot tapping restlessly as he straightened in his chair and started speaking.

"I first realized I had a problem when I threw a chair through a window."

He wasn't the most articulate speaker, but it didn't matter. Wade was transfixed. Everything Darren shared sounded familiar. Losing his temper, feeling irritated all the time. Feeling lost and missing the companionship of his platoon. The night sweats, the dreams so real he couldn't wake up. The anxiety about noise, about losing control in front of others. Getting frustrated easily. Every word provided Wade with another inch of relief. The shared experience didn't fix his problem. He sure as hell wished it would. But at least he wasn't the only one going through it. Was it selfish to take comfort in that?

He heard something else in Darren's talk. Something that wasn't spoken in words but came through anyway. A yearning to get better. To feel normal. To feel like he belonged and could trust himself again.

Wade recognized it. The sense that there was something out there he was reaching for but was scared he wouldn't obtain. He was just reaching for *normal*, and putting a name to it made it feel a whole lot better.

When Darren was finished, Ethan gave them some information about the next meeting and their plans to march in the Veterans Day parade coming up in a few weeks. Then he led them in another moment of silence. And that was it. A quick glance at the old clock on the wall told Wade the meeting was over and he'd survived it. And it hadn't been too bad.

His phone buzzed, and he pulled it out of his jacket pocket. It was a text from Nora asking if he'd made it through.

Yes. Quit worrying, he sent back. And then he relented, adding, It kind of helped.

"Hey." Ethan clapped him on the shoulder with a thump that reverberated through Wade's bones. "What did you think? You gonna come back next week?"

"Yeah, I think I might," Wade told him, almost surprised by his own words. He did want to come back. Even sitting in the room saying nothing helped. Just being near people who were going through something similar to him was healing.

"You'll march with us, right? On Veterans Day? It's a quiet parade. Just the high school band plays. No fireworks or sirens allowed."

Wade remembered Tabitha's sneering comments at church. "A Hoffman marching down Main Street? I don't think Benson is quite ready for that."

"Well, ready or not, you're here and you're a veteran. So they can take their prejudice and shove it."

Wade laughed. Ethan was so totally unapologetic. It was refreshing. "I'll see," he told him. "But I don't know if I'm ready for a parade just yet."

"Well, think about it." He handed Wade a card with his name and phone number written on it. "Call me anytime, day or night, if you want to talk."

"Thanks, Ethan." Wade tried to imagine calling the confident man after one of his dreams. Or after he'd run like a scared kid out of a movie. He couldn't. He shoved the card in his back pocket anyway. "I'd better get going."

"A few of us are heading out for a beer. Want to join?"

"Another time," Wade said. He felt exhausted all of a sudden. Like he'd absorbed too much, felt too much and his skin was too thin. He gave Ethan a wave and headed out the door, welcoming the chill. Ideally it would wake him up enough to get him home to his bed. Anxiety knotted inside him when he thought about sleep. It was unnerving not knowing if it was going to be a good night or bad. Maybe he'd take one of Doc Miller's jumbo sleeping pills just to make sure he got some rest.

He looked up at the stars, shining crystal clear across the autumn sky. He took a breath and let it out slowly, watching it form a cloud around his head. Tonight hadn't changed everything, but it had shifted something inside of him. It was a relief just to acknowledge that things hadn't been going so well.

He thought of Lori and her faith in him. He hoped he was worthy of it. Tonight he'd learned that healing was a long process and could take years. But if he did what he needed to do, he could make progress. And after his panic at the movie last night, one thing was clear. Any step forward was better than staying where he was. He had to make progress, and if he didn't, he had to let Lori go.

CHAPTER TWENTY-ONE

THE STEPLADDER SEEMED steady until Lori climbed onto the last couple steps from the top. Grasping the edge of the white canopy that sheltered the rummage sale tables, she straightened up shakily. She unfolded the banner that would hang along the edge of the canopy and threaded a rope through the grommet at the corner. Her numb fingers felt clumsy as she worked the ends of the rope through the metal loop at the top of the pole.

It wasn't even 7 a.m. and she'd been here for half an hour. One more reason that next year, when the pastor asked for someone to coordinate the rummage sale, she was going to sit on her hands and make sure they didn't wave themselves in the air to volunteer.

But she'd get a break soon. She was in charge of setup and the first couple hours of selling clothes. Then another church member was taking over, and Lori would be free to wander through the festival until it was time to pack up the booth. She was looking forward to wandering. The Benson Harvest Festival was a huge event, stretching down Main Street for several blocks and ending with a big stage and a live band down by Sixth Street. There were a lot of local artists at the fair, and Lori was hoping to find something pretty for Mandy's Christmas gift.

"You look a little shaky up there."

Lori started, then recognized the deep voice below by its power to quicken her pulse. Glancing down briefly, she tried to keep her smile casual. "I'm okay."

Wade was standing at the foot of the ladder. "You look cold. I brought hot coffee. Wanna trade places?"

"I'm good." She tightened the knot and started down the ladder. He held it for her, standing opposite from the rungs so when she got to the ground they faced each other.

"I missed you this week," he said.

"I'm glad." She felt a little shy. The last time they'd seen each other was on their disastrous date. She hadn't meant to avoid him, but she'd welcomed the time away to catch her breath. And to read everything she could about PTSD. "I didn't know you were coming to the festival."

"I wouldn't leave you to deal with the baby stuff. I promised I'd handle it. So here I am."

"But you're not worried? About the crowds? The noise?"

He smiled wanly. "Sure I am. But you're at the quieter end down here, so ideally I won't do anything too crazy."

"You don't have to help," she said quickly. "I'm okay." She was, kind of. She'd loaded everything into her truck on her own, and though she didn't love being around the baby gear, it didn't break her heart anymore.

"Lori." He reached around the ladder and took her hand. "If we're going to spend time together, you have to let me try things. Please don't treat me like I'm broken or try to protect me."

"I'm sorry," she said. "I just want you to be okay."

"I will be. Even if the festival ends up being too much, I'll be okay. Let me try it, all right?"

"Yes, of course," she answered. He was right. If she was going to stick by him, she was going to have to trust him.

"Is one bad date enough to justify a little PDA?" he asked.

"What?" she sputtered, taken totally by surprise.

"Unless you've changed your mind about wanting to date?"

"No. I haven't."

"Well, in that case…" He brought his mouth down to hers, brushing her lips in the faintest of kisses. The kind of kiss that made her want more kisses. "It's nice to see you," he murmured.

"Nice to see you, too" was all she could manage with kiss-scrambled wits.

"I want to help." He gave her a quick kiss on the forehead and went to her truck, pulling out a cardboard box labeled with the word Adult. "Where does this go?"

"Let's put it over here on this table by me, and we'll put the baby stuff over there." She pointed to the table closest to him.

He set the box down and went for another.

She tried not to notice how he looked in his faded jeans, his navy-blue parka and his dark cowboy hat, pulling the boxes out. But how could she not? He moved with such coiled energy, like he was holding some of his actual strength back.

He grabbed another of the big cardboard cartons of clothes. "Try your coffee."

She ignored him and pulled a box out of the truck, dumping it on the ground.

He was grinning at her. "Stubborn much?"

"Back at you."

"We're good that way," he said. "But seriously? You should try that coffee."

She grabbed her cup and took a sip. It was foamy and sweet. "You got me a latte thing!"

"I remembered that you like them."

Well, that was cute. And the drink was perfect for this chilly fall morning. Decadent and hot. She could see the steam rising. "Thank you. I love it."

A now-familiar nose poked her shin. Snack had emerged from snoozing in his bed that Lori had placed beneath one of the tables. Yeah, she was pathetic, bringing along a bed for the little guy. But she'd never had a small dog before. He seemed to get chillier than her old cattle dog had. Was she going to have to buy him one of those little sweaters come winter? She wouldn't even think about that now.

She bent down and scooped him up. "Hey, buddy," she said quietly, and he nuzzled her cheek.

"What the…" Wade reached out his hand and Snack gave a dignified sniff, then allowed Wade to rub his jaw. "Nice fur, little guy," he said. Snack snorted, and Wade grinned. "Is this the dog we talked about in church? He's wild looking."

"He's some sort of terrier," Lori answered. Oh, what the hell. She might as well own it. "He's my dog now. I've had to accept that. He even comes with me on rides."

"He can keep up?" Wade gently lifted one of Snack's furry paws with one finger. "His legs can't be more than six inches long."

"He doesn't keep up. He rides *with* me."

Wade's smile became a grin. "In the saddle? No kidding!" He fluffed up the fur on the dog's head until it spiked like a punk rocker. "Not the dog I'd have pictured for you, but I like him. He has character. What's his name?"

"Snack."

He laughed out loud, and damn, did it look good on him. She stared, trying to absorb it, trying to memorize it, like something she could pull out and ponder on a bad day.

Wade shook Snack's paw. "Good to meet you, Snack," he said solemnly.

Snack huffed and tried to lick his fingers.

"Not polite, Snackeroo." Lori set the dog on the ground. "Go lie down," she told him, and he trotted back to his bed.

"Well trained already," Wade said.

"Working on it," Lori answered. She took another sip of her foamy coffee. "And speaking of working, we have to get this stuff unpacked."

"Sure." He smiled again, and she felt it across her skin. What was going on with her today? She was ogling him like a teenager with way too many hormones. Maybe it was because she finally knew what was really going on with him. He'd always seemed so unshakable and tough that it was a little intimidating. But now she knew he was struggling. She wasn't happy he was hurting, but it did make him seem more human. More approachable.

She went back to setting out clothing for the sale, and Wade wandered off to deal with the furniture. She tried to focus on organizing the booth, but she was restless.

She kept stealing glances at Wade's profile while he was busy neatly stacking toys and baby clothes. He was handsome and composed, but now that she was aware of his condition, she could see the tension in his jaw and shoulders. She wanted to soothe it. Run her fingers over his muscles and help him relax. Her own muscles warmed at the thought. She didn't just want to date him, she realized with a force that had her starting. She *wanted* him.

She felt her face go red and turned her back to Wade. She never felt like this! In fact, she'd wondered sometimes if her libido was broken. Every time she'd dated anyone seriously, she'd felt this reluctance when things started to get too physical. She'd figured it came from knowing the consequences of casual sex way too well. But as the years went on and she didn't change, she'd wondered if maybe she was simply an unromantic person.

But this...it was like the blood in her veins had gotten thicker, warmer, and she was restless. She turned back and stole another peek at him. His lower lip was just a little full. She wanted to kiss it again.

He glanced over, caught her staring and gave her a quick wink. Would he ask her out again soon? Should she ask him out? She wanted to. Well, what she really wanted was to proposition him. But she'd never done anything like that before.

It was disconcerting, how fast things had changed between them. Not too long ago, he'd asked her to dinner and she'd said no. Then he'd asked her out in the parish hall and she'd said no again. But at church, something had started. This need for him grew on her like a vine, attached sticky tendrils to her skin and clung tight. Their one bad date hadn't taken away this feeling that they were meant to be together. That she needed to be with him.

She snuck another peek. He was placidly laying the folded clothes in piles on the table, arranging them by size, just like they'd planned. Totally oblivious to her thoughts.

He turned, a blue onesie in his hand. "Are you doing okay with all this? I can take over the booth for you if you'd rather not deal with it at all."

"Thanks," she said. "I'll stay, but I really do appreciate your help. When I first found out about that load of baby clothes, I thought I was going to have a heart attack."

He came toward her like he was going to give her a hug, but he stopped short. Took her hand in his. "It's been okay, right? Maybe even a little healing." He reached over, grabbed a white baby hat with pink strawberries and plopped it on his head, where it sat at a goofy angle. "I bet together we can face down any baby products that come our way."

She had to smile. She *was* handling it all way better than she'd ever thought she could. The clothes were actually kind of adorable. But an invitation for a baby shower had arrived this week, from a high school friend who'd moved up to Carson City. She'd popped the RSVP right back in the mail with No checked. So she still had a way to go.

She went back to arranging her table, looking for a safer topic. And a distraction from how much she wanted to kiss him. "What have you been doing this week?"

"Working with my new horse, Jackson. The one Todd brought over?"

"How's that going?"

"It's coming along. I didn't think I could do it, but he lets me lead him around now, and touch him, and he's not totally terrified of the saddle pad anymore."

"Hey, that's progress," Lori said. "Baby steps."

"Yup," Wade said and glanced at her uncertainly. "I guess I've been taking a few other baby steps, too. I went to a veterans' support group."

"Seriously? That's amazing!" Her own relief surprised her. Like she'd been holding her breath, wondering if she was going to regret loving him. "I'm so proud of what you're doing," she told him. "With the horse *and* the group."

He took her hand and pulled her gently toward him. "I want to make you proud."

She nodded, her words lodging in her throat. His eyes flickered to her mouth, and something in her fluttered in response. He wanted to kiss her. She knew he did. He stepped closer, still holding her hand. "Lori, I'm so honored that you put your faith in me. I'm going to work hard to get better. I promise."

And her caution was overruled by his words and sweetness and the attraction she'd felt all morning. She was filled with a bone-deep need to be there for him, to be *with* him. She took a step toward him, stood on tiptoe and brought her mouth to his, not willing to go without the taste of him any longer. One kiss, and she'd savor it slowly. One kiss to tide her over. She pulled back, searching his eyes for his reaction.

She'd cracked his reserve. The intensity she craved was there in his eyes—that laser focus on her that left her system humming with anticipation. He whispered her name as his lips found hers again, as his hands cupped her jaw and he angled his head to take the next kiss deeper.

The *heat* he brought! It slid over her skin, melted her fears, had her clinging to his shoulders for support, grateful for the arm he slid behind her back to keep her from falling. All the sounds of people setting up the booths around them faded to a background hum. Her whole focus was riveted on the feel of his mouth on hers, the strength of his shoulders under her hands.

The sound of clapping teetered on the edge of her awareness, then broke through the rushing of her blood. It got louder, and Wade pulled back.

"Uh-oh," he whispered, and she glanced over to see they had an audience. A clapping audience. The dozen or more people who'd been setting up booths around them had all stopped to watch the show.

"It pays to get here early," someone called, and everyone laughed. Wade grinned and pulled Lori in for one more kiss, accompanied by loud cheers. Lori flushed, embarrassed, wondering if it was possible to melt into the pavement. Other ranch owners didn't make out in the middle of a booth at the Benson Harvest Festival. She wasn't exactly conveying the impression of responsible citizen that she'd so hoped to project.

But Wade smiled at her, half shy, half triumphant, and she decided that it didn't matter. Benson would have to take her or leave her as she was, because no way was she not kissing Wade Hoffman again. She clung to his neck and threw herself into another kiss, a feast of heat and need that filled her up like nothing else.

"Damn," Wade breathed when she let him go. "Lori, what the hell did I do to deserve that?"

"You taste good," she said, flushing.

"Right." He looked kind of dazed.

Someone nearby shouted, "Encore!"

"I keep forgetting about all these people," he murmured.

She couldn't even look at them. Because then

she'd have to take her eyes away from Wade, and she wasn't willing to do that yet.

"Do you think we could do a little more of this after the sale?" he asked.

"Yes, definitely," she assured him. "A lot more."

Wade nodded, still looking stunned. Then he turned to face their audience. "Show's over," he called and gave everyone a cheerful wave.

Lori finally looked around. People were smiling. The crowd was happy for them. And she was happy, too. Because maybe things weren't perfect with Wade, but these feelings were real. And no matter what happened next, Wade Hoffman had kissed her breathless in the middle of the rummage sale booth.

The sale! She glanced at her watch. "Oh no, we've only got fifteen minutes to get this all ready!"

"That was awesome," he said, giving her a last soft kiss on the cheek. "Thank you."

They worked in silence, unpacking the boxes and laying the clothing out as fast as they could, and leaning the baby furniture along one side of the booth. When they'd finished, they were a little breathless, but they'd made it. People were arriving for the festival and their booth was ready.

After her first few customers, Lori glanced

at Wade, hoping this wouldn't be too much for him. He needed a success after the movie fiasco.

But it was pretty clear, pretty quickly, that she wouldn't have to worry about Wade having problems. He was too busy talking to all the women. Whether it was curiosity about a member of the dangerous Hoffman family or the fact that a gorgeous man selling baby clothes was irresistible to the female half of the town, Wade was selling the stuff to a line of women ten deep.

Lori would have been jealous if it hadn't been so funny. Some of his customers even requested photos with him and their purchases. Seeing the bemused expression on Wade's face, the mock-pleading glances he sent her way, had her laughing out loud. Watching him be the center of attention, completely accepted by so many locals, had her laughing inside. He was breaking the legacy. He was smiling and joking and making friends and admirers. He looked happy, excited and so different from the broken man under the lamppost. It was relief beyond measure.

"The church should give you a cut of the profits," she teased him as she brought over a pile of bags the ladies could use to carry their purchases. "We're going to sell out at this rate."

"I don't need to be paid." He grinned. "I got a kiss out of this gig."

"A few of them, if I recall." She threw the words over her shoulder as she passed. She set the pile of bags on the table and went to get more, but he caught her arm.

"I'm having trouble waiting for more."

His hand on her arm was making her pulse jump. "Just another hour or so and you can have them."

"Can we go on a date? Spend time together? Just as soon as we're done here?" He looked down at Snack, who had come out of his bed to beg Lori for one of the dog biscuits she'd brought. "With this guy, too, of course."

She tried to contain the smile that broke over her face, to keep it from becoming a goofy grin. "Sure. That would be fun. I'll need to get back here later for cleanup, but we have a few hours. We'd like that, Snackeroo. Right?"

The scruffy dog gave one of his supersonic terrier snorts. Wade started laughing. And laughter looked so good on him, and her new dog was so ridiculous, that Lori started laughing, too. And was still giggling when the line of customers started up again—some of them for her, but most of them for Wade the baby-clothes-selling hunk, who was taking the Benson Harvest Festival by storm.

CHAPTER TWENTY-TWO

"WHERE TO NEXT?" Wade asked. "My truck to dump all this off?" He'd insisted on carrying all of their festival acquisitions, so he was laden with a new bridle he'd won in a raffle and a poinsettia he'd secured for her by tossing a baseball and breaking an old plate. Plus a vase she'd bought from a local artist for Mandy's present.

"Sounds good," Lori said, and they wandered back to his truck, which he'd parked on a side street in the shade of an old pine. She carried Snack, making sure he didn't get stepped on in the crowds.

Wade wasn't sure how he felt about the crowds, either. But he was trying to follow the advice that Dan had given him yesterday morning when Wade had mentioned that he was attending the festival. "Let me tell you about crowds," Dan had said, leaning on his store counter. "Here's how you do it. You need to stay one step ahead of your instincts. When you catch yourself looking for where a sniper might be hiding, stop, take a breath and look for five good, everyday things that you know are positive. Look at a kid playing. Or look up at the sky, or over at the mountains. Breathe in all those little homelike, comforting things."

He'd gone to see Dan almost every day this past week. The guy was a little groovy sometimes, but he gave good advice. Wade looked up. The day had turned warm, and the sky overhead was luminous blue. He looked at Lori. She'd braided her hair into pigtails this morning and put a light brown hat on her head. In her jeans and worn brown boots, she looked every inch the cowgirl, even here off the ranch. He took in her deep blue eyes, the smattering of freckles across her nose. The full pink lower lip he wanted to kiss again.

They put their loot in the cab and then wandered back down Main Street. Snack was still nestled against Lori's chest, and Wade put his arm around them both. It was grounding to touch her, soothing to his overvigilant system. The music got louder as they reached the end of the fair, where a Western swing band was playing. People were dancing in the road. Wade took Lori's free hand and turned her and the dog in a circle under his arm. "I liked dancing with you the night we organized all those clothes," he murmured.

She smiled at him, her eyes shining. "Sometimes something small happens and you know you'll remember it forever," she said. "That night was like that for me."

"Want to dance now?"

"I'm not sure what to do with the dog," she said. "He's too little to be down there with all those feet."

"I have an idea." He put a hand on each of her shoulders. They looked like an awkward couple at a middle school dance, but it worked. He tried to look into Lori's eyes, but Snack poked his head up between them and regarded him suspiciously.

"No offense to the little guy here, but this isn't quite what I pictured when I imagined dancing with you again," he told her.

Lori's laugh went right to his heart. It was so good to see her happy. "I know I look like a crazy dog lady right now, but he seems scared by the crowds. I probably shouldn't have brought him."

He smiled. "Nah, it's good you did. This way he can see that it's okay. Hey, he even gets to dance." He paused, a little embarrassed. "Okay, now *I* sound like the crazy dog lady. But there's something about this little guy."

"I know!" Her eyes sparkled with her enthusiasm. "I'm not totally nuts to have him, right? He's kind of strange and special. He reels you in."

He tugged a lock of her hair gently, loving that he got to do this. Got to be like this with her. "It's cool to see you so sweet on this little stray. You like to be tough, but you've got a soft spot after all."

Lori grimaced. "Well, it took a while for me to get sweet. But he just didn't give up."

"You didn't want him?"

Her cheeks went a faint pink. "He's not exactly your average ranch dog. But then I realized that he can't help his size. I'm pretty sure he thinks he's a cattle dog inside. He has big dreams. Am I really going to crush them?"

"He sounds like someone I know. You. Trying to stand up to all the people who want to judge you because you're a small woman running a big ranch."

She stared at him in surprise. "I guess I hadn't made that connection. But yes. Snack deserves the chance to work on the ranch just like one of the big dogs."

Snack tried to lick his face, but Wade was faster and avoided the long pink tongue.

Lori laughed again, and damn, he loved that sound. He loved *her*. It wasn't some big revelation. He'd probably loved her since they were kids. And here he was with her, right in the heart of the town he was determined to make his own. *This* was the future he wanted. The future he'd dreamed of. And it was here. With her. Laughing and smiling at him.

Someone jostled past Wade, and he started.

Lori stopped dancing. "Are you ready to be away from the crowds for a while?"

"Yeah." He could feel the edges of his composure starting to fray. That was another piece of advice from Dan. *When you feel yourself start to fall apart, take a break.* He was ready for that break.

They walked hand in hand off the dance floor and back to his truck. They'd shopped and danced, so it was probably time to feed her now. He was so rusty at this dating thing. "Where to?" he asked.

She set Snack on the ground and moved in front of Wade. Put her arms around his neck and kissed him on the mouth. Her lips were so soft, so full, and he let her take the lead for a moment, relishing the feel of her, his heart pounding because she really wanted this. Him. As messed up as he was. When he couldn't be still any longer, he brought his hands up to cup the back of her neck, pulling her closer, taking charge of the kiss, opening her lips, deepening their connection.

He took his time. Listening to the tiny catches

in her breath, reveling in the way she clung to his shoulders as if she was holding on for dear life. He knew what he wanted right now. Her. A bed. And a whole lot of time.

And then Snack got his leash wound around their legs and almost tripped them up. Wade held the terrier still while Lori unwound the leash. When they were free, Lori wrapped her arms around his neck and whispered his thought right back to him. "I want to be with you."

He froze. It was like that moment right after you threw a grenade. The seconds of silent waiting before all hell broke loose. Except instead of hell, she was offering heaven.

How could this be happening? He couldn't hide the grin that spread over his face. He took in her inky blue eyes, large in her delicate face, her jaw set in that familiar line that said she'd made up her mind. "Seriously?"

"Seriously," she assured him.

"Where?"

"Your house?" she asked, stepping back and scooping up the dog, ready to go. Typical Lori. She didn't mess around once she was sure.

He pictured his run-down house, his shabby bedroom that he'd made no effort to redecorate because he spent all his time out on the ranch anyway. "It's not good enough for you."

"I'm sure it's fine." She smiled. "I spend most of my time with cattle. I don't need anything fancy."

"My house is far worse than just not fancy. I've never fixed it up. Not yet. Could we go to your house?"

"Mandy might come home for lunch to check on her animals. I'd hate to make her feel uncomfortable."

Wade felt a moment of panic that this thing he wanted, needed, couldn't believe was really happening, was slipping away. *Where could they go?* And then he had an idea. "Would somewhere outdoors be okay? If I made it nice?"

She paused, and he took the opportunity to lean in and kiss her gently on the mouth. Just in case she was changing her mind. That thing between them, that spark, ignited straightaway. He felt her breath catch, and she deepened the kiss. "Okay," she whispered into his lips.

He took her hand and led her silently to the door of his truck. Now that they'd figured out logistics, the reality of it had his heart pounding. The woman he loved wanted to sleep with him. He was torn between doing some ridiculous touchdown dance of triumph and running away in fear. He took a deep breath and felt the anxiety settle. He could do this. He'd done it before when he was only a teenager.

But things were different now. There was so much at stake here because he loved her, because she was there in his every thought, waking to sleeping. Because if she wanted this, then he wanted to make it perfect for her.

They got in the car and he held her hand tightly as they drove, taking it away only when they reached his driveway. Todd had helped him get the old tractor running last week, and he'd borrowed a grading attachment. That plus a massive load of gravel had taken care of most of the potholes.

He glanced over to see if Lori had noticed. She was staring at the drive. "It looks incredible! Such a huge change. And the Keep Out sign is gone!"

Wade shrugged, like it had been no big deal instead of backbreaking. "I decided it was time to make things more welcoming around here."

She squeezed his hand. "It's nice."

Wade pulled the truck up in front of the house, busy making the plans that would make this afternoon worthy of her. He looked down at Snack. "What about this little guy? Do we bring him?"

"I think that's taking this whole togetherness

thing a little far," Lori answered. "Can he crash out in your living room?"

"Sure. I'll take him. Will you wait here for me? For about ten minutes?"

"Sure," Lori said, looking mystified.

"I'll be back." He kissed her once, reveling in the softness of her lips, amazed that this was apparently happening.

Wade picked up Snack and his dog bed and carried them both into the kitchen. He set a bowl of water down. The terrier slurped it up. Then the shaggy beast sneezed and shook his entire body in his own personal earthquake. Stepping into his bed, he circled a few times, collapsed into a ball and tucked his nose under his tail. He looked like a sleepy fox. He'd be down for the count in moments.

Wade hurried around the house, gathering up sheets, blankets and pillows. On the way out the back door he saw a tarp he'd just bought, still in its plastic wrapping. Perfect. He added it to his pile and then remembered *why* they were heading into the woods. He staggered back into the bathroom to scrabble through the medicine cabinet in search of the condoms he'd bought in a hopeful moment on one of his first civilian days.

Then he was tearing back through the kitchen and out the back door, jogging a few yards through the woods to where the creek usually ran. It was dry now, but he headed up-hill along its bank, dodging aspen trees as he followed the route he'd taken so many times as a kid when he fled the house looking for peace and quiet.

The clearing was just how he remembered it—alongside the creek under a canopy of aspens, their leaves bright gold on the trees, darker gold where they carpeted the ground below. Wade spread the tarp, the blankets and the pillows. It looked comfortable. A few aspen leaves drifted lazily down and landed on the dark green blanket. It gave the bed a magical look, like it had grown here right out of the woods. Wade caught a couple more leaves that were falling nearby and scattered them on the blanket as well. They should be rose petals, and this should be a gorgeous bed in a beautiful mansion, but he couldn't offer Lori that. He hoped this would be enough.

He jogged back to the truck to get her. He hadn't done this in a long time. There'd been a woman he used to see when he was on leave, who worked at a restaurant near the base. But it had been casual for both of them. It hadn't meant more than a good time, some human contact and a few moments of much-needed oblivion.

This meant everything.

"Hey," he said, feeling shy covering the last few paces between them. "Your castle is ready, princess."

Lori smiled and held out her hand regally. "For a castle it's really well hidden," she teased.

"For a castle it's pretty small. And it's lacking a few of the comforts of home. Like a roof. And walls."

She laughed. "You have a unique definition of the word *castle*."

"It's got a good view." He took her hand in his, and they walked quietly around the back of the ranch house and through the woods. He watched her tuck her hair behind her ear and bite her lip. "We don't have to do anything," he said. "We can lie around and talk if you want. There's no pressure."

He was trying to be chivalrous, determined to do right by her. But it was sheer relief to hear her say, "I want to. This is exactly what I want."

CHAPTER TWENTY-THREE

LORI WASN'T USED to second-guessing herself. Once she'd thought something through, once she'd made up her mind to do something, she did it. But that didn't stop her from feeling nervous. What if it was awkward? What if it was bad? What if they regretted it? What if there were disastrous consequences, like the first time they'd been together years ago?

But every time she looked over and caught Wade watching her, that same hot desire came back that she'd felt when they were dancing, and when he was holding up tiny baby clothes for the ladies of Benson to buy. And it seemed like she wouldn't be able to do much else, wouldn't be able to think straight, until she got the chance to make love to him.

The aspen tree trunks glowed stark white in the shaded woods. They were almost magical, with the occasional golden leaf wafting down from the fall-jubilant trees. It was so quiet... The creek wasn't running. She felt like she'd stepped into another world after their busy morning at the festival. The perfect place for Wade, where there was peace and stillness.

Then she saw the bed he'd made. The sweetness of it, the rightness of what they were about to do, hit home. She wanted this. And any fears she had because of their history were just that. Fears. It was possible they would come true. But probably not. Because all that was in the past, and something deep inside her believed in this new connection with him. And wanted, more than anything, this chance to honor it.

He pulled her toward him, wrapped his arms around her and hugged her. Buried his face in her hair as if he was breathing her in. She pulled him as close as she could and pressed her cheek to his chest. He smelled faintly spicy.

"This has been a dream of mine for a long time. But now that it's here, I'm so scared I'll mess it up," he murmured.

"I'm nervous, too," she confessed. "But I want this."

He kissed her, ran his fingers through her hair and she felt his shuddering sigh on her mouth. "Me, too."

He kissed her again. She opened her mouth to taste him, to devour him, because suddenly she was ravenous for him. For his mouth crushing hers, for heat and weight, for his strong body and vulnerable spirit. She clung to him, kissing him wildly and pulling at him so he caught her around the back and brought them both down to the blankets.

Leaning away, he kept eye contact, his dark eyes narrowed and intense, his breathing rough as he yanked back the aspen-spangled blankets and lay her down on a soft flannel sheet. She kicked off her boots and tossed them to the side, smiling as he set his down carefully, tidy as always.

She went up on her knees and took his jaw in her hands, kissing him boldly before sitting back on her heels and tugging her thin sweater over her head. It was one of the boldest things she'd ever done with a man, but she forced herself to meet his eyes, to own it. If he saw fear in her, he'd back off. She didn't think she could stand it if he did. He stared at her breasts, touched a finger to the satin of her bra. "You are so beautiful," he whispered.

He rose on his knees, kissing her mouth reverently, his fingers soft along her jaw and neck. Then he reached for the back of his T-shirt, yanking it over his head with one hand while the other reached for her shoulder. Pulling her close, he kissed her again. One arm, hard with muscle, slid to band around her back, offering support. His other hand cupped her breast. Just that intimacy had her gasping, grabbing his shoulders, glad for his arm holding her up. "Wade," she breathed.

"Is it too much?" he murmured, his thumb finding her nipple through the satin of her bra and circling gently.

"It's... I don't know. Just kiss me," she pleaded, and he did, lowering her carefully to the ground with his mouth on hers, pulling the soft blankets over them. She opened her eyes to see him framed in a golden halo of aspen. He pulled back, supporting his weight so he didn't crush her, one thumb tracing her cheekbones, her mouth.

"I can't believe you're here with me," he murmured, and she watched him watch his fingers tracing the outline of her lips, a faint smile on his. "I love you, Lori. I think I always have."

She stared up at him. It was a big confession, but he seemed untroubled, like he'd just reported the weather or something. His fingers were in her hair now, his expression calm and happier than she'd ever seen it.

No one had ever told her that before. Should she say it back? She felt a flash of panic. What was the right thing to do? Then she remembered. She wasn't trying to do everything right anymore. She was trying to do what was right for her. She brought his head down and kissed him deeply, ran her fingers through his short, sleek hair. "I love you," she whispered in his ear and then pulled him in to lie across her so she could hold him close.

She looked up at the aspen with a quick prayer of thanks. He was here, with her. Loving her. A slow, warm feeling came over her. A feeling she didn't recognize at first. A strange, sure confidence that everything was going to be okay.

He kissed her neck, moving slowly along her jaw, sending sensation down to her toes. When he came back to her mouth, she held him there and it was more heated, more urgent. She pulled him closer, running her tongue over his, relishing the way he pressed himself against her, a low groan escaping from deep in his throat.

He slid to one side of her, propped himself on an elbow and hauled the blankets up to make sure she was warm. Then he used that free hand to caress her breast again. He slid his broad palm across her stomach, making the muscles there shudder. She tried to take his beauty in, his sculpted chest and rock-hard abs, tracking the contours with her knuckles, following them down to his belt.

"Can we take off our jeans?" he asked hoarsely.

She swallowed hard. There was something

so sexy about that. Like they were those adolescents again, but this time they knew how to be careful with each other. "Yes, please," she murmured. He pushed away but made no move to remove his own, just stared, transfixed, as she undid the top button on hers and slid the zipper down.

Watching him watch her undress was more erotic than any touch. He bit down on his lower lip just a little, glanced at her face with a smile that had a glimmer of nerves in it. Then she tucked her thumbs under the waistband and shifted a little to get the fabric over her hips. His eyes swiveled down, his gaze locked on to her every move. She had a moment of fervent gratitude that she'd worn her black underwear with the lace trim rather than the silly cowgirl print ones she'd considered this morning.

She slid her jeans down to her knees and brought her knees up to get them off altogether, but his hand stopped her with fingers tracing lines up her thighs to hook into the hem of her panties. "These, too?" he asked.

But then he seemed to get distracted by the silken fabric. His fingers kept traveling over the front of them to stop just above her most sensitive spot. Heat pooled in sensuous contrast to the cooling afternoon air, and she thought she might lose her mind if he kept pressing there so gently.

"Hang on," she gasped, kicking her jeans off. She dove back under the blankets, sliding her underwear down as well. "Your turn." She shot him a grin that seemed to get him out of his trance, and with the same economical movements he used for everything, he shucked his jeans and was naked with her in their woodland bed.

Her heart was hammering in her chest, and she was grateful when he pulled her over him and just held her along his body, letting her get used to his bulk, his unfamiliar combination of softest skin and hardest muscle. But neither of them could be still long, especially skin to skin like this. He reached behind and unhooked her bra so it fell open and her breasts spilled out. He shot her a smile that was some mind-melting combination of joy and desire. "I love this," he whispered. His hands came down her back, over her butt, reaching around and under until all she was aware of was his fingers slicked in her wetness, and her pressing against them like a wild thing until she came right there on his hand. She collapsed against his chest, feeling so thin-skinned, so raw, like she'd laid her soul bare along with her body.

"I've got you," he whispered, cradling her

against his chest. "I've got you always." She tried to breathe, tried to be still with him, but she couldn't. She wanted too much from him. She wanted him to risk, to trust her. So she slid up onto her hands and knees over him and kissed him full on the mouth, needing him to fall apart like she just had. With her raised up like this, he could fill his hands with her breasts, and he did with a hoarse groan. Then he slid one hand down and over her belly, seeking to please her.

She wasn't ready to be so out of control again. She moved away, propped herself up on her elbow so she could run her free hand over his chest, the lines of his abs, stopping just short of where his erection stood. But it was enough to get him thinking of his own pleasure. He rolled her onto her back, his eyes locking on hers. She laced her fingers around his neck and kissed him. His hand came down to find the heat between her legs. "Please?" she gasped, and his hand left her to rummage in the pocket of his jeans.

He handed her a condom. "Would you open this?"

Her hands were shaking when she tore the wrapper, trying not to think about how much she wished they'd used one of these the first time they'd been together. But the thought was there. He knew it, too, and he stopped her hands and took the condom from her. "We should have," he said quietly, caressing the hair back from her forehead. "And we didn't. We were incredibly careless. But I can't regret touching you back then. I can't regret holding you or being inside you. You showed me what it was like to be with someone I loved. And I've held that in my heart ever since, wanting to have something like that again. I just never thought I'd be so lucky that I'd get to have it again with you."

Tears came to her eyes. The mistakes they'd made blended into the love that neither of them had been able to let go of.

He ran his thumb down her cheek, following the track of a tear. "I want you so much. But I don't want to make you cry."

"They're good tears," she whispered, and reached up to kiss him softly on the mouth. He pulled back, and she saw a suspicious wateriness in his eyes as well.

"You have no idea how grateful I am for you. You've been my light for so long." He kissed her again and then brought his mouth to her ear, her throat, making her squirm under his lips. Her hands traveled restlessly over the bunched muscles of his back, his shoulders, his arms and she wondered how she'd ever get enough of him. She felt a movement as he rolled the condom on, and then he was over her, inside her, filling all of her aching want. His skin was hot. She'd been a little chilled but now she warmed, heated, until she was clawing at him, her desire for him burning away all the old regret and shame, and branding something new and breathtaking on her soul.

She cried out softly as she came again, fists digging into the muscles of his back to ground her, to release the torment she'd felt over him for so long, to welcome this new thing. And then, as if he'd barely been holding back for her, his fingers wound into her hair, and he pushed deep inside her with her name on his breath like a prayer. She clung to him as he shook, trying to hold him steady, trying to be there for him, the way he was trying so hard to be there for her.

He kissed her throat, her cheek, her mouth, and there was a tear coursing down his cheek. "You astound me," he whispered as she brushed it away with her knuckle.

He pulled her close and wrapped them both up in the blankets. Lori lay with her head on his chest. A breeze was picking up, and an aspen leaf sailed down and landed on her forehead. She giggled and handed it to Wade, who ran it softly over her cheek, tickling her, making her laugh even more.

He kissed her hair and turned toward her, so she did the same, lying on her side, facing him. He put the leaf in her fingers and ran his through her hair, tucking it behind her ear. "Lori, I love you. What we just did just now? It meant everything to me."

She trailed the leaf idly over his forearm and along his chest, wondering if there'd ever been a more perfect moment. How often in life did you get to do exactly what you wanted and feel healed in the process? How often did you get to hear all the words you'd always longed to hear? "I am so happy," she told him.

He swallowed hard, but his gaze never wavered. Something in his look had her pulse picking up the pace. "I want us to be like this together forever. I want you to marry me."

She stared at him, trying to absorb the unexpected.

"Marry me, Lori. We both know that's where we're going. Let's go there now."

He didn't *look* crazy. She studied him a little more carefully, searching for signs of stress. But he looked earnest. Happy. In love. *Holy cow, he means it.* "Wade, it's too soon."

"It's not. Please, hear me out. When we were young, we slept together, and afterward I let you down in every way. Now we've found each other again and I want to show you that

I've changed. I'll never let you down like that again."

All the shiny newness of making love to him, the fresh-start, new-day sparkle, faded. Because he was making this about what had happened before. Dragging them back to that place and that time she'd only recently felt she was finally leaving. She was cold suddenly and sat up, reaching for her bra and her shirt.

"Lori?" Wade sat up, too. "What's wrong? What did I say?"

Tears were starting, along with a sort of depressed sourness in her throat. Like the tenuous hope they'd been building was disintegrating before her eyes, blowing away with the aspen leaves in the afternoon wind. She took a deep breath, wondering what to say. "You are nice to ask me."

"Nice?" He ran a hand through his short hair, a gesture of pure frustration. "I wasn't trying to be nice. I love you. I want to marry you."

He turned toward her, and their bare legs brushed under the blanket. She shook her head and grabbed her jeans. Needing something between her and him.

"That's not a marriage proposal. It's an apology."

He stared at her in confusion. "Help me out here…"

"You're proposing because you feel bad about what happened when we were teenagers, right? You're trying to make up for what you said to me, and how you left in the morning after we spent that first night together. You want to make it up to me somehow."

He looked genuinely distressed. "I don't mean it like that. Nothing would make me happier than knowing I get to spend my life with you. I thought it would make you feel better about us if I told you now. If you knew how serious I was."

She couldn't be mad. Not when his intentions were so good. But she was disappointed that their golden afternoon was tarnished. "That's nice. But asking someone to spend the rest of her life with you has to be more than nice. It has to be passionate and forward-looking and…" She paused. How to explain when she was just figuring this out herself? "You only recently found out about what happened between us. But I feel like I've been living with one foot in the past every day since college. And when you first came back to live here, I was so angry. Because it felt like the past was taking over everything. But I think you coming back, and me telling you what happened—I think it's actually been healing me. And helping me finally move into the future."

"I'm glad," he said.

"But for the first time, I don't feel totally defined by getting pregnant. And it feels good. It feels new and bright and hopeful and easier than it's been. So I don't want you to propose to make up for what happened in the past. Because then my life—our lives—are *still* defined by that. If you want to marry me, it has to be because you are ready to step into the future with me."

He was quiet. She pulled her jeans on, slid her feet into her cowboy boots, and he sat, just watching her. His eyes dark with some emotion she couldn't read.

"I need to get back to the festival. To pack up the booth. So I'll go on ahead and get the dog," she told him. "Meet me at the truck?"

"Sure," he said quietly.

She started toward the path, then glanced back. He was still sitting in the gorgeous bed he'd made for them, watching her go, his mouth set in a grim line. She went back to him, knelt down and kissed him gently on the mouth. "I loved being with you," she told him softly, looking him in the eyes. "And by proposing, you were trying to make me feel safe, and it was so very sweet of you." The afternoon breeze gusted, sending aspen leaves drifting over them like golden snowflakes. Like bits of hope that she wanted to grab on to and tuck into the pockets of her soul.

WADE WATCHED THE leaves plummeting down through the woods around him. The breeze sent them whispering before they fell, each rustle a little piece of the truth in Lori's words. She didn't want reminders of her past. He'd been enough of a reminder when he first showed up at Marker Ranch.

He'd thought to reassure her today, to let her know his intentions. But instead he'd dragged her backward in her healing.

They were *both* healing. In the past couple of weeks he'd been so focused on dealing with his PTSD that he hadn't thought much about what she was going through. But she was right. She'd changed so much just in the weeks since they first laid eyes on each other again. He could see it now. How much softer she was. How often she laughed now. The way she'd forgiven him so quickly for pushing her away on their date. The way she'd adopted the dog who needed her, and not the kind of dog everyone would expect her to have. How she'd danced with him in front of the whole town with that little dog in her arms. She'd let go of a lot of the emotional weight she'd been carrying—

and he'd just handed it right back to her. *Nice one, Hoffman.*

He grabbed his T-shirt and pulled it over his head. Got dressed as fast as he could and bundled the blankets together. He tossed them on the back porch as he ran by. He'd straighten them up later. Right now he needed to get her back to the festival and help her clean up the booth.

Lori was right. They had no more time to dwell in the past. They had a future to get to. And once he'd joined her there, his feet firmly planted on the ground, he'd ask her to marry him again. Maybe then he wouldn't have to hear *no* for an answer.

CHAPTER TWENTY-FOUR

WADE WOKE UP in the dark, gasping for breath. Vigilant, he went up on his elbows and scanned the room. It was his room, but it looked different. Smelled different. How? Why? Every sense was on alert, scanning for danger.

He remembered, and the tension drained out of him. He'd painted the room a clean white. Tossed out all the ancient battered furniture and bought brand-new, clean, modern pieces. For Lori. For them. A surprise she'd loved. He'd created an oasis in the run-down ranch house. A token room fixed up, a reminder of what the place could be someday.

She shifted in her sleep next to him. She was here, warm and sweet, curled up after making love to him for hours. Like she'd been almost every night for the past couple weeks. He wasn't in the desert. Guns weren't firing. He was breathing. No dying. He covered his face in his hands, wanting a drink of water, not wanting to wake her.

As if sensing his distress, she woke. "Wade, are you okay? Did you have a dream?"

Pride would have him lie, but he was learning that pride wasn't his friend when dealing with PTSD. Honesty was. "Yeah. I think I'll get some water. Would you like some?"

"Sure." She sat up, pulling the sheet to her chin. Reminding him that she was naked under the crisp new down comforter. It was still mind-blowing to ponder. Lori Allen, here in his bed. Naked. He jumped up, needing to get the water, needing to get back to her.

In the bathroom he filled two glasses under the tap and drained one. Refilled it. Splashed cold water on his face, relishing how it brought him into the present and pushed the dream away.

Back in the bedroom, she lay like a sexy angel with her hair spread out around her on the pillow, her eyes solemn on his. "Are you okay?" she asked. "Do you want to tell me about it?"

He had told her about his dreams a couple of times. But it left a bad taste in his mouth when he made his troubles hers. He hated filling her mind with images she didn't need and shouldn't have. They were his to wrestle with. "Nah," he said.

"Then how can I help?" She took the water

he offered and drank deeply as he set his glass on the nightstand and climbed into bed.

"You should get your sleep."

"What if I don't want to?" She set her glass down and turned to face him. Kissed him softly, then deeper, pushing the nightmare further away with every touch of her lips. Because she was light, she was sweetness, she was what he'd always needed. What he needed more than ever now.

She seemed determined to show him that he was okay. She ran her mouth over his again and then started down his neck with little nibbling kisses that almost hurt with their ferocity. That tugged him into the present, back into the reality that was so much better than his dreams. He closed his eyes and let her kisses bring him back to life, gasping when her mouth traveled over his abs, grazed his hipbone and wrapped in velvet softness over his erection.

"Lori." This was new between them.

"Shh… Let me try. I'm not great at this."

Her mouth was firm and soft all at once, sliding over him, gripping him. "Oh, yes you are. You really are."

He couldn't believe she was doing this. He was so damn glad she was. He was losing control, but it wasn't like the dreams that terrorized him. This was heat and melting muscles and all his senses focused on her mouth, the touch of her lips, her warm mouth enclosing him, pushing him over the edge. He could lose control like this.

The pressure was building. She was making him insane. "Lori," he gasped. "I need to…" He expected her to pull away, but she did the opposite, holding him by the hips to steady him, taking him in hungry gasps when he careened over the edge into welcome oblivion.

When it was over, he hauled her up and held her to him as close as he could, burying his face in her neck to say thank you.

"Let me make you feel that good," he whispered, his mind already considering all the possible ways that he could.

"No," she whispered. "Not this time. This time was just for you."

"You're sure?"

"Go to sleep," she said, curling on her side behind him, cradling and protecting him. And to his surprise, he did sleep. And it was long and deep and dreamless.

WADE LOOKED AT the crowd gathering on Main Street. Anxiety prickled his skin, and he turned to Lori. "I don't know if I'm up for this." He glanced at her, afraid of the disappointment he might see in her eyes. But there was nothing but love in those blue depths. The love she'd shown him every night for the past few weeks. Even when his nightmares scared them both, she'd stayed there in his bed, holding him. Making it better.

"You can do this, Wade. I know how strong you are. I know that you are bigger than your thoughts, bigger than the stress."

He gave her a skeptical look. "Have you been reading my PTSD book?"

She laughed. "Busted. But seriously, it doesn't matter to me whether you walk in a parade or not. I'll celebrate Veterans Day with you however you'd like. But I know it means something to you."

God, he hated that he was so weak. Ethan and the other guys were standing around chatting, drinking their morning coffee like it was nothing. And he was shaking at the thought of walking down Benson's Main Street to celebrate the time he'd given to his country.

He'd survived. He had to do this. He owed it to the guys who hadn't come back, who didn't get to be veterans because they hadn't lived through the war.

He flashed back suddenly to a godforsaken spot in the mountains of Afghanistan. They'd parachuted in. Three men in his unit had died that day. He could crumple at the memory and go cower on his ranch, or he could walk in this damn parade for them.

"Give me a minute, okay?"

Lori nodded, squeezed his hand and went to stand by the sidewalk rapidly filling with people out to support the local veterans.

But would they support *him*? Or would he walk down Main Street accompanied by cold stares and snide comments from the people his family had wronged?

Sweat broke out and ran down his back.

"Hey, Wade, how ya doing?" Ethan put a hand on his shoulder. "You up for this?"

"Doing okay." He took a deep breath. He could do this.

"I know this is weird for you. But if you ask me, which you didn't, you need to look this town in the eye and show them that you are your own man—different from your dad and brothers. You don't have to walk today, of course. But I'm a little worried that if you don't, you'll regret it."

He would. It was time. He'd come back here to claim his family's ranch and his spot in this community. If not now, at this parade, then when?

"I'm good. Thanks, Ethan."

"Well, let's go, then." Ethan grinned and gave him a bracing nudge with an elbow. "Stick close to me. I've held this veteran title a lot longer than you. I'll show you how it's done."

"Right. Lead the way, big guy."

A few veterans were in uniform, but Wade was relieved to see that most of the men were just like him. Clean jeans and boots. He'd pulled on his army sweatshirt against the chill.

A couple of older veterans kicked off the parade in a convertible mustang. Then a group on motorcycles rode in formation, their sputtering engines running riot over Wade's nerves. *When a noise feels bad, name it for what it really is*, Dan had taught him. "Motorcycles," Wade whispered. And it helped.

Then the high school marching band got started with a rousing if slightly ragged rendition of "God Bless America." And after that, all the folks on foot started walking. Vietnam veterans marching together. A few from Kosovo. Iraq veterans and Afghanistan veterans marching in one big group, because somehow the borders of those two wars were blurred into one big mess.

Wade found himself next to a man just a few years older than he was who rolled down the street in a wheelchair. "My name's Greg," he said when Wade asked. "Lost my legs to an IED in Iraq." Greg had learned some tricks in his chair and pulled a few wheelies, much to the delight of the onlookers. "God bless America," he said to Wade as the crowd cheered, and Wade couldn't tell if he was being genuine or sarcastic.

Wade wondered whether he'd even be able to joke like that if he was in Greg's nonexistent shoes. How would he feel? He'd gotten off so easy. His wounds were on the inside, in his brain. Technically he was still as able-bodied as the day he'd enlisted. He was one lucky guy.

Someone blew on some kind of trumpet, and Wade just about jumped out of his boots. His wounds might be on the inside, but his skin was still too thin to protect them. He wanted to believe he was getting well, but every sudden noise was a reminder that he wasn't yet.

He heard Nora call his name. She was in front of the Downtown Grocery with Todd, who was barely visible behind his big camera, snapping photos nonstop. Nora was waving a flag and dabbing at her eyes. Crying. "I'm so proud of you, Wade!" she yelled.

And he glowed inside at her words. She'd raised him, been there for him on every leave, even moved back here to help him when he embarked on his crazy plan to resurrect the ranch. He felt like maybe, by walking in this parade, he was repaying her just a little.

And then Lori showed up by Nora's side,

waving at him before she gave his sister a hug. He realized what she was doing. She was quietly making her way down the sidewalk, just behind him in the parade, staying out of his way, but there for him if he needed anything.

He kept marching, eyes ahead for a few minutes, and then glanced over to test his theory. Yup, she was there, just behind him, on the sidewalk, saying hello to a couple with a little boy. He felt like rushing over to hug her, or doing some kind of happy dance, or yelling his thanks to the big sky. True to her word, she was there for him. He might be damaged, he might be weak, but she didn't care. She had his back. And with her, he could face just about anything.

LORI KNEW SHE was probably hovering. Okay she *was* hovering, but this parade was important to Wade. It also presented so many challenges, from noise to unexpected movement to just being in a crowd. Wade seemed strong and tough on the outside, but she'd spent almost every free moment with him these past couple weeks, and she knew that underneath the strong, steady exterior was a soul in turmoil. From the way he started at any unexpected noise or movement to the way his dreams destroyed his sleep, she knew now how desperately he needed someone to look out for him. Even though he'd never, ever admit it.

If he had a hard time, she wanted to be there to help. So she tried her best to stay near him but out of his sight. The upside was that she got to watch him for the whole parade, and she was proud of him. He looked perfect out there, marching with Ethan and some of the other guys she knew. Self-contained, but with the slightest swagger in his step. Owning his survival and what he'd given to his country.

The parade ended at the courthouse lawn, and she stood with Nora and Todd, waiting for Wade to finish backslapping with his buddies. "You must be proud of him," she said to Nora.

"I am. And Lori, if I can just say it, I'm thrilled you two are dating. I can't tell you how happy it makes me."

She blushed, scarlet probably. "It makes me happy, too."

"He's always had a thing for you," Nora told her. "He idolized you."

This was news to her. "Well, I think we always liked each other."

"I feel like I owe you an apology, though," Nora went on. "I pulled him away from you, really abruptly, that summer he moved to Reno with me. I was furious with him. And scared. He'd been getting into a lot of trouble. My dad and brothers were getting more into drug dealing, and I was so afraid they'd drag Wade down with them, too. He wanted to stay in Benson at least a few weeks longer, to spend time with you. I made him leave right away."

"You were looking out for him. I don't blame you."

"It was a hard time for Wade," Nora went on. "And he told me he didn't handle the goodbye very well."

It was old news, old drama, but it helped to know that he really had missed her. That he'd regretted his cruel words to her. "Thanks, Nora. I appreciate you telling me."

"And now I have to ask you a favor."

"Of course."

"I travel a lot for work. Todd tries to check on Wade, but between the machine shop and dealing with his horses, he gets really busy. You'll keep an eye on him, right? And if anything seems off, you'll let me know?"

"Absolutely. Give me your phone number."

Lori had just finished adding Nora's phone number into her contacts when Wade walked up, a wide smile on his face that Lori recognized as relief. Making it through the entire parade was a big victory for him.

Todd snapped a few photos of him until Wade

said, "Enough! You're making me feel like it's my first day of kindergarten or something!"

Nora laughed and gave him a hug so enthusiastic it had Wade staggering backward. "Easy there, sis," he gasped as she squeezed him tight.

"I'm so proud of you." She was wiping away tears now. "So proud that you got out there today and showed everyone how amazing you are."

"I don't know about that," Wade said, typically modest. "I am just glad I made it through without doing anything too crazy."

"You did good." Todd clapped him on the back and then gave him a brotherly embrace. "You even got me teared up. Though not like your sister. Jeez. Next year we're bringing a box of tissues."

Wade guffawed, and Nora smacked her fiancé gently on the shoulder. "Happy tears. And you were a little more than teared up. You could have used a tissue, as well."

It was a side of Wade Lori hadn't seen. She'd always known him as a solitary guy. Seeing the love between him and his sister and Todd was melting away the last of her doubts and worries. Somehow, despite his upbringing, he was a really good guy. He was so strong, battling PTSD every day. And he was a family guy.

And she knew in that moment that she

wanted Wade to be *her* family. She'd told him it was too soon when he'd proposed. Too early to make a lifelong commitment. But watching him with Nora and Todd, witnessing his bravery in the parade today, she had no more doubts about what she wanted. She wanted a life with him. A lifelong bond. She wanted Nora as her sister and Todd as her brother. And Wade as her husband, to love and cherish forever.

Everything seemed to tilt for a moment. Wade was her love. She wanted him for life. And then he was swooping her up in a hug that spun her off her feet. She was laughing and he was kissing her hair, oblivious of her monumental realization. "I saw you," he said, setting her down and kissing her solidly on the mouth. "I saw you all along the route. Thank you!"

She grinned at him. "Anytime. I mean it."

He kissed her again, in front of his sister and Todd, in front of his fellow veterans and the town of Benson. "I love you, Lori Allen. Thank you for being so good to me."

"My pleasure." She hugged him back. And caught Nora's thumbs-up over Wade's shoulder. Everything clicked into place. She was where she should be. Where she needed to be. And it was a perfect feeling.

CHAPTER TWENTY-FIVE

WADE LOOKED HAPPIER and more carefree than Lori had ever seen him as they walked through the crowd at the High Country Sports Bar. Every few steps there was someone new who wanted to shake hands or give him a high five. A few people even thanked him for his service. It was the perfect end to an amazing Veterans Day.

Wade pulled her straight onto the dance floor. "You look beautiful," he said, leading her into a smooth two-step.

She flushed. She was wearing one of Mandy's dresses again. Wade had let out a low whistle when he'd seen it and instantly devoted all his energy to removing it, which had ended with them in Lori's bed and her having to start the whole getting-ready process over again.

Not that she was complaining. The music slowed and he pulled her close, and she put her cheek on his chest and swayed with him. Breathing in his scent, feeling him so perfectly close. A deep contentment settled over her and she sighed.

"You okay down there?" Wade murmured into her hair.

"Doing good," she said. "So glad to be here with you."

She closed her eyes, savoring the feel of him, disappointed when the song ended.

"Want to grab that table?" he pointed to a two-top near the back of the bar. It was perfect. A place where they could retreat and talk, if he needed a break from the day's celebration.

"It's perfect. Will you grab us a couple beers?"

"Absolutely."

But she caught his hand before he could walk away and stood up on tiptoes to brush her lips over his mouth. When she pulled away, he brought his mouth to hers, kissing her a lot harder than she'd kissed him. The satisfying kiss of a man who clearly wanted more. "I'm glad to be here," he said quietly. "But I'm ready to go at any time if you decide you'd like to continue this celebration somewhere more private."

She kissed him again, long and hard, and she was pretty sure, when she pulled away, that his eyes looked a little bit crossed. "Soon," she whispered. "Beer first," she added, giving him a little shove toward the bar, and she went to claim their table.

THE BAR WAS crowded and Wade had to wait a while for the bartender to get to him, but he didn't really mind. It was nice to have a moment in the anonymous crowd to process what had happened today. He'd walked in the Veterans Day parade, and no one had thrown eggs. No one had booed. In fact, the crowd had cheered. For the first time in ages, it felt like his family didn't matter. His PTSD didn't matter. All that mattered was that he'd given his time to his country, and people appreciated that.

And now he got to celebrate that, here with his friends from the support group, and Lori.

A swell of noise behind him had Wade glancing over his shoulder. A whole group of people had arrived, a younger crowd than him. The guys jostling each other, the girls who hung on their arms giggling at all their lame jokes. *It's no big deal. Just loud people waiting for beer just like I am.* But the old instincts reared their hypervigilant heads. The group was like a wall, hemming him in, separating him from the door.

Be logical. There was an exit sign to his left. A few running steps and he'd be out the side door. Not that he'd have any reason to flee.

Their noise seemed to press against his back. One guy made a crass comment about a woman's body, and Wade's annoyance flared. *Not your problem. Just get your beers and get on back to Lori and enjoy your night.*

His heart was pounding by the time he got his order in. He slapped his money on the counter and grabbed the bottles, needing to get away from the press of people.

Emerging, relieved, from the crowd by the bar, he took a few calming breaths and looked for Lori. The table they'd chosen was empty, though her jacket was on the back of her chair. He set her beer down there anyway. Maybe she'd seen a friend or headed for the restroom.

Taking a gulp from his bottle, he idly scanned the dance floor. And saw Lori. She was dancing with some guy. Jealousy flooded hot beneath his skin. The man was dancing close. Way too close. *Don't be stupid*, he told himself. *She has every right to dance with a friend.*

But the friend looked familiar. And then he realized who it was. Seth. The ranch hand she'd fired. What the hell was she doing dancing with him? Wade set down his beer and walked to the edge of the dance floor.

Lori's face came into view, and she didn't look happy. She looked pale and angry. She was enduring this dance, though he had no idea why. Wade watched carefully, trying to catch her eye. When he did, she gave a small shake of her head as if telling him to back off.

Seth grabbed her hand and twirled her innocently enough, except that either he was a terrible dancer or he was deliberately trying to pull her off balance. Lori staggered a tiny bit and regained composure, then said something sharp to Seth. That was all the information Wade needed. He crossed the floor in seconds. "Mind if I cut in?"

"Wait your turn, Hoffman," Seth said. His dark hair looked longer and a little greasy. "Lori and I are having a good time. The song will be over soon."

"Lori doesn't look like she's having a good time." Wade hooked his thumbs into his belt loops to keep himself from punching Seth right in his smug mouth.

"Huh," Seth said. "That's not the impression I have. You okay, Lori?"

"I'm fine," she said, her mouth set in a thin line of something that sure as hell looked like disgust. Why was she dancing with this asshole? "We'll dance the next dance, okay, Wade?"

"Yeah, Wade," Seth chimed in. "Wait your turn."

Wade looked at Seth's beer-blurred eyes, considering how very much he wanted to land a fist between them. But beyond Seth, a few people had stopped dancing and were watching the conflict. Probably waiting to see how a Hoffman would handle it.

"Wade, don't." Lori was pointing at his hands.

Wade looked down and saw that he'd balled them into fists.

"He's just trying to make you look bad in front of everyone." Lori was between him and Seth now. "Don't let him do it."

Seth raised his fists and fake punched the air. "What, all those years in the military and you didn't learn how to fight?"

Wade carefully moved Lori aside. "I did fight. But I also learned that it's not nice to hurt smaller, drunker men." He breathed long and deep, trying to bring down the adrenaline surge that was way too big for this situation. It was combat-sized, battle-sized, filling up his nervous system, putting everything in sharp focus, amplifying all sounds.

Seth stepped up closer to Lori. "C'mon, Hoffman. You can't blame me for asking her. A girl like this? So hot? You're gonna have to get used to sharing her."

"Hey!" Lori turned on Seth. "Don't be gross. Stop provoking him!"

Seth's smile oozed hatred. "I'm just reminding him that he's got some healthy competition. And that his slime-ridden Hoffman blood isn't going to help him much in the race. Come on, Lori, you know you need a real man to make you happy. Not some sniveling son of a criminal."

"Enough." Lori's voice was icy. "I agreed to dance with you because you said you'd fight Wade if I didn't. I danced. So shut up."

"What the hell, Lori?" Wade shoved Seth a step back from her. "You agreed to dance with him to protect *me*?"

She grabbed his arm, gripping tight. "I didn't want him to ruin your night. *Our* night."

"Oh, how sweet," Seth sneered. "You have a mommy, Hoffman. Finally. That must be so nice, since your own didn't stick around,"

"Seth, drop it!" Lori commanded. "You're pissed that I fired you. I get it. But that has nothing to do with Wade."

"Really? Huh. I remember him following me into the barn with a big old attitude. If he hadn't done that, I would have been fine."

"It must be hard, not being able to take any responsibility for your actions," Wade spat out through gritted teeth.

"It must be hard trying to fuck a hot piece like Lori when you're not even a man," Seth shot back. "Here, I'll show you how it's done." He grabbed Lori's hand and yanked her close, shoving his hips toward hers.

Wade's vision blurred around the edges, and his hand was over Seth's face, pushing him away from Lori. Seth let out a grunt as he flew backward and landed on the dance floor. Shrieks rose as people tried to scramble out of the way.

Seth was back up and coming at him, and Wade could hear shouts at his back. He balled his fists, readied himself. But instead of grabbing Wade, Seth grabbed Lori again and put a hand over her breast.

There was a roaring sound in Wade's head, like a wildfire across dry grass, and it brought a white heat with it that blasted everything out of his vision except the other man's weasel face.

He grabbed Seth by the collar and hauled him off Lori. Lifted him and ran him across the room until he was close enough to fling him into the wall. The bastard went down like a rag doll, and Wade let him land hard before hauling him up by the shirt again. He twisted the fabric, balling it tight enough to choke. He wanted to obliterate, to smash his fists down on this vermin over and over.

He was vaguely aware of Lori yelling at him, of the group breath the crowd of spectators took with every punch, of the way Seth went floppy underneath him, of hands clawing at him, trying to hold him back. The shouts, the voices of everyone in the club and the blaring music all blended and pumped through his blood in a primal pulse that told him to kill or be killed.

Huge hands grabbed at his belt, an arm wrapped around his neck and the two bouncers hauled him back. Together they dragged Wade across the room to the front door. People cleared a path, eyes staring wide. All the chaotic noise went silent.

Outside the door was the porch, the steps, the icy darkness, all hurtling toward him as the bouncers shoved him toward the driveway, hard. Wade staggered forward, stumbled down the steps and landed face-first in the gravel below. He rolled twice, back onto his stomach, his mouth full of dirt and blood.

He lay there, welcoming the ground, the pain, his shallow breathing, trying to come back from wherever he'd been.

"Wade!" It was Lori, down on her bare knees in the gravel, a hand on his shoulder. "Wade, are you okay?" She was sobbing. A streak of dirt was smeared over her tear-streaked face, and nausea filled him because he'd brought her to this.

Ethan was there, lifting Lori, trying to get

her to stand back. And Darren from his support group was next to him, eyes wide and scared, asking, "Are you hurt?"

Then the sirens started. An ambulance for Seth and a cop car for him, no doubt. Wade closed his eyes and waited, listening to Lori's sobs, feeling Darren's hand still on his shoulder in silent solidarity. It was a dim spark of kindness and understanding in all the darkness. Then the blue lights of the sheriff's car lit up the night and the deputy's voice barked for everyone to stand back. His spotlight blinded Wade as he ordered, "Don't move."

Wade opened his eyes. Took in Lori's ghost-white face and the firm grip Ethan had on her shoulders. It killed him that Ethan felt he needed to hold her back. Because he couldn't keep himself under control.

A crowd had spilled out of the bar and filled the porch. He lifted his head slightly and glanced their way, all those eyes, all those people. All that judgment. The sheriff approached and clamped handcuffs on, the steel so cold it bit. But it didn't matter. Nothing mattered. Because he'd done exactly what, deep down, he'd always known he was going to do. He'd proved to the town, and worst of all, to Lori, that he was no more than he'd ever been. Out of control. A menace. Just the same no-good

Hoffman kid, pretending to be someone better than he was, and making a fool of himself in the process.

CHAPTER TWENTY-SIX

THE JANGLE OF metal on metal jolted Wade awake. He went from lying down to standing in one motion before he remembered where he was. Puke-green walls, cement floor, a toilet in the corner. He knew the jail cell at the Benson sheriff's office well. He'd bailed his dad and brothers out of here many times.

And now he was the one locked up. His dad would have been proud to know he was keeping up the family tradition.

He hurt, the pain sharp and stinging, on his knees, his palms, his elbow, his face. He backed away from the opening door, heart thudding hard, pieces of last night falling into place. The bar. Seth grabbing Lori. Fury. Throwing Seth. Pulling him up again. Hammering his fist down.

Cold night air and sharp gravel. The circle of onlookers. All those boots surrounding him as he lay with his face in the dirt. Lori crying on Ethan.

He'd tried to be there for her, and he'd messed up everything.

A man in a sheriff's uniform stepped in. Not the young guys who'd hauled him in here last night. This man was older, with graying hair and kind eyes. "Wade Hoffman?" he asked.

"Yes, sir." Amazing how the military training kicked right in.

"Mike Davidson, sheriff." The older man paused and glanced down at the bandages over Wade's palms. "I'd shake your hand, but I don't think that would feel so great."

"No, sir," Wade answered.

"You're in a lot of trouble, son. We're still trying to get the full story. The guy you hit is in the hospital. We had to bring in a helicopter to get him up to Reno."

"I'm sorry to hear that." Wade could barely get the words out through the implications crowding him. All the years Nora had worked so hard to keep him on a straight path. And now he'd be going to jail. Her disappointment, combined with his, threatened to send him to his knees.

"I hear you came back from Afghanistan pretty recently."

"Yes, sir."

"I got a look at your records. You were an army ranger?"

"Yes."

"Your sister put me in touch with your commanding officer. He says you're a good kid. He also says you were in some pretty tight spots. And that you lost a lot of friends."

Wade swallowed hard. "I did, sir. But I'm not looking to make excuses for last night."

"Neither am I. But I am looking for a solution. You'll be assigned a lawyer if the prosecutor decides to press charges. And I suggest you talk to that lawyer about veterans' court. It's a program for guys like you, and it can help you get back on your feet."

"I don't want anyone's charity," Wade said quickly. "I'll face the consequences of my actions." Not like his dad and brothers, who'd fled like cowards when justice loomed.

"I get it." Mike nodded. "But I see it differently. They say the hardest part of fighting in a war is coming home. Veterans' court isn't charity. It's a way to manage the thousands of guys just like you who are ending up in court because their minds are affected by what they went through over there."

At least his brand of crazy had plenty of company. It was stark comfort. "Thank you, sir."

"For now, you're free to go. Your girlfriend posted your bail. She says she can guarantee that you'll stick around until we get this all sorted out. In other words, don't leave town. Understand?"

"Yes, sir." Wade wondered if he could just stay here. The squalid cell would be better than facing the disappointment in Lori's eyes. But Mike was waiting, so he squared his aching shoulders and followed the sheriff out the door, past a few battered old desks covered in paperwork and into a shabby waiting area.

Lori had her back to him, staring out the window at the street outside. Her hair was loose down her back, and she had a shearling coat wrapped around tiny frame. She turned, and he saw her pale skin and the shadows under her eyes. He'd done that to her. He'd put that look of exhaustion and worry on her pretty face. She crossed the room in a few steps, throwing her arms around his neck.

He wanted more than anything to hold her close. But he'd lost that privilege when he lost control last night. So he closed his eyes and inhaled her warm, sweet scent one last time. And took her wrists and removed her hands, setting her away. It felt like something inside him was bleeding when he said, "No. We can't."

LORI WAS DESPERATE to hold him. To feel for herself that he was safe. "Wade, what's wrong?"

He glared at her with hollowed eyes. "We just can't. Not anymore."

His hair was on end, his face and clothing filthy. "It's okay. I don't care about the dirt, or anything." She reached to hug him again, but he stepped back. There were scrapes on his nose and cheeks from falling last night. She wanted to touch them, to touch all of him, after a night of worry so sharp she'd thrown up twice.

It was torture, knowing he was hurt, locked up, probably scared and in pain and—knowing Wade—berating himself for fighting. "It's okay," she said again, hoping to reassure him. "They're letting you go. That's what matters. Let's go home and get you cleaned up."

His face was etched with new lines as if one night in a jail cell had aged him years. He moved away again, out of reach of her touch. "I appreciate you getting me out of here. But that's it. We need to end this thing between us *now*."

Her tortured stomach wrenched, and for a moment she thought she'd be sick again. "What do you mean, *end* this? We're a couple. We'll deal with this together."

"We can't *be* a couple," he said hoarsely. "We can't be together anymore. It was a mistake to try."

His words were hitting her and sliding off. Impossible to take in. "We *love* each other. That's not a mistake."

"Love isn't enough. Not with someone like me."

She stared at him, aghast. "What do you mean, *someone like you*? Wade, you are the person I love. We've gotten through so much. We'll get through this."

He ran a bandaged hand over his gaunt face, misery in every move. "There's something wrong with me. You know it. You saw it last night."

Tears were starting. She swiped them with her sleeve. "But you're working on it. You've been trying to get better."

"And I'm *not* better. I'm worse. I couldn't stop hitting Seth. What if I turned on you that way?"

"You'd *never* hurt me like that." She hated that her voice was quavering. "I know you wouldn't."

"Well, *I* don't know it. I don't know anything anymore, Lori."

"You know you love me. And I love you."

His jaw muscles tensed, and she felt the words before his rough voice sliced into her heart. "I don't even know that. You need to move on from me. It's time."

A sob tore at her throat. "It's *not*. You don't get to tell me when it's time."

He glared at her. "I can tell you when you're wasting yours."

His words were too familiar. Sickeningly familiar. "Really? You're doing this *again*?" Her bitter laughter startled them both. "This is the thing you do when you're scared, right? Like you did back when we were young? Where you push me away from you with as many cruel words as you can find, because you're not sure what's going to happen next?" She stepped up to him with fists clenched, wishing she was taller so she wouldn't have to look up to meet his eyes. "You're *such* a coward, Wade. You think you're acting all grown up and manly right now, trying to protect me, but you're doing *exactly* what you did to me when we were eighteen. Haven't you learned *anything* since then?"

She saw the glitter of tears in his eyes. But she also saw the mulish line of his jaw.

"I'm a mess, Lori. But I won't be *your* mess. I won't ruin your life with my problems. You deserve a hell of a lot better than I'll ever be."

The tears were streaming down her face as she stared at him, willing him to give in. But he shoved his torn-up hands in his jacket pockets. "Go," he said quietly. "Go on. I'll find my own way home."

She took a step away. It was hard to trust that the floor was there, or the door, when everything felt so unreal. So shattered. She hesitated, looked back at him, but he shook his head. So she stumbled forward and shoved her way outside, shuffling blindly into a world she no longer recognized, because everything had changed in just one night.

WADE LEANED ON the pasture fence, watching Jackson graze. He hadn't worked with the mustang in a couple of days. He was probably losing ground. Losing the trust they'd been building. But so what? That was how he lived his life, apparently. Took a couple steps forward and slid all the way back again.

If he didn't end up in jail, he was thinking of leaving. He'd dreamed of reviving the ranch, of redeeming the Hoffman name in Benson. But he'd failed. Spectacularly. Because he'd been trained to be violent, trained to kill. And here, back in society, there was no place for a killer.

He'd always thought the guys who committed suicide after they got home from combat were nuts. Why survive a war just to die once you got home? But now he understood perfectly. There was no home for them anymore.

Not in their hometown, not in their country. And when you had nowhere you belonged, ending it all might seem like a logical option.

Not for him, though. He wasn't a suicide, but he *was* considering reenlisting. Even if he just got a desk job somewhere, at least he'd be around people who understood a little about who he'd become since Afghanistan.

He looked around idly. The heifers would need a new home before he could go. He'd give them to Lori and Mandy. Todd would take back JM and Jackson, of course. Nora was staying in the area now that she was marrying Todd. Maybe Marker Ranch could become part of the sanctuary they were trying to create for wild mustangs?

The idea of living somewhere else felt bleak. But staying here as the local loser felt worse. And living next door to Lori, watching her move on with her life? The pain of that stabbed at his guts.

The rumbling of an engine had him backing up a few steps to where he could see Nora's Jeep rattling down the driveway. Instinctively he looked for somewhere to hide, like he'd been doing every time she or Todd or Ethan or anyone else tried to pay him a visit.

But some voice in his head told him to man up. It had been almost a week since the fight, and he'd have to face his sister sometime. So he went back to the fence, stared at his horse and waited.

"They're not pressing charges," Nora said quietly as she walked up. "They probably realized it would be hard to build a case when so many witnesses saw Seth grab Lori like he did."

No jail. Anxiety loosened its grip for a moment. "Thanks for telling me." His voice came out hoarse. He couldn't remember the last time he'd spoken.

"How have you been? I get that you don't want to see anyone, but I've been worried."

"I texted," he said.

"Yeah," she said flatly. "Thanks for that. The words 'I'm still alive.' That's real informative. So reassuring."

Her sarcasm masked her hurt. He knew that. But he had nothing to give her.

"Have you talked to Lori?" she asked.

"Nope."

"She's been calling me. She's worried, Wade. She cares about you."

"We broke up," he told her. "So it's not her job to worry anymore."

"I don't think telling her she's not your girlfriend is going to change how much she worries. She loves you. She needs to know if you're okay."

"Just tell her I'm fine."

Nora looked like she wanted to punch him. But she settled for kicking a rock down the lane. "You're being such a fool. You two are meant for each other."

"No, we're not. I'm doing her a favor by ending it. Someday she'll be grateful that she's not saddled with all my problems."

"Wade, you lost control for a couple of minutes! When you were *seriously* provoked. Seth grabbed Lori. He *assaulted* her. You had a reason to fight him."

"I would have killed him if I could have."

She shrugged. "Don't you think we all have those instincts? If I'd seen him grabbing Lori like that, I would have wanted to kill him, too. And I'm sure Lori would still like to kill him. Have you thought of that? Of how *she's* feeling right now?"

"Of course." It's all he thought about. "Look, you might have the instincts, but you don't act on them. I do. I went somewhere in my mind where I couldn't stop."

Nora took his hand. "And you probably need some help with that. So go get it. But also remember all the times lately that you *have* kept your instincts in check. You've made so much progress, going to that support group and talking to Dan about stuff. Overall you've been getting a grip on this thing."

"By spending a night in jail? Putting a man in the hospital?"

"No, of course not. But I'm telling you not to give up."

"I'm not giving up," he protested.

"What else do you call what you've been doing this past week? Oh, wait, I know. It's called wallowing in a big hole of self-pity and pride."

He shook his head, thinking of the rage, and the dreams that even Lori's love couldn't stop. "You don't know what this is like."

"No, I don't. Ethan does, though. And he wants you to get your butt back to the support group and call these people." She pulled some folded sheets of paper from her coat. "He wrote it all down for you. Counselors and psychiatrists who specialize in helping ex-soldiers. Hotlines for veterans. Call these numbers, Wade. Get some help now. Before you lose everything you've worked so hard for."

He took the papers, feeling like that messed-up kid again, the one she always had to jump in and rescue. He folded them small and shoved them into his back pocket. "I'll look at them later."

She shook her head in disgust. "Because

you're so busy right now? Come on, Wade, think about it! We worked our whole lives not to let our family define us. To be something better than them. But here you are, letting this stupid PTSD define you! If you don't get help, you're letting it win."

He looked out over the mountains, at the peaks that had always represented freedom for him. She was right about one thing. He was so tired of being trapped—imprisoned by his own mind. "It's not easy to beat."

"Most good things don't come easily." She looked defeated all of a sudden. "Look, if nothing else, think about the men and women who died fighting in Afghanistan. They won't get a chance to finish their lives, but you will. So do what it takes to live a great one. If nothing else, you owe it to those fallen soldiers to fight this!"

There were tears in her eyes, and she swiped them with her sleeve as she climbed into her Jeep. She slammed the door behind her and gunned the engine, leaving a cloud of dust around him as she drove out.

He watched her go, welcoming the silence. Welcoming a break from all the hard truth in her words. He was so damn tired. Maybe he should just go inside and sleep for a while.

A noise had him turning to face the pasture. Jackson had made his way over to the fence and stood just a few feet away, reaching out his funny reddish speckled nose to snuff the air between them. Taking a hesitant step closer, he nibbled at Wade's sleeve with his lips.

Wade felt his heart jump a little. It was the first time Jackson had ever sought him out. Slowly he reached out and stroked Jackson's velvet cheek and jaw. The red horse took another step closer so Wade could scratch his neck. Another step and Jackson was leaning his head and neck over the fence to rub his forehead on Wade's shoulder, almost knocking him off balance.

"Hey, big guy," Wade murmured, bracing himself as Jackson used him as a scratching post. "Glad I can help you out here."

The horse stopped scratching and whuffled his ear. Wade smiled, the expression so unfamiliar after the past week that his face felt stiff. "You want to do some work, Jackson?" He pulled the halter off the fence post, slipped it gently over the horse's nose and buckled it behind his ear. "Want to go for a walk?"

Wade climbed the fence slowly so as not to startle the horse, but Jackson didn't seem worried. He waited patiently while Wade dropped to the ground next to him and fastened a lead rope to his halter. He walked quietly by Wade's side as they started off through the big field.

The quiet presence of the big horse walking alongside him was more soothing than any of the drugs in Dr. Miller's arsenal. The rhythm of his muffled hoofbeats slowed the panic corroding Wade's spirit. Jackson didn't see him as broken. As long as Wade was calm and gentle, and fed him and worked with him, the horse was happy.

A thought stole over Wade's unquiet soul like a snowfall covering rough ground in soothing white. He might not be able to have Lori and the love he'd dreamed of. And he might never be totally accepted by everyone in Benson. But he could have *this*. This trust and friendship with Jackson. This chance to help a wronged animal adjust to its new and unfamiliar life.

He could do some good here. It wasn't everything he'd wanted, but it was something. A reason to put another foot forward and keep going. Because Nora was right. It was time to start fighting—for his sanity, for this horse, for this ranch, for everything he'd clung to in his darkest moments during the war, those moments when he'd wondered which of his next breaths would be his last. He'd survived, he'd lived, but now he needed to figure out how to start actually living.

CHAPTER TWENTY-SEVEN

ONE OF THE steers Lori had brought down from the mountains was limping. Half-wild from his summer in the mountains, he was not at all interested in letting Lori near him to take a look. She kept her distance for now, walking slowly behind him, trying to decide if the problem was with his hoof or his leg. Or it could have been something up in his shoulder, in which case it might just resolve itself in the next day or so.

She glanced at her watch. Ten minutes before she was due to meet the feed supplier down at the barn. Maybe she'd ask Jim or Ethan if they could get up here and look at the steer and see what they thought.

She called Snack, and he pulled his nose out of the hole he'd been digging, dirt coating his muzzle and clinging to his haphazard fur. The little dog tore himself reluctantly away from whatever rodent he'd been after and followed her through the gate, then sat patiently, tail wagging, while she latched it behind her. At her whistle, he jumped into her arms. She set

him up on Dakota's saddle, swinging up behind him. She'd be a few minutes late getting
back to the barn, but that was okay. The more
packed her schedule was, the less time she had
to think about Wade.

Not thinking about Wade had become the
driving force in her life. When he'd kicked her
out of his life, she'd decided to fill up every
waking hour, from dawn until midnight, with
work. That way there'd be no time for worrying or wondering. And hopefully, with enough
time, her feelings for him would just dry up
like a neglected garden in a summer drought.

Unfortunately it had been almost a month
and her efforts hadn't made much difference.
She still thought about him way too often. She
still missed him with an endless dull ache. But
the ranch was looking great, all repaired and
ready for winter, thanks to the extra hours she
was putting in. And eventually she'd *have* to
stop missing Wade. Somehow.

Mandy kept telling her to call him. Or write
him. To try one more time to make their love
work. But she was done. A girl could take only
so much rejection.

Nudging Dakota down the dirt road, she
passed the water tank. And glared at it because it was a reminder of that fall day when

she'd found it empty and gone storming over to Marker Ranch to find Wade there.

And how they'd fought, and then become friends and eventually more.

And how he'd promised to love her forever, and then told her it was all over, because he couldn't let himself lean on anyone.

He had too much pride and an independent streak a million miles wide. She got why. He'd practically had to raise himself because his family had been so messed up. If he hadn't had that independence and pride, he might never have made it.

Maybe she understood him because she was similar. She'd had a lot of time to think lately. About her own pride. Her own determined independence. That maybe her single-minded focus on being a great rancher had been a way to avoid thinking too much about the hard stuff, like losing her mom.

Had she ever really faced her mom's death? Of course she'd cried, but as her dad and Mandy retreated into their individual, isolated grief, she'd seen that it was up to her to keep the family going. She'd managed the ranch, paid the bills, studied harder than she needed to and jumped into every school activity. It had been easier to keep herself busy than to think or feel.

Which was exactly what she was doing about Wade now. Trying not to feel. And that hadn't worked so well the first time around with him. All her old feelings had come pouring out the moment she saw him again.

She held Snack tightly as Dakota picked her way down a steep, narrow path that served as a shortcut to the barn. It was time to do something different. It was time to stop hiding from the hard emotions.

Lori glanced at the mountains behind her. There was still a lot of daylight left. She'd go meet the feed delivery and then clear her schedule. It was time to break the pattern. It might be depressing, but she was going to do something she should have done a long time ago. Take the last trail her mom had ridden. Face down the sorrow and grief that was there. And maybe, by facing that old pain, she'd find a new way to deal with the heartache of losing Wade.

LORI GUIDED DAKOTA across a dry creek and up the trail. Here the arid eastern flank of the Sierras gave way to graceful aspen groves. The trees peppered the air with the crisp rattle of their dry leaves, reminding her of the day that Wade had made them a bed in the woods. When they'd made love with the golden leaves wafting down around them.

It had been so magical and sweet. But that was the problem with sweet stuff. It always left you wanting more, even though it was bad for you. What if she was never able to look at an aspen tree without remembering that day? Without wanting more of what they'd had?

What was she thinking? She'd been in the mountains for only an hour and she was already going a little crazy. Maybe this pilgrimage was a bad idea.

Or maybe it was good to finally think about things. She scratched Snack's head, and the little dog looked up at her with his strange, black-rimmed eyes. "You doing okay, buddy?"

Snack wagged his tail. He was perched in his usual spot, in front of her on the saddle, looking thrilled with his wilderness adventure. His ears were perked up and he turned his head back and forth, snuffing the wind, trying to take in everything around them. She was glad he'd insisted on coming with her.

As Dakota's steady hoofbeats took them further up the ridge, past the aspen and into the pine-pocked high country, Lori scanned the surrounding hillsides. Here the real mountains began, with granite boulders piling up around her as if tossed by some giant hand. It was wild country, not good grazing land, so she rarely came here.

In its stark way, it was utterly beautiful. Above her, the granite peaks shot straight up into the sky, jagged and foreboding and a testament to the fact that Lori and her problems were just a tiny part of it all. She needed that reminder.

Forty-five minutes later, she and Dakota crested the ridge, and Lori's heart beat a little faster. The trail descended with a treacherous scree slope on one side—a vast steep field of broken rock stretching from the trail to the edge of a cliff. Every time she'd ridden this trail, she'd made a point to stare straight ahead here and never look down.

But this trail led to the rock that looked out over the Ten Lakes Valley. And just before the lookout was where her mom had died.

The wind was picking up, finding its way in between the seams of her parka. The temperature was dropping, too, and Lori scanned the sky. It couldn't be more than three in the afternoon. She should have time to get to the lookout, pay her respects and still get back to the ranch before dark.

She pulled her hat down lower and slowed Dakota a little, encouraging the mare to pick her way more carefully down the slope. The horse was sure-footed, and soon the trail flattened out. This was it. The place where her mom's horse had spooked and her mom had fallen.

Suddenly it was hard to breathe. Lori reined Dakota in, and the obedient mare stopped immediately. Tears blurred her vision, and Lori scooped up Snack, letting the little dog nuzzle her face, offering his own brand of snuffly terrier comfort. Why had she thought this would be a good idea?

Because she was trying to face things. To feel things. To stop running. Setting Snack down on the saddle, she forced herself to calm down. What happened here was horrible. Terrifying. Devastating. But what else? She listened beyond the pounding of her own heartbeat to the quiet rushing of the wind in the pines. To the stillness of the high country.

There was more here than just fear. She remembered her mother's smile. So quietly beautiful. How she'd worn her straight blond hair in a ponytail most days, but there were always a bunch of wisps that escaped and framed her face. How she'd lie in the hammock her dad had hung in the pines by their house on Sunday afternoons after church and read a book for an hour. Her mommy-time, she'd called it. How she'd loved to dance, and cook, and garden and ride. She'd put Lori and Mandy on horses as soon as they could walk, and she loved to get the entire family out for trail rides together as often as possible.

Cozy blanket forts in front of the fire, birthday cakes and the huge Christmas party she threw every year. Church committees and girlfriends and board games and laughter. Memory after memory came spilling out like gems from a treasure chest that Lori hadn't realized was hidden in her heart.

Her mom might have died too young, but she'd lived and loved so well.

And ever since her death, Lori had traded those kinds of rich experiences for rigid goals. She'd let her fears rule her choices, and they'd kept her from so much. From friendships, connections, hobbies and all the small, fun adventures her mom had brought to their lives. And now they might steal her chance at a deep and generous kind of love.

When she got back home, she was going to write Wade Hoffman a letter and tell him one last time that she loved him, and why he'd made the biggest mistake of his life when he told her to go. She was going to ask Mandy if she wanted to go to the movies. She was going to put on a nice dinner for the ranch hands. She was going to start living.

"Thank you, Mom," she murmured to the empty sky, to the woman who'd taught her so much, and continued to teach her right here on this mountain path. "I love you. And I miss you."

Turning Dakota, she started back up the trail. The afternoon was a little dimmer, the air was getting colder and the mare was eager to get home, walking in a fast jerky rhythm that would get her back to her warm stall as fast as possible. Lori felt the same way and let her set the pace.

The path was steeper now, and the scree slope and the cliff dropped off on her left. Lori kept her eyes ahead, glad that with this pace, they'd soon be past it. Dakota, too eager to oblige, stumbled. She lurched forward, twisting her body suddenly to avoid the slope. But her back legs went over the edge, and she scrabbled frantically in the loose rock.

Lori reached for Snack, throwing him uphill, away from the drop and free of the falling horse. She kicked her feet out of the stirrups and used the pommel to vault off, shoving herself away from Dakota so her leg wouldn't be caught underneath if the mare fell.

She missed the path and hit the scree shoulder first. The steep slope took her, rolling her over and over. She scrabbled frantically at rocks as she went, searching for a handhold, but each one was as loose as the last, coming away in her hands. And then she saw the cliff, and made one last desperate, useless grab before she slid over. There was a sickening feeling of falling. Rocks loomed and she twisted, trying to right herself so she'd hit the bottom feet-first, shielding her head with her hands. And then there was nothing.

WADE WAS GROOMING JM when his phone buzzed. Seeing the unfamiliar number light up the screen, he ignored the call, letting it go to voice mail while he cleaned the gelding's hooves with a pick. It was soothing, work like this. Simple and straightforward.

It was easier to think when he had something to do. And right now he had a lot to ponder. It hadn't taken more than a few appointments with his new counselor, a long talk with Dan and a few beers with Ethan to realize that he'd made a terrible mistake with Lori. That he'd fallen right back into his old ways of handling crisis—making sure he handled it alone. It came from his childhood, his counselor said. He'd been rejected by everyone when he was growing up—his parents, his older brothers, even his town. So he had no faith that anyone would be there for him. When things got scary, he pushed people away to avoid the rejection he was sure was coming.

In other words, he was royally screwed up. Thanks, Dad. Thanks, Mom.

But whatever the reasons for what he'd done, he'd hurt Lori in a big way. And he had no idea what he was going to do to try to win her back. Ironic, because the one thing in his life most clear to him was that he loved her—and he wanted a life with her.

The late-afternoon light filtered through the stall door. He'd given JM some grain, and the sound of the horse's contented chewing filled the air. Until it was interrupted by the phone buzzing again—the same unknown caller.

Shoving the hoof pick into his back pocket, Wade picked up his phone and answered. It was Mandy, talking fast, the panic scrambling her voice. Lori had gone for a ride in the mountains. And Dakota had come back without her.

Wade hit Speaker and set the phone down so he could slide a halter over JM's nose. "I'm trailering my horse, and I'll be over in fifteen minutes. Can you have some supplies ready for me?" He listed off anything he could think of, picturing his pack when he was in training to be a ranger. Food, first aid, emergency blankets, fleece clothing, rain gear and rope. Really long rope. Flashlights. A gun, or bear spray. A fresh horse for Lori.

By the time they were off the phone, he was

at his truck, backing it up to the trailer. He lowered the hitch down at record speed, slapped the chains on and ran back to the stall to get JM. Ten minutes later he was pulling up to the main barn at Lori's ranch with a mantra in his head: *please let her be okay.*

Mandy came running toward him, tossing a few coils of rope onto the heap of gear on the ground. "She went up toward the Ten Lakes lookout. The trail starts near the well and heads southwest. She took her little dog with her, and he isn't back, either."

"Why did she go up there?" he asked, unlatching the trailer door.

"I don't know. She said she just wanted some time to think."

Guilt shot through Wade. He'd certainly given her plenty to think about lately. "I promise you I'll bring her back."

"I know you will." It was a flawed vote of confidence. Mandy's voice was shaking, and she looked white as a sheet. Wade knew it wasn't just fear for her sister that had her falling apart. Her mom had died on that trail.

He opened the trailer door and backed JM out. He set down the bucket of grain JM hadn't had the chance to finish in the stall, and the horse ate while Wade opened a side compartment and grabbed the saddle and the thick pad.

He settled them carefully over JM's back, taking his time to make sure his horse would be comfortable.

When the cinch was tight, Mandy handed him a pair of stuffed saddlebags. "There's a chestnut in the corral just on the other side of the barn. His name is Teton. The saddle is on the corral fence."

Wade nodded, taking the halter and going over to swipe a handful of grain from JM's bucket. He jogged around the barn. Teton was a big guy, almost sixteen hands high, perfect for this situation. He could carry a bunch of the gear out and bring Lori back home again. *I hope.* Wade shoved the words away before they sickened him.

Teton snuffed up the grain while Wade slid his halter on. He had the chestnut saddled by the time Mandy came back with the rest of the supplies. They worked in silence, tying on the last of the saddle bags.

Wade swung up on JM, and Mandy handed him Teton's lead rope. "I'll bring her back, Mandy. But it's getting late. I've only got a couple hours of daylight left, so I probably can't get her home tonight. Call the sheriff and tell him to have search and rescue head up first thing in the morning in case I need help with her."

"Can you help her? If she's hurt?"

"Until a few months ago, I was an army ranger. We're trained for pretty much anything. I can do this." God, he hoped so. The anxiety inside was eating at him, fraying his composure. It would be so easy to lose it. To rage at whatever twist of fate had gotten Lori into trouble. But he wouldn't allow the fear and anger out, no matter how hard it burned. He could control it. He just had to use what he'd learned from his counselor the past few weeks. He took a deep breath like he'd been taught, and let it out. He could do this. He had to.

He turned JM toward the mountains, giving Mandy a quick wave. Teton trotted along next to them through the ranch and along the dirt track that would lead them out of the ranch. He passed Lori's well, dry now thanks to him, and stepped the horses carefully over the irrigation lines they'd run from his well to her land.

Water sharing. It had seemed so complicated at the time, but he'd give a lot to have that be their only problem now.

A DULL THROBBING pain filtered in through the darkness. Awareness flickered, disappeared into blackness. Flickered again. Her head hurt. *Where...?* Lori tried to organize her thoughts, but they kept floating out into the blackness again. Was it dark? Were her eyes open?

She forced her mind back from the darkness. *Focus on just one thing. Open your eyes.* She found the muscles eventually and opened her eyes, surprised to see that it was still light out. Not bright, though. Evening. Or early morning. She could see dirt, and a rock right in front of her. It hurt to look. She closed her eyes. The blackness came back and she welcomed it.

A sound penetrated her oblivion. Someone was shouting. Or barking. There was an echo in her brain. Or was it in the mountains? She opened her eyes again. It was her name. *Lori.* Someone was yelling "Lori."

She lifted her head, and her forehead throbbed. She tried to bring her hand up to touch it and gasped at the stabbing pain in her wrist. Broken for sure.

She had to yell back, had to be strong and get help. Taking a deep breath, she forced herself to roll onto her side. It hurt. But at least her mouth wasn't in the dirt anymore. "I'm here," she tried to call, but it came out as a whimper. She took a breath that hurt going in and tried again. "Here!"

The sound bounced off the walls of the canyon. *That's right.* She'd slid down the slope. Over a cliff. Was she at the bottom?

She heard frantic barking. Snack? She'd had

him with her. Pushed him away from Dakota. The last thing she remembered.

"Lori, I heard you! Where are you?" That deep voice. *Wade.* A rush of relief had her eyes tearing up. No, she couldn't lose it. She had to stay strong and calm.

She sucked in another breath and it was a little easier this time, thank goodness. Ribs bruised, but maybe not broken. "Down the scree slope!" She had to stop and catch her breath before she could shout again. "Over the cliff!"

"Are you hurt?"

"Yeah." Every time she yelled, her ribs radiated pain.

"I'm going to lower some gear before I come down there. Is there space for it?"

She raised her head out of the dirt a few inches. She was on a sizeable ledge. "Twenty feet wide. Only ten deep," she yelled up to the sky above. *Ouch.*

"Got it. Don't move."

Don't move. Ha. Not really a problem. Could she even move her legs? She tried, and her right ankle shot pain. Broken?

She closed her eyes and was just getting comfortable in the blackness again when a pebble hit her on the forehead. Dirt followed, raining down. "Oh, ugh." She heaved herself out of the way, spitting out dust as a large bundle hit the ground next to her.

"Do you have it?" Wade called. "Just pull the tail end of the rope. It should untie easily."

Lori used her right hand, the only one working at the moment, and did as he said. As the rope came loose, the wool blanket wrapped around the bundle opened, and all kinds of gear spilled out. Tarps, sleeping bags, clothes and a small duffel bag. An overwhelming wave of gratitude washed over her. He'd found her. She wouldn't make dying out here a family tradition. She closed her eyes, saying a silent prayer of thanks, trying to block out the pain.

Wade was coming. And he knew what to do. It was going to be okay.

CHAPTER TWENTY-EIGHT

WADE WIPED THE sweat out of his eyes. How could he be sweating? It was about thirty degrees out and the temperature was dropping with every inch the sun slid down to the horizon.

But he knew the answer. It was always the same answer these days. Stress. PTSD. His own mind betraying him.

He needed to stay in reality. Keep the facts in front of him. Lori was okay, thank God, but she needed help. He had really good supplies thanks to Mandy. He'd done mountain rescues before, so he knew how to help her. He could do this.

Plus, he had Snack to offer some comfort. The terrier had been here when he rode up, sitting on the edge of the trail and looking intently down the slope to the cliff. When he saw Wade he went nuts, barking like crazy and jumping so high Wade was afraid he'd be the next casualty over the edge. He'd cut a piece of rope and leashed him just in case, relieved to see that the dog appeared to be unhurt.

Wade walked over to the flat area on the opposite side of the trail where JM and Teton were grazing on a rough patch of dry grass. He pulled their saddles off and set them down in the trail where they'd be easy to spot. Just in case he couldn't get Lori back up again and needed a rescue.

Ideally the horses would stick around, but he was going to free them so they could get away from any predators. He was going over that damn cliff, and he wouldn't be here to protect them if they were hobbled.

He glanced around quickly. What else would he need? What had he wished for when his buddies had been hurt and dying around him out in the godforsaken mountains of Afghanistan?

He looked down at the dry dusty ground. It was like being back there. But he had to remember that this was different. No one had been hit by a shell. No one was firing at him. All he had to deal with was the mountains this time. And Lori was talking, which meant she wasn't dying.

Still, his blood felt uneasy in his veins. He brought his hand up behind his neck to ease the ache of knotted muscles there. He had to keep things in perspective. That's what his counselor kept telling him. His reactions were calibrated to the trauma he'd gone through. His nervous system tuned to life-and-death situations. His mind locked into memories of the cruelest and worst kind.

Next steps. Focus on next steps. That's what they'd drummed into him during his training. What if she needed a stretcher of some kind? Or a splint? He needed wood. Grabbing the tools he'd thrown into a bag, he ran down the trail to a few spindly pines trying to push their way up through the rocky landscape. Using a small hatchet, he hacked at their trunks one by one until they fell. It took a few more minutes to strip away the branches. Then it was back to the rope, and he tied them on. He added the second set of saddlebags and the backpack with the first-aid supplies. And lowered them down to wherever the hell Lori was. He wished he could see her.

"Lori, can you pull the rope again?"

Silence. *Oh, damn, silence.* "Lori?" He called again. Nothing. Had she blacked out? Was she hurt a lot worse than he'd realized?

Working quickly, he tied his end of the rope around the base of a big tree across the trail so the supplies he'd sent down wouldn't tumble farther down the cliff. Then he pulled another coil of rope off his saddle. He needed to get down there fast.

He spotted Snack, sitting quietly where he'd been tied, watching his every move. He couldn't leave the dog here or he really would be a snack. He untied him, leaving the rope attached to his collar like a leash, and scooped him up. "It's a good thing you're so small, little guy." Unzipping his parka, Wade loaded the terrier inside and zipped it back up again so just the dog's head was peeking out. "Gonna need you to stay really calm," he told him. "No wiggling or freaking out. I haven't done this in a while. And I've never done it with a dog stuffed in my clothes."

There was nothing more to do but get himself and Snack down the cliff. He tied one end of his rope to the tree, then emptied his mind of everything but his basic training. *Step over the rope. Bring it behind the leg, across the hip, over the opposite shoulder. Down across the back. Don't think, just do it.*

He backed over the edge of the scree slope, leaning back, forcing himself to let the rope take his weight. It was counterintuitive and damn, he'd forgotten how much it hurt. The parka helped pad his back where the rope carried a lot of his weight. But his braking hand was gonna get some serious rope burn.

One step, then another down the treacherous scree, not trusting his feet on the sliding surface, trusting the rope, trusting his skill, trusting the hours of training and his experience. His heart pounded, but he kept up a steady dialogue with himself, just like his counselor had taught him. Yeah, it was scary, but he'd done this before. And bonus—it wasn't even dark yet. He had to keep it in perspective. This was easy. People did this for fun all the time.

Under his feet, the scree slope was turning into sheer cliff, and he winced. Lori had gone over this. He could see her now, lying crumpled on her side on a ledge. Thank God for that ledge. Otherwise she'd be at the bottom of the gorge below, dead for sure.

His heart hammered against the walls of his chest, and panic started to rise. Sweat coated his back, his stomach, and the wide skies around him seemed to close in. Snack shifted in his coat and whined. He didn't want to go over this cliff, either.

"Steady, Snack," Wade cautioned. The dog was picking up on his anxiety. He had to keep it under control or the little guy might squirm right out of Wade's jacket. He took a deep breath and let it out. *Do what's in front of you. The rest is just noise. Just anxiety. Push it back slowly, calmly. It's unnecessary. Unimportant. Just noise.*

His breathing calmed. His feet found purchase on the cliff edge, and he lowered himself easily. Butt down, boots on rock, brake hand searing hot and throbbing, but he was doing it. For Lori. For her ridiculous dog. He could be strong for them.

His feet hit solid rock below. He was on the ledge, wanting to kiss it with gratitude. He'd done it, PTSD and all. He'd stayed in control.

Making sure he had his balance, he unwound the rope from his body and unloaded Snack, tying the dog's rope to his belt loop so the excited animal wouldn't go too close to the edge. The terrier ran for his mistress, straight for her face as if checking for her breathing. When she didn't respond, he brought a paw up in consternation, looking back at Wade with wide eyes as if saying, "Do something."

Wade scrambled to get the first aid backpack untied from the rope he'd lowered it on, then went down next to Lori, registering the cool, pale skin, the shallow breathing—the first signs of shock. Grabbing the blanket from under the pile of supplies he'd lowered down first, he covered her, then unrolled a sleeping bag and threw that over her, too.

He brushed the dirt off her face and searched

through her matted hair for the wound there. It wasn't bleeding much now. He pulled out a neck brace, slid it under her and poured a little of his water over the wound. It ran red for a moment, but at least it took some of the dirt with it and allowed him to see that the cut wasn't bone deep. Good. Now to pray that there was no fracture under there.

She opened her eyes, looking up at him hazily. "Wade? You're here."

"I sure am. Listen to me. You've had a bad fall. You've got a bump on your head. Don't move."

One of her hands went up to feel the neck brace. "I'm okay. I can move. I already did, to get out of the way of all that stuff you dropped on me."

"Sorry about that. I couldn't see where you were from up top."

"It's okay. I'm just glad you're here."

Snack whined and came around Wade to snuffle her face. "Snack? Did you fall, too?"

"He was up top when I got here," Wade explained. "Waiting for you to come back up that cliff, I think. I had to bring him down in my jacket so he wouldn't be alone up there all night."

She smiled as the little dog licked her cheek. "Thank you."

The wind was picking up, and gray clouds were rolling in low. He had to get moving. It was dusk already and would be full dark soon. He lifted up the blanket and scanned down her body. No blood pooling anywhere. "What hurts?"

"My right ankle. And my other wrist. And I think I have some scrapes and bruises."

Pain was good. Her spine was intact. "We'll start with your head and work our way down."

"Sounds nice." She gave him a half smile.

"Dirty jokes at a time like this?" He couldn't help but smile back.

"Hey, we might be out here for the night. Might as well have some humor."

She tried to push herself up to sitting and grimaced.

He eased her back down. "No moving until I say so. You probably have a concussion."

He cleaned her head wound a little more and placed a gauze bandage over it, wrapping more gauze around like a headband to hold it in place. Then he moved to her wrist. Broken, clearly, but no bones sticking out. He cut a few branches from the saplings he'd lowered and made her a splint. Her face glowed white in the dusk and she bit her lip, but she took the splinting like a champ. Man, she was tough.

And then the ankle. Sprained badly, as far as

he could tell, though there could be a chipped bone in there somewhere. He wrapped it in an elastic bandage and made a splint to hold it steady, avoiding her ankle bone just in case.

At least she was more awake now. He rummaged in the first aid kit for the packet of drink mix he'd seen earlier and added it to one of the water bottles, shaking it up. He put the duffel bag against the rocks behind her and helped her lean on it to sit up. Her ribs were bruised for sure, but they didn't feel broken. "Drink this." He put the water bottle in her good hand.

She drank deep. Then swallowed down the painkillers he offered. "Thank you. For coming. For bringing all this stuff. For climbing down here to hang out with me."

"Hang out." He grinned. "Literally. I have the rope burns to prove it."

She reached for his hand and turned it over, palm up. And winced. "Ouch."

"It was fun. It's been a while since I rappelled down a cliff."

"How long since you climbed back up one?" she asked.

"About as long." The light was almost gone. "We definitely have to sleep here tonight. I can't get you up the cliff and back down the mountain in the dark."

"How did you get all this stuff up here?"

"JM. And I hauled a bunch of stuff on Teton, too. Both horses are loose at the top of the cliff. I figure either they'll stay here or head back to the ranch tonight, or JM will revert to his formerly wild ways and take Teton with him."

"Sounds about right." She smiled at him, and it was the most reassuring thing he'd seen.

"I have some food that Mandy packed. She's let the sheriff know to send up a rescue in the morning, so this cliff dwelling of yours isn't a permanent thing."

"Oh, good. I thought it might suit, but the driveway was a little treacherous."

He smiled. "Just a little." He knew what she was doing. Joking to keep her fear away. And he appreciated it, because he wasn't much looking forward to spending the night on a cliff, either. Especially with the temperature dropping and the sky clouding up.

"I think we'll get some snow."

"You've got to be kidding." Lori studied the sky. "You know, I think you're right."

"I'm gonna rig us a shelter with a few of these tarps."

"You're a useful guy to have around, aren't you?"

He laughed bitterly. "It depends on what you want done. Build you a shelter on a cliff? A no-brainer. Take you on a date to the local bar? Not so useful."

"Good thing I don't like bars much."

"Good thing," he agreed. He pulled out one of the tarps he'd brought and then grabbed rope and started threading it through the grommets. Soon he had the tarp tied to outcroppings in the cliff above them and anchored with rocks on the ledge. It was just a lean-to, but it should keep them fairly dry if it started snowing.

He felt something light and cold on his face. Correction: *when* it started snowing. As in now.

CHAPTER TWENTY-NINE

WADE HAD MADE them a nest. He piled up sleeping bags and blankets for them to sit on and burrow under, and he'd helped her put on so many clothes she felt like she was in her own personal cocoon. Snack was nestled down in the blankets, and it was snowing outside.

It wasn't a perfect setup. Every once in a while, Wade had to get up and flap the tarp of their lean-to so the snow wouldn't build up and take the whole fragile shelter down with it. But they were warm enough and mostly dry, and they had Mandy's food and even flashlights. Lori was pretty sure that falling off a cliff in the wilderness had never been so luxurious.

Wade opened another of Mandy's saddle-bags. Sandwiches, muffins and fruit spilled out. "Have I told you how much I love your sister?" Wade asked, staring in awe at the loot.

"I swear she is the angel of food," Lori breathed, reaching for a sandwich with her good hand.

Wade helped her with the wrapper. The painkillers he'd provided had taken the edge off, but her broken wrist still throbbed enough to make her eyes water. That was fine. Because she was alive. She was going to be okay.

"I just can't believe that you're here," she said. "That you came to my rescue."

She could feel him smile in the darkness. "Don't get ahead of yourself. I haven't actually rescued you yet."

"It's a good start, though. So much better than it could have been."

They were both quiet for a moment. The horror of just how bad it could have been was so big, Lori couldn't even think about it without panic clogging her throat. She could easily have died, and she was glad she hadn't.

Better not to think and just focus on the present. She nibbled on her sandwich, taking small bites because of her sore jaw.

"Are you going to tell me what you were doing out here?" Wade asked.

"I went to see where my mom died. I know it sounds morbid, but I just felt like I needed to. Like I never really had closure."

"Did it help?"

She flushed in the darkness. "It helped a lot. I came to a big decision."

"What's that?"

She took a moment to sort it out in her

thoughts. "I guess what I realized is that I haven't been brave enough to reach for the life I want. Except for ranching. I made that happen. But all the other things that make life rich—friends, fun, really celebrating holidays—I think I've missed out on a lot of that."

"So your decision is to have more of the good stuff?"

"Yup," she said. "I want all the good stuff." *Including you*, she wanted to add, but didn't. It would be too awkward if he rejected her again, and they had to spend the night on the cliff together afterward.

"When I was in Afghanistan," he said quietly, "I think I had a lot of similar thoughts. All I wanted was to come home and build this brand-new life for myself, full of all the things I missed so much. It seemed so simple back then, but when I got to the ranch and saw the mess there, and figured out that my brain wasn't really working too well…it just got way more complicated."

"Tell me something about when you were at war," Lori said. "If you don't mind."

Wade was silent for a moment, and she worried that she'd been too intrusive. She was just about to tell him not to answer when he spoke.

"My squadron went on a mission up in the

mountains. We parachuted in. Our orders were to clear out a small group of Taliban fighters."

It sounded terrifying, and he was only on the first sentence. He paused. Lori set her sandwich down on the blanket, reaching out to touch his arm with her good hand.

His big, warm hand covered hers. "I was second in command. Our leader was killed on the way down. A sniper picked him off. Turned out they'd been expecting us. A few more guys in my unit were shot. My best friend was one of them. We hit the ground and hauled him into a cave. We hid there for hours. He died in my arms."

Her heart ached for him. So much pain and fear in his curt sentences. "I'm sorry, Wade. That must have been devastating. How did you get away?"

"We waited until dark, then left the cave, and I radioed for a helicopter to pick us up. But it couldn't come to our location or the Taliban would open fire, so we agreed to meet on the other side of the mountain. We slid on our bellies from rock to rock, up and over the mountain in the dark. And the whole time I was crawling, I was pretty sure I'd be shot any minute. So I decided I wanted to die thinking about the things I loved most. I thought of these mountains. The way they look in the early morning when that pink light comes over the valley floor and slowly hits the granite peaks. How the air smells like the pines. How great it feels to jump into one of the lakes in summer or snowboard down the slopes in winter. And I realized that this area—Benson, Marker Ranch, all these peaks and valleys—is my home. And that whatever happened to me growing up on my family's ranch, whatever bad experiences I endured, they at least made me strong enough, and stubborn enough, to crawl up that Afghan mountain range."

"You were brave," she murmured. He'd been through so much horror. No wonder he was having such troubles.

"But it wasn't just the mountains I wanted to come home to. It was you."

"Me?" Lori's thoughts whirled even faster. "Why me?"

"I was in love with you, Lori. All through high school. And I never forgot our night together."

Her cheeks went hot. "Oh, that."

"Remember how it came about? The way you found me so upset? I was hitchhiking out from town, remember? Right at the end of the school year. And I'd just found out that I was expelled, and I wasn't going to get a diploma because I hadn't passed enough classes. And you drove up, and I stuck out my thumb."

She laughed softly. "I remember that. Of course I do."

"You made me laugh and feel better about everything."

"And then I agreed to meet you," she said, wondering at her teenage self. How blithely she'd walked into that night, with no idea how it would change everything.

His grip on her hand tightened. "And you gave me the most amazing night. You were loving, generous. And even though I was a complete jerk when it came time to say goodbye, I cherished that night. Crawling through those mountains, convinced that I was going to die any second, *that* is what I thought about the most. Your beauty, your generosity, and what it was like to hold you and laugh with you. I wanted those to be my last thoughts."

She was silent, trying to take it in. All those years, she'd hated him for leaving her, while he'd clung to what had been good between them. "I'm glad they weren't," she finally said.

He laughed. "Trust me, I'm glad, too. And by the time I got to that helicopter, I knew I was going to come back here and find a way to make this place my home. And somehow, I'd find a way to see you again."

"But you *didn't* see me. You got home, and you never told me you were here."

"That's what I meant when I said the reality of coming back was a lot more complicated. I must have driven up to your driveway a dozen times when I first got home. But my anxiety was bad, and I just couldn't face you all shaking and nervous like that. I'd had this idea that I'd come home this confident soldier. That's how I wanted you to see me. Every time I tried to visit, I realized I wasn't that guy, and I just turned around and went back home."

They sat in silence. It was so quiet Lori swore she could hear the snow falling on the rocks around them. If she ignored her wounds and the fact that somehow she was going to have to climb up a terrifying snowy cliff tomorrow, it was really peaceful. "If you had such a crush on me in high school, how come you never did anything about it?"

"You were gorgeous, smart, kind, talented Lori Allen. And I was Wade Hoffman, the local drug dealer's son. I never felt good enough for you. Or imagined you would care about me."

"That's kind of the same thing you told me in the sheriff's office."

He was quiet for a moment, and when he spoke, his voice carried a low note of intensity that carried straight to her heart. "I guess it's my fallback excuse when I get scared that I won't get what I want."

"And what *do* you want?" she whispered.

He reached over and softly tucked her hair behind her ear. It was pitch-dark, but she could feel his warmth near her and it was pure comfort.

"I want you, Lori. For the rest of my life. I want you and our families and friends and kids. I want our ranches to thrive and I want cattle, horses, pets and adventures. I want to go to church with you, and I want to find my place in our town, and I don't want to be so scared to reach out and make those things happen anymore."

He leaned over and kissed her softly, carefully, on the lips. "I'm so sorry I was a fool. I shouldn't have pushed you away."

"I didn't go far," she whispered against his mouth. "I was next door the whole time."

"I know I don't deserve another chance with you. I know that deep in my heart. But I'm begging for one." He pushed himself up off the sleeping bags and turned around awkwardly so he was on one knee. "Lori Allen, will you marry me? Once we get up this damn cliff?"

She giggled even though her ribs hurt. There was just too much joy inside her to not laugh. "Wade Hoffman, if you can get me up this cliff, in the snow, with my dog and a broken wrist and a bum ankle, you'll be an even bigger hero to me than you are now. And I will be so happy to marry you."

"Consider it done." He kissed her sweetly, bringing a heat that had nothing to do with all of their blankets. And when he was done, she felt him smile against her lips. "Hey, I just thought of something," he murmured.

"What?"

"All this snow. And it's only November. Do you think the drought could be ending?"

Lori grinned. "It will certainly help," she said, giving him a kiss on his lower lip. "It might even put some more water in that well of yours."

His laugh rang out in the silent night, and Snack lifted his head out of the covers in alarm. "Well, I'll be happy to share it," he assured her. "And now, can you try to get some rest?"

He helped her slide down into the blanket nest, shielding her broken wrist and sore ankle with some of the extra clothing. And then he lay next to her, warm and solid in the dark. She thought about what he'd told her, about Afghanistan. And the long, complicated, sometimes heartbreaking path they'd taken to get to this moment. "Life isn't simple, is it?" she murmured into his chest.

Wade kissed her hair. "Nope. And I can't promise you simple. I'm not healed. I'm working hard at it, and I'll keep working hard, but I'm not all better."

"I'm done trying to make it all perfect," Lori said. "I feel like I haven't been brave enough to reach for what I want. But I know I want you, Wade Hoffman, PTSD and all. I loved you when you were the tough kid next door. I love you now, when you're getting used to life after combat. And I'm sure I'll love you when you're just a peaceful old rancher with a bunch of grandkids on your knee."

He laughed against her cheek. "And all the days in between?"

"We're going to make them amazing. I'm sure of it."

It wasn't simple. It wasn't perfect. But it was exactly what she wanted. Despite her aches and pains, Lori closed her eyes and welcomed sleep, knowing she was as safe as she could possibly be on a ledge halfway down a cliff in the wilderness with snow falling all around. Wade was here, and he'd brought ropes, and soon it would be morning. All they had to do was climb this cliff, this one last obstacle, and they could head down the trail toward home.

* * * * *

LARGER-PRINT BOOKS!

GET 2 FREE LARGER-PRINT NOVELS PLUS
2 FREE GIFTS!

♦ HARLEQUIN®

Romance

From the Heart, For the Heart

YES! Please send me 2 FREE LARGER-PRINT Harlequin® Romance novels and my 2 FREE gifts (gifts are worth about $10). After receiving them, if I don't wish to receive any more books, I can return the shipping statement marked "cancel." If I don't cancel, I will receive 4 brand-new novels every month and be billed just $5.09 per book in the U.S. or $5.49 per book in Canada. That's a savings of at least 15% off the cover price! It's quite a bargain! Shipping and handling is just 50¢ per book in the U.S. and 75¢ per book in Canada.* I understand that accepting the 2 free books and gifts places me under no obligation to buy anything. I can always return a shipment and cancel at any time. Even if I never buy another book, the two free books and gifts are mine to keep forever.

119/319 HDN GHWC

Name	(PLEASE PRINT)

Address	Apt. #

City	State/Prov.	Zip/Postal Code

Signature (if under 18, a parent or guardian must sign)

Mail to the **Reader Service:**
IN U.S.A.: P.O. Box 1867, Buffalo, NY 14240-1867
IN CANADA: P.O. Box 609, Fort Erie, Ontario L2A 5X3
Want to try two free books from another line?
Call 1-800-873-8635 or visit www.ReaderService.com.

* Terms and prices subject to change without notice. Prices do not include applicable taxes. Sales tax applicable in N.Y. Canadian residents will be charged applicable taxes. Offer not valid in Quebec. This offer is limited to one order per household. Not valid for current subscribers to Harlequin Romance Larger-Print books. All orders subject to credit approval. Credit or debit balances in a customer's account(s) may be offset by any other outstanding balance owed by or to the customer. Please allow 4 to 6 weeks for delivery. Offer available while quantities last.

Your Privacy—The Reader Service is committed to protecting your privacy. Our Privacy Policy is available online at www.ReaderService.com or upon request from the Reader Service.

We make a portion of our mailing list available to reputable third parties that offer products we believe may interest you. If you prefer that we not exchange your name with third parties, or if you wish to clarify or modify your communication preferences, please visit us at www.ReaderService.com/consumerschoice or write to us at Reader Service Preference Service, P.O. Box 9062, Buffalo, NY 14240-9062. Include your complete name and address.

HRLP15

LARGER-PRINT BOOKS!

REQUEST YOUR FREE BOOKS!
2 FREE WHOLESOME ROMANCE NOVELS
IN LARGER PRINT
PLUS 2
FREE
MYSTERY GIFTS

HEARTWARMING™

Wholesome, tender romances

YES! Please send me 2 FREE Harlequin® Heartwarming Larger-Print novels and my 2 FREE mystery gifts (gifts worth about $10). After receiving them, if I don't wish to receive any more books, I can return the shipping statement marked "cancel." If I don't cancel, I will receive 4 brand-new larger-print novels every month and be billed just $5.24 per book in the U.S. or $5.99 per book in Canada. That's a savings of at least 19% off the cover price. It's quite a bargain! Shipping and handling is just 50¢ per book in the U.S. and 75¢ per book in Canada.* I understand that accepting the 2 free books and gifts places me under no obligation to buy anything. I can always return a shipment and cancel at any time. Even if I never buy another book, the two free books and gifts are mine to keep forever.

161/361 IDN GHX2

Name	(PLEASE PRINT)	
Address		Apt. #
City	State/Prov.	Zip/Postal Code

Signature (if under 18, a parent or guardian must sign)

Mail to the **Reader Service:**
IN U.S.A.: P.O. Box 1867, Buffalo, NY 14240-1867
IN CANADA: P.O. Box 609, Fort Erie, Ontario L2A 5X3

* Terms and prices subject to change without notice. Prices do not include applicable taxes. Sales tax applicable in N.Y. Canadian residents will be charged applicable taxes. Offer not valid in Quebec. This offer is limited to one order per household. Not valid for current subscribers to Harlequin Heartwarming larger-print books. All orders subject to credit approval. Credit or debit balances in a customer's account(s) may be offset by any other outstanding balance owed by or to the customer. Please allow 4 to 6 weeks for delivery. Offer available while quantities last.

Your Privacy—The Reader Service is committed to protecting your privacy. Our Privacy Policy is available online at www.ReaderService.com or upon request from the Reader Service.

We make a portion of our mailing list available to reputable third parties that offer products we believe may interest you. If you prefer that we not exchange your name with third parties, or if you wish to clarify or modify your communication preferences, please visit us at www.ReaderService.com/consumerschoice or write to us at Reader Service Preference Service, P.O. Box 9062, Buffalo, NY 14240-9062. Include your complete name and address.

HW15

LARGER-PRINT BOOKS!
GET 2 FREE LARGER-PRINT NOVELS PLUS
2 FREE GIFTS!

(H) HARLEQUIN®

INTRIGUE
BREATHTAKING ROMANTIC SUSPENSE